HIDDEN
BONES

OTHER TITLES BY VIVIAN BARZ

Forgotten Bones

HIDDEN BONES

A DEAD REMAINING THRILLER

VIVIAN BARZ

THOMAS & MERCER

Text copyright © 2020 by Vivian Barz
All rights reserved.

Published by Thomas & Mercer, Seattle

www.apub.com

Amazon, the Amazon logo, and Thomas & Mercer are trademarks of Amazon.com, Inc., or its affiliates.

ISBN-13: 9781542005784
ISBN-10: 1542005787

Cover design by Shasti O'Leary Soudant

Printed in the United States of America

For Mom, who never complains when I want to discuss murder. Again.

Prologue

"It works kinda like a slingshot in reverse," said Gus, who favored being known simply as the Man Who Gets Things Done—in these parts, where personal information left you as vulnerable as a double-wide in a tornado, the less anyone knew about you, the better. "See, 'stead of flinging up, the bottom part of the trunk snaps down after you make the cut—kinda like a big manhole cover. Most people don't realize trees leave craters in the ground when they fall over, specially these old redwoods. They're rooted deep, so everything gets yanked out. Could drop a car down into some of the holes I've seen."

A car. Yah, *right*. Wouldn't that be nice?

"Is that so?"

It was a question delivered with an impatient sigh that might be construed as threatening, if one's ears were attuned to such things. Gus's ears sure as hell were perked for danger, but it was a detail he was not going to let anyone in on. Just as with personal information, a smart man didn't go offering up his opinion in situations such as these, and he, though a far cry from what hoity-toity folks over in Seattle might call an "intellectual," was no dummy.

"Yup." Gus's knees popped as he hoisted the machine from the soupy mud that squished around his worn rubber boots like diarrhea. It was a heavy mother, the Eversharp 298X. American tough and built to last, toothy steel nasty enough to gnaw straight through a man's thigh if he didn't watch what he was doing.

"You got lucky with that big storm last week," Gus continued, yelling to be heard over the wind. It had picked up something fierce, screaming blasts of ice against earlobes, the clouds blackening swirls overhead. If he didn't get the show on the road, they'd be standing around in pissing rain. "A few more fell down that way, in an area that's, um, privater." Gus jerked his stubbly chin toward the opposite end of the trail. "But this sumbitch is the heaviest, so I figured it'd work best. In the long run, you know. Course it's up to you."

"Best get to it, then."

Gus nodded to show that he was on it, though he didn't make eye contact, fixing his attention a little higher, on brows and forehead. There was something about that reptilian gaze that made him uneasy, its unapologetic indifference. A gaze that would probably hold the same expression at a carnival as it would at a day care massacre, the infected brain behind it absorbing the world with the kind of cruel detachment only a true psychopath was capable of.

Gus spat a gob of chaw from the side of his mouth and then swiped his cleft lip clean on his shoulder. It was a dirty habit, chewing tobacco, but it was an improvement—albeit a slim one—over the cigarettes he'd recently quit smoking for what could easily be the fiftieth time in his adult life. He used the chain saw to gesture toward the crater. "I'm going to need the, uh, the thing."

"Go," the Boss barked at one of the two lackeys in attendance for the festivities—there were three if Gus included himself, which he didn't—a twentyish kid who used to play for Clancy High's football team. Not too bright, but he had a decent arm. Not decent enough to get a scholarship to UW, though, like some of his teammates had. Kelly something. Now Kelly stocked shelves down at Ah, Nuts *and* Bolts!, the town's only hardware store, owned and operated by one pun-loving Gilly Bolts.

2

Kelly the failed football player trotted a few yards to the beat-up van they'd arrived in ("they" not including the Boss, who might have materialized right there among the evergreens like a forest goblin for all Gus knew) and yanked the back double doors open with a screech. He hollered down the cab at the loafing driver, who had uttered not a single word during the ride over and who Gus was unfortunate enough to know firsthand stank of onions and motor oil. A real piece of work, that one. More rotten teeth than good, more zits on his face than clear flesh. Gus would suspect the stringy-haired creep had been helping himself to five-finger discounts of Pop C, but he was too much of a fat ass to be on uppers; the van rose almost a foot now as he oozed out from behind the wheel.

Not to mention, that shit would never fly. Even *think* about stealing from the Boss, and you were as good as dead.

The two flunkies went about unloading the cargo with a series of grunts and profanities, their incoordination jarring the van to and fro. Gus nearly broke out in crazy giggles as he thought of those bumper stickers he used to see plastered all over shaggin' wagons way back when he still had a full head of hair and was too young and stupid to concern himself with trifling matters like the long-term effects of smoking cigarettes. *If this van's a-rockin', don't come a-knockin'!*

He always did that, lost it at the worst moments. Times like when he was scared out of his ever-loving mind. He swallowed hard, not particularly relishing the notion of getting himself killed—and he had no doubt that he *would* be killed if he took it upon himself to suddenly crack up in present company.

The cargo was a lumpy mass of duct-taped shower curtain. It was transparent plastic but decorated with a cartoony theme that would be best described as ocean disco: sparkly seahorses, eyelashes comically long; octopuses swinging platform-heeled tentacles; goldfish la-la-laahing into microphones. A dead yellow eye winked out between two contorted starfish that were meant to be dancing. Gus couldn't bring himself to look away. What he could manage was a gnash of teeth to the inside of his cheek. The tang of copper flooded his taste buds, and he commanded himself to please, oh dear God, *not scream*.

Because to scream would be worse than laughing.

The two men set the mass down at the edge of the crater with an oof, both wiping their hands on the fronts of their jeans straightaway, as if they were disgusted at having to touch the thing. Gus wished he could wipe his brain clean down the front of *his* coveralls, since he was disgusted, too, with everything he had and was about to witness— disgusted with himself for even being there. But it wasn't as if he had a choice in the matter, now did he? He was hardly in any position to make demands. Or refuse any.

Kelly produced a buck knife from a sheath at his hip and went to work slicing apart the cheap plastic. It didn't take long, and might have even taken much longer if his greasy sidekick had offered a hand. Which, of course, he hadn't.

He couldn't have been more than nineteen, the dead Native boy who gaped up at them with an erupted volcano for a face, mouth frozen in a coagulated shriek of gore. He was naked, scarred all over, and mus- cular in a cage fighter sort of way, with *Fuck da Haters* inked in wobbly cursive across his chest. He was, Gus saw, missing both his kneecaps.

And his tongue.

Probably some kid from down on the rez. Gus had heard that older boys were being recruited—*older* open to interpretation much the same way *recruited* was, but word on the street was that the ripe picking age was sixteen—despite the futile efforts a few of the braver elders were making to keep young tribal members from turning to a life of crime. It was all about the money, honey, and in Clancy, with a population hovering just below six thousand, legitimate, decent-paying jobs were few and far between. The boys worked as Pop C manufacturers, mainly, cheap chemicals destroying lungs before they'd even had the chance to finish developing. Sometimes they worked as dealers, like this kid probably had, spreading addiction across neighboring reservations like cancer.

Gus could sense the Boss's gaze smothering him, squeezing him like a vise, assessing his behavior with a mistrustful eye. Had someone in town said that he'd been flapping his gums? Because he damn well hadn't. He knew what happened to those who ran their mouths about the operation; he only had to look at the brutalized kid in the mud if he needed a reminder. He also knew what happened to the ones they loved—sisters, brothers, husbands, wives, children—which was the scariest prospect of all.

Aware that he was being watched, he studied the kid with blandness that took great effort to feign. At least *this* poor bastard was dead, which wasn't always the case. Losing a tongue and kneecaps was something Gus never wanted to experience in this lifetime or the next, but he imagined being trapped alive beneath a two-ton tree trunk, waiting days for death to come, would be the worst punishment of all. A man would lose his mind, praying for the bliss of suffocation.

Grunting, he pulled the cord. The Eversharp sputtered defiantly in a plume of unhealthy gray smoke and then growled to life—the thing was almost as old as he was, and it would probably outlive him by a hundred years. He nodded at the stinky driver.

Mr. Personality stepped forward, planted his work boot firmly on the dead kid's hip, and kicked him into the hole. Gus swept an arm out, indicating that everyone should take a few steps back. He then cut the tree about six feet up from the roots. Its stump snapped back down over the hole, just as he'd said it would, sealing the boy forever in a forest tomb.

The Boss nodded in approval and then silently walked off into the trees.

Slowly, Gus let out his breath. He felt bad for the kid—sure he did. But, still, he thought: *Better him than me.*

CHAPTER 1

Had Eric Evans still been at Warrenton, the large private university he'd been employed at back in Philadelphia once upon a time, he would have been thrilled to see that the enrollment numbers had spiked into the triple digits for his Introduction to Geology course for the upcoming semester. But, for his latest teaching gig at Perrick Community, a tiny Northern California college with a student body barely reaching one thousand, it was a different story.

The number, in fact, prompted a jerky double take at the computer screen, resulting in a few slops of coffee launched from his **GEOLOGY TEACHERS ROCK** mug onto the desk. He mopped it up with a curse and the paper towel he'd been using as a makeshift plate for the towering stack of Girl Scout cookies he'd just inhaled. He deposited the soppy mess into the wastebasket, sat back in his creaky desk chair, and stroked the stubble on his chin he'd been too lazy to shave during the past week despite Susan's protests that it was starting to feel like sandpaper when they kissed.

Eric's first thoughts were of the faculty at the college, who'd been far more gracious than one would expect them to be in their treatment of him following the traumatic events at Death Farm, where he'd nearly met his demise at the hands of a serial killer. Most had offered commiserations when the press began showing up on campus and chasing him with video equipment and microphones, screaming questions as he strode, and on some days *ran*, across the quad to do the job he'd been paid to do. How they'd learned of his involvement in the infamous case remained a mystery, since he and everyone else involved had remained tight lipped about the situation.

As the harassment continued and later expanded to other faculty and his students, the commiserations were replaced with put-out questioning—*When will it stop, do you think?*—as if he'd personally invited reporters to be there. Eventually, the vultures, with fresher tragedies to exploit, stopped circling, and his colleagues began to warm to him once more. But now, lo and behold, here he was testing their patience again by poaching their potential students, albeit unintentionally—because no way *that many* individuals had awakened on enrollment morning with a sudden and urgent need to study geology.

Really, it shouldn't come as a surprise, he thought sourly. With today's youth being as celebrity obsessed as they were, anyone with a modicum of fame was thought to be worthy of attention, even a pseudocelebrity like a college professor purported by the press to have psychic abilities. Eric snorted at the notion, closed out the enrollment screen, and returned to the mystery novel he'd started to pen at his therapist's behest.

So far, the only "mystery" was why he'd thought it would be a good idea to begin with. He was only three thousand words in, which may sound impressive to a layman but was actually minuscule considering that an average commercial mystery novel comes in at about seventy to ninety thousand words, give or take. At the rate he was going, he'd have it finished sometime around his fiftieth birthday. Having a creative outlet was supposed to relax him, but so far it was having the opposite effect.

Eric had concluded that seeing a therapist for treatment might not be a bad idea once he could no longer count on the digits of both hands and feet the number of wakeful nights he'd suffered since he'd been held prisoner, never mind the brutal nightmares that came once he *did* manage to sleep. Then there was the unrelenting anxiety and his latest fixation: three little seconds. Not thoughts of the ghostly dead boy who'd haunted him day and night, and not of the insects that had crawled all over his flesh down in the darkness—but of the idea that, had police arrived only *three seconds later*, he would be dead.

He obsessed over all the activities he was unable to do in less than three seconds on any given day: Pouring a cup of coffee, *four seconds*. Dead. Tying his tennis shoes, *six seconds*. Dead. Buttoning his shirt, *nine seconds*. Dead. Peeling an orange, unlocking his office door, running a comb through his hair . . . dead. Dead. Dead.

Susan, who'd been staying over so much lately that she was practically a resident at Casa de Evans, had no idea about the three-second thing. He had no intention of letting her find out. His schizophrenia was already scary enough for her to deal with, he imagined, and she had plenty of trauma on her own plate—though she always swore that she was fine, just fine, whenever he asked.

He was about halfway to the kitchen to grab what few cookies were left in the box when his phone blurted to life on his desk. "What's up, Prof?" It was Jake.

"Mr. Bergman, haven't heard from you in a while. I almost thought you'd forgotten about your dear old professor now that I no longer have grades to lord over you," Eric teased.

"Sorry," Jake said, but not flippantly. "The band's been practicing a ton—we've even gotten a few new songs written."

"You've got to strike while the iron's hot."

"Exactly. We've also booked a couple shows up north, which is kind of why I'm calling."

"Do tell."

"First, how are *you*? Bonnie says that I can sometimes be a little self-centered, so now I'm making a point of asking about others first before I start yammering about myself. I'm not self-centered, am I? *I* don't think *I* am," Jake said. "That last part was a joke, me asking about being self-centered. See what I did there?"

Eric chuckled. Bonnie was the girl Jake had been seeing for the past month or so. She had flaming red hair and stood a good foot and a half taller than the dwarf violinist, but he thought the two made a cute couple. Maybe not a *forever* couple, but cute enough for the time being. "Must be the musician in you, accustomed to the spotlight," he said, and Jake made a guilty oops sound. "How are things with Bonnie, anyway?"

"Eh." Now Jake *was* being flippant. "We'll see how it goes, but if I were you, I wouldn't go investing in any wedding china for us. Just sayin'."

"Noted. And, since you asked . . . I'm fine-*ish*."

"Reporters showing up at your house again?" Jake guessed.

"Thankfully, no, but I've got a ton of students enrolled in my class next semester. Funny, since before all this hoopla, I had to practically beg students not to drop the class."

"Can't say I didn't see *that* one coming."

"I don't know why *I* didn't, though, not after the way I was stalked on campus."

"Some psychic you are."

"Good one. So, what's this about your shows?"

"Oh," Jake said, as if he'd forgotten why he'd called. "We've booked a show in Clancy!"

Outside, a plane flew by overhead, sounding close enough to shave a few shingles off Eric's roof. Surely there was some kind of law against that. California, he'd found, had laws against many things that might seem arbitrary in other states; a person could find themselves on the receiving end of a hefty fine if they didn't watch what time of day they watered their lawn, for example. There was also a head-scratching amount of Proposition 65 cancer warnings he couldn't seem to escape no matter where he went: *This coffee / paint / salad bowl / tennis ball* (take your pick here of almost anything at all) *contains chemicals which are known to the State of California to cause cancer and birth defects or other reproductive harm.* Californians, it seemed, were especially susceptible to cancer.

"You sound excited," Eric said. "Am I supposed to know what Clancy is?"

And there it went again, another tremor of an airplane overhead, except this one was accompanied by an ear-shattering crack and sounded on the verge of touching down. Impossible. His little rental cottage was almost forty miles from the nearest airport, San Francisco International. An ugly image fizzed through his brain, lightning fast: smoke, fire, bodies strewn about, the tail section of a 747 sticking out from the top of his home like an ugly hat. He'd been having more gruesome visions like these lately than he'd care to admit.

Jake huffed an incredulous breath down the phone. "You've never *heard* of Clancy? Clancy, *Washington?*"

Eric turned his attention back to the conversation, ignoring the bad feeling in his stomach. "Should I have?"

"Hell-o! It's only where all the Darkest Thrills novels take place—*and* all the movies based on the books!"

"Okay, that does ring a bell. Spy stuff, right—like actiony, blow-everything-to-smithereens, macho-guy kinda thing. Kincaid something."

Jake made a choking sound. "You're not . . . oh my God . . . don't tell me you've never seen *any* Dylan Kincaid films! *Night Smoke, Darkest Sunrise, Revenge Fire* . . . there's like a *bajillion* of them!" Jake prattled on about his favorite film in the series, *Darkest Sunrise*—which, despite its title, took place primarily in an underground bunker.

"Not really my kind of flicks. You were saying about your show in Clancy?" Eric prompted before Jake had the chance to further launch into the many ways Dylan Kincaid had kicked ass and taken names in *Night Smoke.* Maybe the books were better than the movies, which, judging by the billboards he'd seen, had more CGI-enhanced explosions and chisel-chested eye candy than quality acting.

"We're heading up to Clancy for a show—next week, actually. There, and then Seattle, which is just a few hours away. It was kind of a last-minute booking, but it just so happened that we called at the perfect time. We were initially trying to book a Seattle gig a couple months from now, but the original headliner for next week bailed because of some issue with the lead singer—he fell off the wagon again and was whisked off to rehab. The club's even throwing us some extra cash for being so accommodating."

"And because your band is getting to be pretty big now, too, right?"

"Sure, sure," Jake said, endorsing what was only a fact. Augustine Grifters had recently had a lucky break when lead singer Madison's brother, a big-time advertising executive in Los Angeles, used a sample from one of their more popular songs, "Loverbot," in a sports car commercial that had run nationally for a few weeks during prime-time television. The number of downloads the band had on the first night alone exceeded all the sales they'd had in the entire six-month period prior.

"Anyway," Jake continued, "we figured that, since we were heading to Seattle, why not also book a show in Clancy. Madison also has a friend there, named Darla, who she wants to surprise with a visit. The two were pretty close up until a couple years ago, when Darla took up with some loser none of her friends—Madison included—approved of. She left the Bay Area and moved up to Clancy with the dude. They lost touch with each other but still occasionally stayed in contact on Facebook. You know how it goes."

"Sure."

"Things didn't work out so well with Darla and the deadbeat—surprise, surprise—and he drained their bank accounts and took off on her. Now, she's kind of stuck with no money or job in Clancy, which, apparently, is painted a lot nicer in the Darkest Thrills series than it actually is in real life. The town's pretty dead end, from the sound of things, and a lot of local business owners are riding out the Kincaid fame for as long as they can with tourists. But even that's dying off."

"What a shocker. The movies seem like such gems," Eric said dryly, and then he could practically see Jake rolling his eyes.

"*Anyway*, Madison's hoping she can convince Darla to come to California, though 'convince' is putting it lightly—it's like she's on a crusade. All I care about is doing the touristy stuff in Clancy before it disappears. There's a couple Dylan Kincaid–themed bars and restaurants on the main drag that sound fun—you know the sort of thing, where the waitstaff dress up as characters from the films and the burgers have spy-lingo-y names."

"I can see where that would be fun," Eric said carefully. He was feeling uneasy about his friend's plans, though he couldn't pinpoint why. "But is Madison even sure that Darla will want to come back with her?"

"Madison's pretty sure she will. It doesn't sound like she's got too much going for herself in Clancy. But that's kind of why I'm calling too."

"Oh?"

"See, we're trying to caravan up there in two cars. As it is now, we're pretty full with just the van, with all the gear and equipment we've got to haul around with us."

"Okay . . ."

"So, I'm wondering if you'd be up for a little road trip—you and Suze?"

"To help haul your gear?"

"Well, yes and no. We *do* need the extra space of your Jeep, but I also thought you might want to get out of town for a minivacation, given all the recent drama. You're off work now, anyway, right, with the semester being finished?"

"I'm off now, but, hmm, I don't know . . ." Eric rubbed the slight hump his nose had developed courtesy of the face-first, ten-foot drop into a hole he'd taken while in captivity. He glanced at the novel on his computer screen and let out a long sigh. Maybe it *would* do him some good to get out of town for a few days. "I'll have to talk to Susan first. She only went back to work this morning."

As if on cue, Susan's keys were jingling at the front door. Eric said goodbye to Jake and went to meet her. Immediately, he was taken aback by how miserable his girlfriend looked. She shrugged off her coat and hung it on the wonky coatrack pegs he'd been meaning to tighten, not bothering to pick it up when it fell to the floor.

"What's wrong?"

She gave him a short answer. "Everything."

Eric wrapped his arms around the woman he had come to consider not only a lover but also a best friend. "Want to talk about it?"

She shrugged underneath his grasp. "There's not much to say. It's just . . . I don't know if I can be here anymore. Here, in Perrick."

"Bad day at work?"

"The worst. It was so bad that I was 'informed' that I could—more like *should*—take more time off."

"How much time?"

She shook her head. "They didn't say; they just want me gone— they'd probably be happiest if I stayed gone forever. You won't believe this, but somebody carved *traitor* on the top of my desk, like I had something to do with what happened . . . on the farm." Her voice, Eric had noticed, always took on a strange tone when she talked about the place. "I wish we could pack up everything; leave this petty, small-minded, backstabbing place; and never look back . . . why are you smiling?"

"Because I can make your wish come true. Maybe not forever, but at least for the time being."

CHAPTER 2

"Well, well, the mayor of Clancy herself. I'm honored," Jake said, taking Mayor Julia Moulden's hand into his own.

The mayor smiled amiably as they shook hands. "I'm the one who's honored. Been a fan of you guys for years, since 'Neon Skies.'"

Jake was impressed. He took a long swig of his rum and Coke, a freebie from the bar's owner for a performance well done, happy to note that the bartender had poured heavily—nothing worse than a weak mixed drink. The crowd and band were also happy, which meant that he was happy too. He nodded. "Our first album, from way back in the day. Most of our listeners in Perrick—that's where we're from—haven't even heard of it."

"We *do* have the internet up here," Mayor Moulden said coyly and then flipped her hair back from her shoulders.

She was attractive in a dignified older woman sort of way—what was older for *him* in his late twenties, which placed her in her midforties—with dark eyes and a heavy raven-colored bob with severe bangs. Mayor Cleopatra, he dug it.

He was wishing that he'd ended things with Bonnie before the trip, and not just because he thought the mayor was cute. Something told him that she wanted it to be over, too, but didn't want to be the one to strike the first blow. Nobody ever wants to be the bad guy—or girl—in a relationship.

The mayor introduced herself once more as the rest of the band—Chuck, Madison, and John—joined them. Madison raised her eyebrows at Jake in a manner that suggested she had noticed his admiration of the mayor and approved. She then gave him a thumbs-up as she took a drink, as subtle and embarrassing as a stage mom at a toddler's beauty pageant. He gave her the sort of threatening *quit it* look only close friends are allowed to give each other with no hard feelings attached. This only seemed to encourage her. "So, Mayor Moulden, are you single?"

The mayor threw back her head and let out a loud *hah!* Without skipping a beat, she said, "I *am* married—to my job!"

"So, single, then," Madison persisted. "Good." She gave Jake an encouraging look that the mayor would have to have her eyes closed to miss. Had they been sitting at a table, he would have kicked his friend hard in the shins to shut her up.

Luckily, Chuck swooped in to change the subject. "Do you have another job—most mayors in smaller towns have second jobs, right? Our mayor back in Perrick also owns a feedstore."

What a weird thing to ask, Jake thought. Then again, because he was a musician, people were forever asking him if he also had a "real" job. That, or his other favorite, *You make enough to live on* just *being in a band?*—as if rephrasing what boiled down to the same question made it any less crass to ask.

The truth was that Jake technically wouldn't need to work a single day in his life, if he budgeted just right—or at least not for a very long time—thanks to the large inheritance he'd gotten from his maternal grandfather at age twenty. But what would be the fun in that? He liked to stay busy, and he enjoyed the feeling of putting in a hard day's work. His great-grandfather, grandmother, and father had all been jewelers, so naturally it had been presumed that he would join the reasonably lucrative family business—three stores in Northern California, one in Orange County, and an online shop. While he didn't want to make hawking jewelry a full-time gig—when it came to rocks, he, like Eric, preferred geology as a whole—he helped out when needed.

"You're right. I'm also a freelance accountant," Mayor Moulden said.

Jake was about to utter something flirty yet borderline corny— *smart* and *beautiful*—when a drunken jackass with a long ponytail and an embroidered pot-leaf beanie came up on his side and coiled a sweaty arm around his shoulder, sloshing half the rum and Coke down on his shoes.

"Dude!" the guy shouted as an opener.

Jake was not happy, but he also couldn't be too rude, given that the idiot had dropped fifteen bucks to see him play. His smile was all gritted teeth. "Hey, buddy, you mind watching what—"

"You're from that California murder town, right? The one where they found all those dead kids?" He grinned down at Jake like he'd just won the lottery. "Man! That shit was *insane*."

The interloper was far too cheerful, acting like the murders of twenty-one children were the punch line to a big joke. This did not endear him to Jake, who was accustomed to people in Perrick speaking of the Death Farm tragedies with appropriate solemnity. He didn't know what to say, but he knew what he *wanted* to say to the guy: *Get out of my face before I slug you.* He might have been small, but he was strong and could hold his own in a fight. He'd learned how to handle himself early on, around the time he discovered that he would not be joining his fellow classmates in their physical growth. Nothing catches the attention of the schoolyard bully quite like being the runt of the litter.

Ponytail was off again, inebriated to such an extent that he swayed to and fro. His armpit was nose level to Jake, and no amount of patchouli oil in the world—and this guy was wearing a bucketload—could mask body odor so pungent. "That's the hot cop over there, right—the one who worked with the FBI? And that psychic guy! Oh my God, this is unreal! Think they'd autograph my shirt for me? Do you know them?"

Jake saw that he was pointing to the bar area, where Eric and Susan were chatting amiably with a couple of young twentysomethings in flannel button-downs, a staple among the crowd. The dipshit was being about as subtle as a ten-alarm fire, talking so animatedly that people were starting to stare, despite the boisterous sounds of the crowd. Eric and Susan looked their way, frowning. Now, Jake was getting angry; his friends were getting upset, and they'd been having a nice time up until their uninvited visitor started running his mouth. Being drunk did not give *anyone* a free pass to be disrespectful.

The mayor looked as if she was getting upset too. She glanced at the bouncer helplessly and signaled him to come over. He was as big as a house and looked mean enough to eat rusty nails for breakfast—the last person anyone would ever want to encounter in a dark alley.

"What do you think you're doing?" Madison asked coldly as Ponytail pulled out his cell phone and aimed it at Eric and Susan. "Hey, stop!"

"Come on, man—that's not cool," Jake said, moving his hand in front of the phone so that video couldn't be taken.

Ponytail moved the phone out of Jake's reach. "It's a free country," he simpered.

Jake was about to deliver a few choice words when a behemoth arm whizzed past his face. "Yah, grab this jackass," he heard Chuck say, and then Ponytail was lifted off his feet as the bouncer seized him roughly by the collar, tearing most of it clean from his shirt.

"You can't touch me! Hey, help!"

"It's a free country," Jake sang, enjoying the show. He couldn't help himself. The guy *did* have it coming.

Ponytail let out an incredulous yelp as the bouncer began rooting through his pockets and pulled out his wallet, removing the driver's license. "You're not from around here. Thought so." He grabbed Ponytail by the shirt again and began dragging him toward the exit—an easy feat, since he was three times the kid's size. "I think it's time you head back to Olympia, partner."

"I didn't do anything! You can't—"

The drunk's head flew back as the bouncer cracked him hard on the nose. Within seconds, the front of his shirt was saturated in blood. Jake and John gasped at the overreaction, and Madison let out a quick, sharp shriek. Ponytail fell to the ground dizzily; the bouncer hauled him to his feet using a fistful of hair, punching him in the gut when he stumbled, and resumed dragging him away.

Jake was starting to feel sorry for the guy. He'd only wanted him to go away, not be pummeled.

"Jesus, is that really necessary?" Susan hollered as she and Eric approached.

Jake glanced at the rest of the crowd, caught off guard by their strange reaction. As a musician, he'd witnessed his fair share of drunken bar brawls, yet never one that had escalated as quickly as this. Usually, the crowd stared at the display as if it was being provided for their entertainment; sometimes, they'd even hoot and holler. If they had a bit of class about them, they might even try to break up the fight, or at least attempt to talk some sense into the brawlers.

This crowd, though, was pretending not to notice the violence unfolding before them. They sipped their beers and quietly continued their conversations, life as usual, just another normal night out in Clancy. Some turned their backs on the display altogether. Incredibly, a few shifted, and just when Jake thought they were going to intervene, they turned sharply and headed for the door as if fleeing from a fire.

The few who dared look over appeared to be experiencing the same horror that Jake felt, yet they seemed reluctant to speak up. They shot nervous glances at the mayor, the band. Nobody wanted to say anything.

"Guess you guys don't like outsiders much," Chuck prattled nervously.

"Not when they act like that," the mayor said distractedly. Her attention was focused on the bouncer and Ponytail, who was being hurtled out the front door. "There's a sign posted right on the door which states that photography is prohibited in the bar."

"Guess he missed it," Susan said, making her displeasure evident. "If that guy had any sense about him, he'd file an assault charge."

The mayor turned to look at Susan, as if suddenly coming to her senses. "Of course," she said, shaking her head. "I'm going to have a talk with the owner about his staff. That was totally unacceptable. I'm sorry you had to witness that." Mayor Moulden extended a hand and introduced herself to Eric and Susan.

This seemed to soothe Susan's anger. "It wasn't like you were the one who did the punching," she said with a half smile.

"I just don't want you to get the wrong idea about our little town." The mayor pulled a small leather pouch from her purse, pinched out a few cards, and distributed them to everyone in attendance.

Jake couldn't help thinking of a greasy used car salesperson. He stared down at the card awkwardly; the font that identified Julia as mayor was three times the size of her accountant title. This did not surprise him. She seemed the sort to engage in politics even when she was off the clock, a bigger politician than she was an accountant. He found this icky yet strangely admirable. She had passion, at least, even if it was grossly misplaced. Because, without passion, what did a person really have?

"Is it true what he said?" the mayor asked Susan, casual yet still businesslike. "I heard about those murders down in California. Terrible stuff. Were you really there?"

Susan took a long sip of her beer. "Afraid so."

The mayor made a show of shivering. "I didn't really put two and two together until the kid with the ponytail said something; otherwise, I wouldn't have ever known. You and your town were all over the news."

After a beat, she nonchalantly asked, "Do you still have a bunch of journalists following you around?"

"Not unless they're good at hiding," Susan said with a chuckle. The mayor didn't seem to share her amusement. "No, they've been leaving me alone for a while, thank God. Why?"

The group watched as the bouncer sauntered back through the entrance. There was enough blood on his hands to be seen from clear across the room. "There's something seriously wrong with these people," Madison whispered at Jake's side, and he nodded in agreement. Something was definitely off at the bar, maybe with Clancy as a whole. During his brief exploration of the town earlier that day, the locals were hardly what anyone would call warm. The crowd had been a little better during the show, but, after the one-sided brawl he'd just witnessed, he'd be lying if he said he wasn't eager to move on to Seattle.

The mayor sipped her drink. Jake could practically hear the gears in her head turning as she crafted the perfect statement. "I love Clancy and the people who live here. We may be small, but we have a lot of pride in our town. Most of us strive to bring us closer to modernity, and we welcome visitors from out of town because it keeps many of our businesses afloat. A few folks in town, however, are a little . . . unhappy with all the attention we've received from those Kincaid movies." She smiled. "It's nothing personal against tourists like yourself; sometimes people in small towns get a little too used to their privacy."

"Okay," Susan said guardedly.

Mayor Moulden smiled good-naturedly. "Don't look so worried. All I'm trying to say is that I would consider it a personal favor if you didn't mention the incident with the bouncer on social media or to the press."

Susan shook her head. "Oh, I wasn't—"

"And maybe you also shouldn't advertise that you're here. I'm truly very sorry about what happened in your town, but you can probably understand why we wouldn't want Clancy associated with child murders, even if it's indirectly. A lot of folks would be unhappy if the press came up here looking for you." She glanced at Eric. "And you. I hope I'm not offending, but I wouldn't be doing my job if I didn't do my best to look after Clancy."

"You couldn't get me to talk about the murders if you paid me," Susan said.

Eric said, "Ditto."

"Good." The mayor relaxed. "I know it sounds paranoid, but I have to show the people of Clancy that I'm *hearing* them and have their best interests in mind. Sometimes, it can be hard to make everyone happy."

Eric and Susan both made polite statements about taking no offense, but Jake suspected that they just didn't care. They'd be out of there in no time, and he was willing to bet that they were as eager to get to Seattle as he was.

"Hey, wasn't your friend Darla supposed to come and meet us?" Chuck asked, filling what had become an awkward silence.

"She sure was," Madison said. "I wonder why she didn't come. She used to be so reliable, but that was before she took up with that deadbeat."

Jake let out a loud yawn. It was considered poor form for members of a headlining band to depart the hosting venue shortly after a set. But, he figured, the rule no longer applied once it was revealed that the venue's staff had a propensity toward beating out-of-town visitors to a bloody pulp.

"How long will you guys be staying in town?" Mayor Moulden asked lightly. But, after her previous comments, her sentiment was clear: *How long until you're gone?*

Not soon enough, he thought.

CHAPTER 3

"It's like the aftermath of the apocalypse," Susan commented as she and Eric drove down the one road that led to downtown Clancy, where they were in search of thicker socks that would better accommodate her brand-spanking-new hiking boots. Which, according to Eric, was a rookie mistake.

"Right. It's weird—where are the people?" he asked. "Does nobody walk in this town?"

"More like: Does anyone *live* in this town?" She took in the bleak surroundings, made all the more ominous by the murky Pacific Northwest sky overhead—she wondered if the sun ever shone in Clancy. The cheerless surroundings indicated the negative. It would be difficult to stay optimistic in such a place, though it didn't seem that the locals had much to be happy about.

Vacant houses dotted the outskirts of the town square with all the appeal of busted teeth. The majority of them had faded **FOR SALE** signs staked into overgrown front lawns. Without stepping foot in any, a buyer would already know that the inside reeked of mustiness—the air on the Olympic Peninsula was so damp it was like breathing steam.

The main drag itself was no better. Every other shop was out of business, with dusty front windows boasting vacancy signs as faded as the ones they'd seen on the houses. "When was the last time you saw one of *those?*" Eric asked as they passed a DVD rental shop that, oddly enough, seemed to still be functioning; a gigantic Dylan Kincaid cardboard cutout sat in front of it on the sidewalk. Still, it was hard to tell which businesses were truly open, since there were no crowds inside them or even on the street. There were only a few stragglers scattered about, most middle aged and looking down on their luck. "Have you seen any kids here?"

Susan shook her head; come to think of it, she hadn't. No young moms pushing strollers either, which one would expect to see on the main drag of a tourist town. Also no teenagers hanging at the tables of coffeehouses, though there didn't seem to be many of those either. All she'd seen was a drive-through coffee stand a mile or so down from the hotel. "I haven't seen any old people either, have you?"

"No. What demographic does this community serve—what do people *do* here, do you think?" he asked. Having been raised in Philadelphia, he probably had a hard time conceiving of a world so small, even after living in Perrick, which in comparison to Clancy seemed as big as Los Angeles.

Susan shrugged. "There's got to be *some* kind of long-standing industry here. Think of all the younger people who were at Jake's show last night. Logging, maybe?"

They parked the car and went into a touristy drugstore called Clancy Fancy. The inside was a peculiar mishmash of camping supplies—hiking poles, propane stoves, bug spray—and Dylan Kincaid memorabilia: Darkest Thrills novels, Dylan Kincaid action figures, and "Mrs. Kinkaid" T-shirts. The middle-aged man inside greeted them warmly and introduced himself as Ben Harvey, taking both their hands into his as if they were old friends. He wore round wire-frame glasses, a sweatshirt with a logo for Clancy Fitness—*"Come sweat it, you won't regret it!"*—and glaringly white high-top tennis shoes straight from the eighties.

Immediately pegging them as outsiders, he asked if they were in the market for a Dylan Kincaid tour. "I've got a van stocked with all the complimentary snacks and cold drinks you can eat. I'll take you around town to spots featured in both the books and the films."

Eric held his hands up. "We're only in the market for hiking socks for the lady. Her boots are brand new."

"Ouch, breaking in new boots on a hike? I hope you like blisters." Ben made a pained face, and Eric gave Susan a look—*told ya!* "Yah, I didn't peg you two for Darkest Thrills fans, but I had to ask anyway. Could use all the business I could get." He looked around his empty store, emphasizing his point.

"Business slowing down?" Eric asked, and Susan shot him a look. It didn't seem polite to ask, particularly since the answer seemed apparent.

Ben didn't seem to mind. "Oh, hell yes. I'm sure you've heard that they're not making any more Kincaid films. Books either, with that writer fellow dying four years ago—which, coincidentally, was about the time my business started going to pot—imagine that." He gave the pair a wry smile.

"I'm sorry," Eric said.

Ben flapped a hand. "Nah, got other businesses keeping me afloat. I'll be good."

If you say so, Susan thought.

They made polite chitchat about their travel plans and the weather back in California as Susan picked out long wooly socks that were thick enough to use as a pillow—take that, blisters.

"Know of any good hiking spots?" Eric asked while they were being rung up. "Locals only?"

"Do I ever!" Ben brought out a map from underneath the register. He looked like he was winding up to provide lengthy descriptions of each spot. Susan hoped this wasn't going to take forever; their time in town was limited, and she was eager to enjoy some fresh air. He flattened it out and pointed at various spots along the peninsula. "This one's the prettiest. Lots of fauna, and the trail is quite challenging."

Susan let out a quiet groan. "*How* challenging?"

Eric chuckled. "We're not trying to get too crazy."

"Right, no K2 trails today," Susan seconded.

The man laughed, moved his finger north along the map. "Of course, if you're not looking to exert yourself, you should try this one. It's a poky little trail, but you'll see some pretty views. There's also a waterfall near the end."

Eric and Susan peered at the map. She asked, "These seem a long way out of town. Aren't there a bunch of trails right in this area? I thought that's what you guys were famous for—besides Dylan Kincaid. It seems every tourist website I saw about Clancy mentioned the forests here; they're world famous."

The man's smile wavered. "Oh, well . . ." He waved a hand dismissively. "Nah, the trails around here are no good. They'll be crowded, and unfortunately, many of them are littered with trash from tourists who aren't as nice as you two."

Susan was dubious about the crowd thing, given how desolate downtown was. She would feel mean pointing this out to Ben, though, given his earlier comments about his dying business that was rooted in tourism. "We're not fussy. Really, we just want to stretch our legs. We don't want to drive too far."

He rooted around below the register and pulled out two small pieces of paper that looked like tickets. "If you're looking for exercise, here's two free passes to Clancy Fitness. I own it."

The couple took the passes and thanked him. "Maybe we'll come in after our hike," Eric said.

Ben frowned. "Oh, I thought you'd come and work out at the gym instead of going on the hike."

Susan said, "I'd never hear the end of it if we did *that*," and Eric grinned. Ben seemed displeased by the statement. "Do you want your passes back or . . . ?"

Ben shook his head and provided them a smile that seemed forced. "No, no—of course not! Just . . . watch yourselves on the hike. Don't stray off the trail, you hear?" he said, making it unclear whether he was delivering a warning or a threat.

◆　◆　◆

"Everyone might be weird in this godforsaken town, but the nature sure is on point," Susan said, spinning around at the opening of the Mugachopee National Forest, her arms spread wide. They'd driven only a couple of miles from Clancy Fancy, yet it felt like they were in a different world.

She took a deep breath, inhaling the crisp, clean scent of what she thought might be redwoods—she wasn't exactly versed in the names of tree species in the Pacific Northwest, but she knew that redwoods were big and that these trees were *huge*. The emerald green that enveloped them was so vivid it almost hurt her eyes: ferns sprouting every which way down low, as if trying to caress her legs; moss cascading down from high up in branches; the earth beneath her feet, squashy and damp, like walking on a rain cloud. Orange and purple mushrooms popped up in clusters. Somewhere in the distance, an animal of indiscernible species called to its mate.

She asked, "This doesn't seem real, does it? It feels like we're in a surrealist painting. Have you ever seen anything so beautiful?"

Eric wriggled his eyebrows at her. "You."

"You sap," she ribbed, though she was secretly pleased, and not only because of the compliment. Eric had been acting strange since their arrival in Clancy, and he'd only been getting moodier. It was comforting to see him behaving lightheartedly.

In the time they'd been dating, he'd never once hidden the details of his schizophrenia from her—at least, she didn't *think* that he had—but lately she'd been wondering if he didn't sometimes downplay his symptoms, perhaps in an attempt to spare her from pitying him. Or save face. Eric, she'd found, had a lot of pride in this regard; he loathed the idea that anyone might feel sorry for him because of his illness, which he liked to think he had under control.

She believed that he did, typically, but she'd also been reading up on schizophrenia via online forums, and it seemed that a common complaint among sufferers was the sudden onset of depression. She suspected this could be the case with Eric, whether because of the ordeal he'd suffered through at Death Farm—*she* might have felt okay, but that didn't mean that *he* did or even should—or because he was simply despondent in general. She knew that she was unique in this regard, her ability to let most things roll off her back.

Whenever she'd tried to broach the subject with Eric during the last few weeks, he'd cheerfully assured her that he was fine, just fine. His actions lately, however, suggested otherwise. She'd felt him tossing and turning in bed next to her night after night, yet in the mornings, he'd pretended that he'd slept well.

What was more concerning was Eric's behavior in Clancy. He was upbeat when he was aware that he was in her sights, yet he allowed his expression to fall in relief when he believed she wasn't watching, as if he'd been wearing an uncomfortable mask of happiness that had been pinching his face. He'd been candid with her about recently switching his meds, so perhaps his odd behavior was a by-product of the adjustment.

It also could have been Clancy itself that was making him behave strangely. After watching the drunk kid get the daylights beat out of him by the bouncer the night before, as well as the standoffishness they'd been confronted with by every single person they'd encountered in town, she wasn't too fond of the place either. She was looking forward to heading to Seattle, where they'd hopefully face less hostility; she had to stop herself from counting down the hours, she was so eager to leave. If it wasn't for the natural beauty laid out before her now, she might consider their stay in Clancy a few days of vacation wasted. But, Eric seemed happier today, so she would take what she could get.

"You ready to get the show on the road?"

Eric jogged up to her side and playfully paddled her behind with both hands. "Let's hit it. I'll race you!"

"Whoa, there—you just simmer down, Flash!" She laughed. "We've got all day."

He winked at her. "I like to show off. Lead the way."

Her heart sank when the pinched look slowly returned to his face. She hesitated, wanting to ask if he was okay, ultimately deciding that she did not want to spoil the mood by quizzing him. Not yet, anyway. She began hiking up the sloping trail, already feeling her lungs tightening in exertion. Every so often she peeked over her shoulder to see how he was faring. He looked sweaty and ashen, as if he was struggling to keep up with her leisurely pace. "You good back there?"

He gave her a thumbs-up, his mouth spreading into another phony smile.

About a mile in on the trail, she could no longer stay quiet when he began massaging his temples. He squeezed his eyes shut, as if in real agony. "Are you okay?"

"All good!"

"It's not, though," she said, stopping. She rotated around and cocked her hip. Enough was enough. "You're as white as a sheet. What's going on—are you sick?"

He waved away her concern. "Okay, my head *might* hurt a little. Nothing to be concerned about, just a tiny migraine."

"I *knew* something was wrong. Do you want to go back to the car? I won't mind if you want to."

"Nah, I'm fi—"

CHAPTER 4

Eric was not fine.

The pressure in his head was so great that he felt as if his brains might squirt out his ears at any moment, like a geyser releasing built-up steam. He coughed, trying to get a handle on his breath, clawing at his neck as his throat started to close. He moaned, an ugly, startled sound.

"Oh my God!" Susan shouted from a galaxy away. "Eric!"

A terror like none he'd ever felt seized him as the world around him went pitch black. "I can't see!" he shrieked, crying out as he rubbed at his eyes and discovered them still open. "I've gone *blind*! Help me!"

"Hold on—I'm calling an ambulance!" And then: "*Shit!* I don't have any reception! I'm going back—"

"No! Don't leave me here! Don't leave—"

His knees gave out, and he dropped to the ground on all fours. He scrambled off the trail in a panic, his hands and knees going cold from the dank earth. The ground fell out from beneath him, his body pitching forward at a slope . . . and then he was tumbling, tumbling, shrubs lashing his face, branches clawing at his body, biting into his flesh. He groped every which way, grabbing fistfuls of air, his screaming mouth filling with moss and muck.

"Susan!"

His skull vibrated like a gong as he headbutted a tree trunk, halting his descent. He held his aching skull, dizzy and sick, hearing voices—an argument in the distance, getting louder, louder, as if he was tuned in to a staticky radio station far away but was quickly closing in on the tower.

(. . . *wasn't me! I swear I didn't do it!*)

(Quiet, you filthy beaner!)

Suddenly, he could see.

But it was all wrong—*he* was wrong.

He was down in a crater in the earth, gazing up at two men he did not know and could not recall ever meeting before in his life. This might have had something to do with their figures, which were blurry and shifting, like wet watercolors smeared by a paintbrush. Yet, he could sense them staring down at him coldly as he continued shouting up at them in a voice that was not his own.

(*Don't do this. Please!*)

He tasted blood, smelled it on his skin. He dabbed at his lip, and the tips of his fingers came away bright red. Fear strangled him as he noted that one of the men held a chain saw.

The other a rifle.

The man with the chain saw made a move to power up his machine and—

"Kill me first!" Eric screamed, back above ground in the real world. *His* world. He snapped his head back, blinking, his cheek wet with moss and tears, the earthiness in his mouth comingling with the raw tang of terror.

In the distance came Susan's frightened shouts. "Eric? Eric!"

"Here! I'm down he—"

Back in the hole, his sobs intensifying. He looked to the shape with the chain saw and clasped together two dark-brown hands that belonged to another man. He raised them as he fell to his knees.

(*Please, oh God, please! I'm begging you!*)

"Sorry, amigo, but there ain't no way around it," Rifle Man said with a snort. Unlike *his* own voice, the voices of his captors had an echoing, synthetic quality, as if produced by a machine. *Sorrrryyyyy, ammmmigooooo* . . . It was like seeing hallucinogenic-induced trails, but . . . inside his ears. He clutched at his head, dizzy.

(*Kill me first!*)

No-no-no, Eric thought dully.

(*Shoot me! Please, have mercy! Shoot me!*)

No! I want to *live*.

Soft mumbling from above, and then Rifle Man said to his partner, "Boss said no." Then, regarding the man in the crater who was Eric but also wasn't: "You're a snitch, Miguel. And snitches don't get last requests."

(*But I didn't do it! Whatever you think I did, I didn't do it! I swear to Christ! Don't make me die like this! I'll go crazy!*)

Chain Saw Man placed the machine at his feet and then made a move to seize the rifle, a Sailor Jerry–style pinup girl tattoo on his bicep peeking out from beneath his sleeve. It melted and swirled as he moved.

Rifle Man shrugged. "Doesn't matter either way to me. But it's your ass if anyone finds out." *Yooooooooooooour asssssssss* . . .

Chain Saw Man nodded and accepted the rifle. Eric, who hadn't attended a day of church in his entire life, began reciting the Lord's Prayer. In Spanish. The words felt foreign on his tongue, yet he was able to recite them flawlessly.

Chain Saw Man brought the rifle to his shoulder and aimed it down into the hole.

He closed his eyes.

Bang!

"Eric!"

Bang! Bang!

"Eric!"

Eric blinked up at Susan, who was crouching above him, poised to give his shoulders another shake. Her face was contorted into a helpless twist of terror. He groped at his chest, surprised to see that his hands came away blood-free. He wrapped his arms around her and pulled her close, his body trembling against hers.

"Are you hurt?" She pulled away, smoothing her hands down his face and body. "Anything feel broken? Can you see—you said you couldn't see?"

"Do you have any water?" he croaked.

She fished into her pack and hauled out a bottle before ripping the cap away and thrusting it at his lips. Her shaking hands spilled the first few sips down his chin. He took the bottle from her, swiping at his chin with the sleeve of his shirt. He felt better after a few gulps.

"I can see. I'm . . . I . . ." He made a move to sit up and then stand. "I actually feel *okay.*" He dusted off the seat of his pants, which was wet and caked with muck, and then looked himself over. "I'm not hurt. I might have a bump on my noggin tomorrow, but I'm fine. Totally fine." He let out a chuckle that sounded a little strangled. "Am I glad for *that!*"

Susan was staring at him like he was an animal she was afraid might take flight. "What *was* that?"

"You tell me. I was gone."

Susan frowned. "What do you mean, gone? Like fallen down the embankment?"

"No, I mean I was *gone*—like somewhere else . . . like I had jumped back in time or something. Like I was . . . in a different dimension."

Susan was fretting. He could practically see the light bulb dimming, brightening, dimming above her head. She seemed to be running through each response she could give, searching for the right words. She must have been having difficulty locating them, because she remained silent.

"Look, I know how crazy I sound."

"Do you?" she asked ever so slowly. "And I'm not saying that you *are* crazy—"

He barked out a harsh laugh, which did not help his cause, and she jumped. "But I *am* crazy, Susan!" He shook his head. "But not about this. I was *there*. I'd stake my life on it."

"Where? Help me understand. Because I'm not following you. *Whatsoever.*" She rubbed at her eyes; she was upset, understandably. And scared. "Is this . . . could this be your new meds? Are you having some kind of *episode* maybe?"

Could this be the case—*was* it his meds?

Medicating a schizophrenic, as every single doctor he'd seen had explained during the seventeen years he'd been living with the disease, was a delicate affair. Each sufferer reacted differently to the chemicals, so what worked for one schizophrenic might send another spiraling down into the deepest of depressions, or even exacerbate his or her symptoms to the point of psychosis. His new physician in Perrick had recently tweaked his medications because of the anxiety he'd been feeling, and he'd known when he'd agreed to come along to Clancy that he was taking a risk by traveling. If he'd had it his way, he would have waited a week or two to see how the new medications affected him before hitting the road. But, time and tide wait for no man, as the saying went, and so now here he was in Clancy with Susan, who was starting to look pretty anxious herself.

But, no, blaming his meds was bullshit. Would he be questioned as much if he wasn't schizophrenic? Doubtful.

"If I didn't know you better, I'd say you looked almost afraid of me," he said, surprised by the anger in his voice, which was merely a mask for the hurt he felt way down deep. He could take prejudice in stride from strangers and, on occasion, acquaintances, but not from the woman he loved. And he *did* love Susan; he'd known it for some time, yet hadn't mustered the nerve to tell her. He'd been left a little gun shy after his own brother had run off with his wife.

Now, it sounded as if *she* was the one getting angry. "I'm not afraid *of* you! Of course I'm not. But I'm not going to lie; I am afraid *for* you.

Eric, you have a legitimate disease. It's not your fault, and I'm not trying to blame you for any—"

"I don't think I'm explaining it right. It's like before, with . . ." He swallowed hard. "It's like when I started seeing Lenny Lincoln." Even now, he had a hard time discussing the boy, who'd been both his terrorizer and his savior. Though he'd mentally drawn a line through the experience, residual fright he suspected would never fully vanish still effervesced someplace down deep in his belly whenever his ghostly little friend's name was dropped.

Susan let out a long, throaty breath and sounded calmer as she asked, "Okay, in what way?"

"I'm trying to think where I should begin." He raked a hand through his hair, which had taken on a few twigs during the tumble. He plucked a leaf from a strand and watched as it swirled to the ground lazily. "Okay, do you remember when I told you a while back that I sometimes get a 'sense' of objects?"

"Like the steamer trunk Lenny was in?"

"Like that, yes. But also sometimes with other *things* too—recently, places."

"How so?"

"I sometimes get a sense when something bad happened in a specific location."

"Example?"

"I almost don't want to tell you, because it sounds so . . ." His bottom lip pulled down, exposing a row of teeth that were slightly crooked. "It makes me sound nuts, all right?"

"Try me."

"You asked for it. You know Davie's down on Fourteenth Ave?"

"That coffeehouse? Sure. It's been open in Perrick for as long as I can remember."

"Right, but did you know that there was a fire there back in the twenties—when it was an ice-cream parlor?"

She shook her head. "I had no idea."

"I didn't either. But—and here's where the nutty part comes in—when I started going there, I'd always get a tickle in my throat and smell smoke. The first time it happened, I actually asked the girl at the counter if they'd burned something in there. None of the staff had any idea what I was talking about. Nobody could smell it but me.

"The next time I went in there, the smell of smoke was stronger, and I could have sworn that I heard sirens, but they sounded far away. Then, the third and final time I went in there, the smell of smoke was so strong that I couldn't stand in line long enough to order coffee. I couldn't stop coughing—my eyes watered and I felt like I was choking, like I couldn't get enough air. Then, I heard the faint sound of screaming. A man and a woman."

Susan didn't say anything, so he kept going.

"After that third visit, I worried that—just like you suggested before—I might be getting sick. It's not uncommon for me to hear things even on a normal day, as you know, but I typically only *smell* things right before I have an episode," he explained. "But the funny thing was that I only smelled smoke *inside* Davie's. Plus, there were the physical symptoms, the coughing and watering eyes."

She asked, "Could it have been a type of psychosomatic response?"

"The thought *did* cross my mind. But, as soon as I was out on the street, all the physical symptoms disappeared, the screaming stopped, and I was perfectly okay."

She thought for a moment, as if trying to formulate a theory. "Maybe there's a type of coffee they're using that smells like smoke," she said in a tone that indicated that even she didn't buy what she was saying. "Maybe you're allergic to its smell. Like—what's that coffee?— Café du Monde. That stuff has chicory in it, doesn't it—could it be something like that?"

He was shaking his head before she'd finished talking. "I *drink* Café du Monde—the stuff is delicious. And, trust me—I'll take a coffee allergy over a schizophrenic episode any day."

"Hmm."

"For shits and giggles, I ran an internet search on Davie's, not really expecting to find anything. Imagine my surprise when I read that the building had burned down back in the day. What's spookier is that the owners died in the fire, a husband and wife."

"That's odd; I'll give you that," she said. "But why am I only hearing about this now? I've taken a leap of faith on you before, haven't I? I like to think that you know I'll always hear you out."

He shrugged. "Honestly, I kind of pushed it to the back of my mind. I had enough on my plate with teaching my classes, and then this all started happening around the time reporters started hounding me. And what was I going to do about it, anyway?"

"Sure, but you could have told me. You know I'm here for you—what's the point of me being your girlfriend if you don't talk to me about things?"

"I guess I didn't want to believe it myself. I always knew that I had a connection with antiques. At least I thought I did, but I never really took it to heart. Honestly, I assumed it was the sort of BS I told myself as a justification to keep buying more junk. Lately, though, I've started to suspect that I might actually have a . . ." He flapped a hand, annoyed. "I don't want to say *gift*, because it sounds so hokey—like I really *do* think I'm psychic, which I absolutely do *not*. But I don't know what else to call it. A *sense*, maybe."

Susan's eyebrows were almost to her forehead. "Are you saying that you don't think you have schizophrenia—"

"And that these visions are coming from elsewhere?" he finished for her.

"Yah."

"No. God, no. I'm not saying that *at all*. I will always be schizo-phrenic; there's no way around that. But, given what happened just now, and with everything that went down on the farm—plus a few other odd things I've noticed since then—I can't help but wonder if maybe my disease makes me, I don't know, *susceptible* to things more mentally sound people are incapable of detecting. Maybe I'm sensing—dare I say *spirits*—who have died but are maybe not at rest." He chuckled lightly. "Which, I don't even know that I *can* believe, being a scientist *and* an atheist. Thinking like that goes against everything I've come to believe and stand by in my adult life."

"You're saying that you have a sixth sense because of your schizophrenia?"

He couldn't help snickering at the expression on her face, which was incredulous to the point of being comical. "Okay, well it sounds nuts when you put it like *that*. All I'm saying is that I've been sensing things more strongly after what went down. It's like that whole experi-ence unleashed something inside my head that I didn't even know I'd been keeping locked up."

"So, what *did* happen just now?"

Eric quickly outlined what he'd seen down in the crater, starting with a description of the two men—as much as he could describe them with their blurred faces and the Sailor Jerry tattoo—and ending with how he'd recited a prayer he didn't know in a language he knew even less.

"And you experienced this through the eyes of somebody else?"

"That's right. A man named Miguel, who I believe is buried under there," he said, pointing to the tree stump he'd headbutted. "He was shot three times in the chest. There is no doubt in my mind that it happened. I can't tell you exactly *when*, but I get the feeling that it hap-pened very recently—maybe because of the vividness of my vision, or how quickly I'd been overtaken."

"You got a last name for Miguel? Or even the names of the men who were keeping you—him—prisoner?"

"Unfortunately, no. It was kind of like before with Lenny. And, I guess, with the fire-in-the-coffee-shop stuff," Eric said. "I've been thinking a lot about this, and the best explanation I can come up with is that maybe the dead don't communicate the same way as the living."

"How so?"

"Well, like with Lenny. He didn't come right out and say who killed him, or that two children were being held hostage. Instead, he showed me all kinds of things that I would've rather not seen—like his rotting horse, for example. And, at the time, I couldn't understand why I was seeing it. Later, though, it was the horsehairs that had been planted on the kids that helped lead you to the killer, and it all added up. And, like with the coffee shop, it was the smell of smoke and screaming that led me to investigate a fire."

Eric paused to take a sip of water.

"And, now, with this Miguel guy. Wouldn't it have just been easier for him to say: *My name is Miguel So-and-So. I was held hostage and murdered by two men, and their names are . . .* Why wouldn't he say that, if it meant finding his body and bringing his murderers to justice? He would, right? So the fact that he didn't tells me that maybe he *can't*. Maybe there's some cosmic law that prohibits the dead from coming right out and saying what's on their mind. If they could, think of how many open murder cases would be solved."

Susan nodded. "So, you're saying that the dead leave clues?"

"Sure, in a sense. But, I don't think they're doing it *consciously*, if you know what I mean. I think it's more of a necessity or a default mode, maybe because they're simply incapable of communicating the way the living do. Maybe because they fade in and out of existence, their concept of time and their thoughts—if they're capable of having thoughts—are jumbled. Or, maybe they're not 'ghosts' in the traditional sense, but rather imprints that have been left in space and time."

He broke off with a laugh. "I'm no physicist, so I wouldn't be able to describe it without sounding like a crackpot—although, with all this other stuff I'm saying, I might already be there."

"I don't think you're a crackpot," Susan said. "But, you have to admit, it is a little out there."

"Oh, it's more than *a little* out there. And, believe me when I say that you'd be hard pressed to find anyone on the planet who's a bigger skeptic about this"—he raised his hands and wiggled his fingers—"*woo-eee-whoo* stuff than me. At least, I used to be, until it started happening to *me*. As crazy as it all sounds, it would be crazier of me to continue ignoring these things when they're right in front of my face, or causing me to go blind, or leaving splinters under my nails, the way Lenny Lincoln did.

"Some of these things are probably of no consequence, like the coffee shop that burned down. Really, what am I supposed to do about that now? But, with the farm murders, just imagine if I would have ignored the clues Lenny had given me, those kids . . ." He broke off and shook his head. "What if there's a couple murderers out there who keep killing because I was so stubborn and close minded that I couldn't even *consider* that I might not know everything about the afterlife? Is my pride worth more than the deaths of innocent people?"

"Nobody knows what happens after we die. And anyone who claims to know is full of it, because the only way to know such a thing would mean being dead," she said sensibly. "So, I suppose it *is* good to keep an open mind."

"And this forest, it feels *wrong* to me. Despite its beauty, it feels . . . evil."

Susan began to walk the surrounding area, examining the foliage near the stump. "Do you happen to know when it rained last?"

"No clue, but it wouldn't be too difficult for us to find out." He took his phone out of his pocket and scowled. "Once we have cell reception."

"It *does* look like somebody has been up here recently, I'll give you that. The branches look broken, here, here, and here," she said, pointing. "And . . . oh my God."

"What?"

"Come over here and look at this!" She'd moved closer to the stump and was staring down at the ground directly in front of it. "You said there were two men, right? And one of them had a chain saw, which he set on the ground?"

Eric was seeing it too. Two sets of footprints, so large and flat that they could only be men's work boots, and . . .

"That's what I think it is, right?"

"Looks like it to me," he said, studying the chain saw imprint that had dried into the mud, teeth and all.

CHAPTER 5

Sitting at the top of 916 Glenham Avenue like a swear word delivered at the beginning of an offensive statement was a decrepit one-story ranch-style dwelling with curled shingles and white paint faded to the color of pus. The swear word in question was the home of Darla Manns, she of terrible taste in men and one vanished deadbeat boyfriend; the offensive statement was the rest of the fifteen or so ratty houses that continued down either side of the street, dead-ending at a vacant concrete lot that might have served as a garbage dump at some point in history.

Most of the lawns, enclosed in sagging chain-link fences, were littered with rusty barbecues and neglected toys: moldy pedal cars, flat-tired bikes, squashed soccer balls. The walkways boasted cracks deep enough to trip a person up if they didn't look down at their shoes as they strode. A shirtless, barefooted boy of about five stood in the yard of the third house down, its crown jewel a rickety old swing set with a disintegrated seat and broken chains that gave it all the appeal of a medieval torture device. In the house next door was a dog of indeterminate breed with an incessant bark thunderous enough to be heard from inside the van with the windows rolled up and the engine running.

Perhaps it was because Madison had insisted that they first stop by Darla's before heading downtown to embark on a much-anticipated Darkest Thrills tour, but Jake was not getting good vibes from the neighborhood. As she cut the engine, he rolled down the window to get some fresh air, the van still smelling of Madison's stinky menthol cigarettes, fast food, and stored-up farts from their journey up from Perrick. It seemed their funk had permeated the seats. He wasn't all too surprised to discover that the air outside smelled worse. An overflowing garbage can nearby clarified why.

He watched as the boy picked up a clod of dirt, lobbed it at the dog next door, and coughed as the wind blew it back into his face. He was doing it all over again a moment later with much the same result, as if coughing had wiped his short-term memory. A moment after *that* came an aggressive *Shut up, you worthless piece of shit!* shouted from the house with the dog, followed by a beer bottle hurled out the front door. Across the street, the "curtains"—two mismatched beach towels—jerked open, and out peeked a woman's snarling face, her hair screaming away from her scalp like she'd spent the morning sticking butter knives into light sockets. Wanting to know what all the blasted commotion was about. She could've been twenty-five or seventy; it was hard to tell with a mug like that.

Jake shook his head. "Holy shit," was about all he could think to say. That and, "Where *are* we?"

Beside him in the back seat, Chuck, the band's drummer, let out a whistle. "Hey, Mad, are you sure this chick is still here? This place looks as if it hasn't been lived in since . . ." He paused, presumably to think of something clever to say. "Since I lost my virginity."

"Oh, I think it's been abandoned *a lot* longer than a month," Jake cracked, and Chuck pulled a face at him.

"I've actually been dating your mom for *two* months," Chuck countered, and now it was Jake doing the facemaking.

"You guys are worse than two adolescent boys," Madison grumbled from behind the wheel.

True, they were behaving like children. They were tired from last night's show, grumpy from the bouncer's savagery they'd witnessed. That, and all the driving they'd done prior—630 miles from Perrick to Portland, Oregon, then another 250 miles from Portland to Clancy.

Why Madison had been so adamant about heading to Darla's *right away* and before the Kincaid tour, like it was some big emergency, was beyond him. Like a couple of more hours would have mattered.

But, her van, her rules.

"I'm sure. At least, this is the last address I have for her, and I *know* she doesn't have the money to move."

"Why would anyone want to ever leave this utopia?" Chuck said with a snort.

Madison made a move to get out but then hesitated, probably not wanting to be murdered by any creepers who might be lurking in the shadows. Or hit with flying beer bottles. "Anyone want to come with?"

"Take John."

At Chuck's suggestion, Madison and Jake both made a displeased *humph* sound. During the drive up there, John had been about as useful as a surfboard in the desert, having slept the majority of it. Even with the farty smell and the dog's barking, he now snored away blissfully in the front passenger seat, mouth gaping open and chin squelched against his neck in one of the least flattering poses any human could possibly make. The drive from the hotel to Darla's had taken less than ten minutes.

"We should leave him on the sidewalk," Chuck said with a wicked gleam in his eye. "Let him wake up in *this* hood at the stroke of midnight—that'll serve him right."

"We want to scare the guy, though, not kill him," Jake pointed out. "Who knows what would happen in this hellhole."

"Which is why I need someone to go with me," Madison said, turning around in the front seat so that she could face Chuck and Jake. She flashed them a sugary smile. "Any takers?"

Jake and Chuck played a quick game of rock, paper, scissors. "Dammit," Jake said and then exited the vehicle.

In Darla's yard—if a few patches of weeds, a frostbitten rosebush, and a random smattering of mismatched stones constituted a "yard"— Madison hissed, "Be nice!" as Jake recoiled, having barely sidestepped a petrified bird carcass. The house, missing about every other panel of siding, was even worse up close. Half the windows were cracked, the exposed concrete foundation was crumbling, and flecks of what was unquestionably lead paint were scattered all over the straw that had once been grass; eat some of that, and you'd be dead before you even realized you'd started dying.

Madison gave Jake a nervous smile and then rapped her knuckles on the splintery front door. "See, nobody's home," Jake said after two whole seconds had passed. "Can we go on the tour now?"

"Shhhhhhhhhh!" Madison shushed. "I think someone's coming."

The door cracked open, and an eyeball peered out at them. "Who is it?" a woman demanded, suspicious, as if it might be Death himself on her doorstep.

"Darla!" Madison squealed. "It's me! Open the door!"

The door did not open.

"It's Madison . . . from Perrick?"

Now, the door creaked open slowly, and there stood a living stick figure. Darla peered at the two of them distrustfully, her mud-colored brown eyes narrowing as she closed the door behind her and stepped onto the porch. "What are you doing here?" She twirled a flyaway strand of dishwater-blonde hair around an ear that jutted out from her skull with an effect that was almost cartoonish, because of how thin she was. She folded inward as Madison threw her arms around her while she awkwardly patted her friend's back in return.

"You didn't come to our show last night." Madison pouted.

"Oh." Darla frowned. "Yah . . . after I thought about it, I realized that I couldn't afford to go."

"I told you that I'd leave a free ticket for you at the door. And you know you could've put all your drinks on my tab!"

Jake imagined that Madison could have left fifty free tickets and a case of beer at the door, and Darla still wouldn't have shown. She hardly looked thrilled to see her old friend.

"Why did you come to my house . . ." She stepped back from Madison and peered down at Jake. "Hey, you're *short*."

And you're a walking scarecrow, Jake thought with some aggravation. Unfortunately, this wasn't the first time he'd encountered such bad manners. He opened his mouth, saw Madison give him a pleading look, and so he closed it.

Finally, he opted for sarcasm over indignation instead, which he'd found to be the best way to deal with the ignorant, who were often too stupid to understand that they were being mocked. "Am I? I haven't noticed!" He raised a hand to his heart and looked around dramatically. "Thank you for telling me."

She didn't laugh.

Darla peered at the houses behind them and then craned her neck so that she could see down the street. Jake turned around and saw movement behind the windows of a few of the homes that were still occupied. The ones that weren't appeared permanently deserted, with abandoned beater vehicles, tires rotted and flat, in a few of the driveways. He imagined half-eaten meals decaying on dinner tables and radios blaring with nobody to listen, as if the occupants suddenly walked out the front door one day and never returned. In a place like this, he could hardly blame them.

They were being watched. Some of the gawkers—like the scowling woman with the beach towel drapes—didn't bother to conceal their nosiness, as if they felt entitled to know the business of utter strangers. "*People* seriously need to get a life in this town," Madison said with obvious passive aggression and loudly enough that a few of the closer neighbors could probably hear. Darla shushed her.

She looks almost . . . worried, Jake thought. But why? Was she really that concerned with maintaining cordial relationships with what neighbors she did have? They didn't seem the types to get together for barbecues and block parties. Her distress only seemed to heighten once she spotted the van.

Madison seemed to notice too. "Oh, that's just the rest of our band," she said and gave Chuck a little wave. Thankfully, he smiled and waved back in lieu of offering up an obscene gesture, which he'd been known to do on occasion. Maybe he could sense their struggle on the front porch. "Don't worry—there'll be plenty of room for you."

Darla made absolutely no attempt to disguise her irritation. "Room for me? What are you talking about?" *Leave me alone. Go away,* her eyes said. If they didn't get out of there soon, it would be her lips expressing the same thing, and probably a lot less kindly. "Why are you here?"

"I've come to whisk you away!" Madison said in a cheerfully shrill voice that Jake only heard her use when she was acutely uncomfortable, like when fans—the male ones in particular—got weird with her back-stage after shows. At least she was on the same page as him now: their unannounced visit was not wanted or appreciated. It would have been worse—more embarrassing—if she *still* hadn't cottoned on.

"Away from what?" Darla asked, though Jake thought it was obvious. Look around, Toots.

Madison's smile strained. She looked to Jake, as if to seek help, and he looked back at her blankly. *You're on your own on this one. I wanted to go on the Darkest Thrills tour, remember? And didn't I tell you that ambushing Darla might be a bad idea?*

"I—we—came to help you move back to California. Remember all those times you told me that you wanted to come back?" Madison prompted.

"I never said that!" Darla snapped, peering nervously at the houses behind them. "You're talking *really* loud."

Jake had to disagree; to him it sounded like normal conversation. He was in a band, though, and musicians had notoriously bad hearing. Maybe she *was* yelling.

"We could go inside?" Jake suggested, though that was the last thing he wanted to do. If the outside looked this bad, what must the inside be like?

Darla gave him a look that would be more suitable had he suggested they hand out razor blade–laced candy to schoolchildren. She shook her head violently. "No, that's not a good idea."

Madison persisted, "If it's about the money, I can help. You wouldn't even have to pay me back—"

Darla opened the door and stepped into the house. "I can't go with you, I'm sorry. Please leave. Not just my house but Clancy." Her voice was nearly a whisper as she hissed, "It's not safe here for . . . tourists."

"Darla, if you'd just—"

"I'm sorry, I can't! You need to *go*!"

And at that, the door was slammed in their faces.

Madison's mouth dropped open, and she let out an incredulous breath.

"Geez," Jake said. "So . . . that went well. Talk about awkward. Are you sure we got the right house? That chick is your *old friend from way back when*, right, like she actually *knows* you? You didn't just choose this address randomly out of the phone book? Because she was acting like she hardly knew you."

Madison made a move to knock on the door, but then Jake seized her hand gently and pulled it back. He felt bad for his friend, as well as embarrassed for her, knowing how eager she'd been to bring Darla home. "I think she made her stance very clear. I'm not seeing a trip to California any time in her future, are you?"

"I don't understand. She always made it seem as if she was dying to get out of here. I thought she'd start packing her bags at the sight of me. I thought I was doing her a favor." She looked around pointedly. "Why would she *want* to stay here?"

"She's got dinner delivered right to her front door," Jake joked while pointing at the dead bird, hoping to lighten the mood.

"Shut up. Let's go." Madison was not amused.

CHAPTER 6

"I don't think just the two of us are going to be able to get it to budge," Susan said.

They'd been trying to move the stump from various angles for the past five minutes, with pitiful results. "This thing must weigh over a thousand pounds." She was reluctant to break the news because of how determined Eric was. But one of them had to speak up, or else they would have spent the whole day in the mountains killing themselves with fruitless exertion, until blood vessels in their faces burst and their backs snapped in half like branches.

"I know, you're right," he finally admitted. "What should we do, then?"

"I don't know how much good it'll do us, but we can go into town and make a report with the sheriff's department."

"Think they'll believe us?"

"Would you?" she asked and then pursed her lips. "But that doesn't mean we can't try."

"We also have the photo I took of the footprints," Eric said. "If they need proof."

That's some flimsy proof, she thought, but said nothing. They remained silent for most of the hike back.

"Think we should say something to the band? I can call Jake," Eric said once they reached the Jeep.

Susan mulled it over and then said, "Better not. They'll be getting ready for Seattle, and I don't really see the point." *And I want to spare you the embarrassment,* she thought. While she had no doubt that Eric *believed* he'd seen what he had, she wasn't wholly positive that a dead man named Miguel with three bullets in his chest was buried underneath a stump in the forest he'd just happened to blindly stumble upon. Literally.

Sure, he *had* been right about a lot of things at Death Farm. At the time, his claims hadn't seemed that far fetched, as they'd turned out to be accurate, for the most part. Weeks later in retrospect, though, it all seemed so . . . coincidental?

She felt ashamed for thinking doubtful thoughts about the man she loved. He'd always had her back, and he'd believed her about a lot of unbelievable things. He was her boyfriend, and that's just the sort of things boyfriends did. But, now that he needed her, she wasn't returning the favor. Some gratitude.

There was always the possibility, however slight, that he could be right about the stump. She couldn't see the harm in filing a report, if only to make him feel better. The footprints and saw indentation were one hell of a coincidence, though; she had to give him that.

"They're probably on a Dylan Kincaid tour, anyway," he said. "I think that's where Jake said they were going. I wonder if our buddy, Ben Harper, will get weird on them too."

"John's pretty weird, so they'll probably get along well."

Eric smiled. "Good point."

"How about this: If the sheriff's department comes up with anything substantial, we'll tell Jake. Until then, we'll keep it between us?"

"Deal."

Twenty minutes later, they were pulling up in a desolate parking lot that housed only a single unit, an L-shaped modular block with a long ramp that ran up its side. It made Susan think of the sort of structure a fly-by-night telemarketing firm would use to sell nonexistent insurance policies as a ploy to steal identities. With just a small single window, it was painted a nondescript taupe color, and at the ramp's base was a handwritten sign made out of the backside of a used manila envelope. **PUBLIC OFFICIALS' OFFICES:** DEPARTMENT OF TRANSPORTATION, SHERIFF'S DEPARTMENT, FISH & GAME, FORESTRY, it read. All arrows pointed in the same direction, to a single door at the top of a ramp that was propped open with a large rock.

"Kind of low rent, don't you think?" Eric said grimly. "Is this normal for these types of offices?"

"This place makes Perrick PD look like Buckingham Palace," she mumbled under her breath, cognizant that someone could be listening. They were making the only noise in the entire parking lot, which sat off a similarly quiet road. That was small towns for you. "And, no, I've never seen anything like this—having federal and state officials working together out of a *trailer* is just plain weird."

"And so many different departments." Eric tapped the envelope. "But the sign sure is fancy."

"This is like something you'd hang up on a telephone pole to advertise a garage sale," she said with a quiet snicker.

"Let's get this over with and get out of here. Seattle can't come soon enough."

During the drive over, they had decided to keep things simple as far as their story was concerned.

Which meant lying.

It had been Eric who'd been first to suggest that the truth would paint them as lunatics. She hadn't argued. She'd been worried about the same thing and had been relieved when he'd broached the subject first. Unlike Eric's mortifying visit to Perrick PD back during the farm murders, here there would be no talk of psychic dreams or even borderline crackpot gut feelings. They had a straightforward cover story, and they'd made a pact to stick to it.

The inside of the building was a single sprawling room. Several desks were placed sporadically throughout the space, with old metal filing cabinets used as makeshift dividers. There was only one employee present, a handsome lad of about twenty-five who wouldn't have looked out of place fronting a boy band. Eric lightly nudged Susan with his elbow when he saw her admiring his gym-toned physique as he trotted toward them from the opposite end of the room in a forest ranger's uniform that was so tight fitting that it was almost camp. The fabric probably would have ripped clear from his bulging biceps if he'd sneezed.

"What?" she whispered innocently.

"Give the guy a stereo and a thong, and he could be a strip-o-gram," he muttered and then gave her a peep of a smile to show that he was only teasing. Eric was far from the jealous type, which Susan appreciated.

"How can I help?" Mr. Park Ranger 2019 asked. He appeared a good fifteen to twenty years older up close than what Susan had previously estimated, with an easy smile and intelligent eyes. His name tag read P. Clausen.

"I'm not sure we're in the right place," Eric said, looking around at the empty space.

"Oh, I bet you are, I'm afraid. It's pretty ragtag, isn't it?" Clausen said and then winked. His voice had a soft, calm twang—possibly Southern—that caressed the ears like pure cashmere, and he exuded the sort of disarming energy that puts one instantly at ease. Susan liked him, and she could tell that Eric did too.

"No comment," Eric said and let out a laugh that was genuine, which further relaxed her. He didn't seem like he was tottering on the brink of another episode—which, though unaware of it, she'd been fretting about because of how abruptly the last one had seized him.

"We had a big fire here in town," Clausen explained about the space. Susan asked, "When?"

"Oh, it was about four months ago, down on Pitts Court. Wiped out most of the block, including four separate government buildings, which was where we all"—his arm swept out at the desks as he said this—"used to work."

"I never heard about it," Susan commented. "The fire."

"Why would you have? I'm guessing you two aren't from around here," Clausen said easily. "Though you do seem kind of familiar. You guys aren't actors or anything?"

Both Eric and Susan chuckled and shook their heads. "Far from it," Eric said. "It sounds like you aren't from around here either."

"Nope. Born and bred Texan, but we all have crosses to bear, don't we? Had just accepted the transfer when the fire took place, if that isn't rotten luck—not so sure I would have been so keen to get up this way, had they told me I'd be working out of a trailer. Anyway, if you've been touring around, you've probably seen that we aren't exactly a metropolis here in Clancy. Which is fine. I'm from Dallas, and the whole reason I moved was to acquaint myself with *real* nature—that and the cheap house prices—but it's also a nuisance when you've got two dozen or so displaced government employees. This is the best they could find on such short notice. It was *this* or the county library, and I don't want to imagine how unfun it would be, having those librarians shushing us all day."

"But where is everybody?" Eric asked.

"Until they repair the fire damage—and Lord knows when that's finally going to happen, I'll probably be retired by then—most everyone is working remotely from home. Everyone on the low end of the totem pole, that is. Those of us with seniority have to come and work in this box all day, which is strange, right, because you think it'd be the other way around? I don't mind too much, though, because I'm usually out in the woods. We try to make it so that we aren't all here at the same time, since it can get stuffy—have you ever tried making a phone call when there's six other people in the room yammering all around you?"

"Can't say that I have," Susan said. The guy could sure *talk*, but she found that she didn't mind so much. His lulling voice had the easy hypnotic effect of a rocking chair. He would have killed it in a career reading children's audiobooks, she thought. Had she been five years old, she would have been curled up in a ball at his feet, snoozing.

As if reading her thoughts, he said, "I guess it's about time that I ask why you're here. Pardon my chattiness—I work by myself about ninety percent of the day, so I get excitable when there's real live *humans* to talk to."

Eric and Susan waved off his worry. "We're here to report a possible crime," Eric said.

"A crime? You probably want Sheriff Stogg, then. Neal should be back any minute—I'm actually waiting for him, too, so I can head back out into the woods. His desk is just across from mine, if you want to come and have a seat."

They followed Clausen and then sat down at the two chairs in front of Sheriff Stogg's desk. "You guys hungry?" Clausen asked. "Got some Twizzlers in my desk. No promises on how fresh they are."

Susan was about to tell him no thank you for the both of them (Eric loathed licorice, as did she) when a hard-looking large man with a dour face came stomping through the door, making the trailer's hollow floor vibrate under their feet. He frowned when he saw her and Eric. *Please don't let this be—*

But then she clocked the name tag: Stogg.

He sat down heavily in the squeaky metal chair behind his desk, casting his wrapped sub sandwich—it smelled like meatball—aside with a thump. "Guess lunch'll have to wait," he said disappointedly, not quite looking at them, as if they'd come in to file a report for the sole purpose of spoiling his meal. A few beats of awkward silence later, he asked Eric, "What can I do for you?"—ignoring Susan altogether.

So, he's one of those, she thought. *This'll be fun.*

He was far too young to exhibit such apathy toward the public. Usually career law enforcement waited until at least fifty before they let the cracks show through their deep-seated hatred of the job and for humanity in general. This delightful soul looked as if he was only in his late thirties.

"*We're* here to report a potential crime," Susan said.

Now he looked her way. He had a jowly, droopy-eyed face that likened him to the bulldog breed. "Potential? Either it is a crime or it isn't."

She half expected him to tack on *sweetheart* at the end of his statement, but he only sat staring at them disinterestedly. His gaze shifted, and he eyeballed the sandwich like he was entertaining fantasies of making sweet love to it. He fingered the edge of its wrapper, sighed.

She gave Eric a nudge, and he began providing Stogg the song and dance they'd concocted in the car on the way over. The outcome was the same—dead man in a hole—but how they reached it . . . well, that was a different story entirely.

"So, just before our hike, I went into the bathroom at the foot of the trail. I was in the last stall, you know, taking care of business, when these two guys came in, having a conversation. From the way they were talking, I could tell they were bad news."

"How could you tell? What were they saying?" Stogg asked.

Susan was impressed by how smoothly Eric answered. "You know, like drug stuff, robberies—bragging about some guy they mugged a couple months back."

Stogg glanced down at the notepad on his desk and clicked his pen, though he didn't write anything down. "Go on." He sounded as defeated as a stowaway walking the plank toward shark-infested waters. He stared at his lunch longingly.

"They started talking about a body they'd buried off the trail in Mugachopee National Forest, which was where we were."

"A *dead* body?"

No, a live one—what else, you moron? Susan thought scornfully.

Eric leaned back in his chair. "I assume so. I didn't ask them for clarification or anything—"

"I got it!" Clausen whooped behind them from his desk, causing Stogg, Susan, and Eric to start.

Stogg groped his chest. "Christ, Clausen, why'd you have to shout like that?"

Clausen ignored the sheriff. "I figured out where I know you two from! You're *her*. You're the cop who saved those kids—*and* brought down a serial killer." He looked to Eric, snapped his fingers, and pointed. "And you helped. Stogg, we've got ourselves a couple of big shots here! Well, I'll be!"

Normally, Susan would have changed the subject, but the look on Stogg's face was too priceless. He no longer looked as if he was famished; he looked like a man who'd accidently smashed his thumb with a hammer because he hadn't been paying attention to what he was doing. "That's right," Susan said, more to Stogg than to Clausen, the subtext being: *In your face.*

"The FBI publicly thanked her too," Eric said, beaming with so much pride that it made her blush.

"I didn't recognize you two," Stogg said quietly. "But I'm familiar with the case."

"Guess that goes to show that you never know *who* you're talking to, doesn't it?" she replied with the thinnest of smiles.

"He's supposed to be clairvoyant or something, right?" There was no mistaking Stogg's feelings on *that* subject, given the way he'd said *supposed to be.* Not surprising. He didn't strike her as the type to give credence to matters of the otherworldly.

"I'm not supposed to be anything," Eric commented.

Susan shook her head as something dawned on her. She turned around and asked Clausen, "You're federal, right, as a forest ranger?"

"Correct. Got me a gun and everything." *Everythang.*

Susan got to her feet and prodded Eric to do the same. "Actually, I think we should be talking to *him*, then," she said to Stogg. "Because this is a body buried in Mugachopee National Forest. That's federal land, if I'm not mistaken?"

"This okay by you?" Stogg asked Clausen, who was already on his feet and ushering them over. He couldn't get rid of them soon enough.

After running through the standard bevy of questions typically asked about Death Farm—*How did you become involved? What are you working on now? Were you really almost killed?*—all of which Susan side-stepped with the standard "We're not really allowed to talk about it," P.

"Call me Pete!" Clausen got down to business. Unlike Stogg, he showed enthusiasm, and it appeared as if he was taking them seriously. Or, at the very least, he was willing to hear them out. He took several notes.

Eric outlined how the criminals in the bathroom detailed where the body of a man they called Miguel was buried.

"That's strange, isn't it?" Clausen commented. "That they discussed the exact spot the body was buried?"

Eric didn't skip a beat. "They'd forgotten to conceal their tracks. Guess they realized it once they'd already left," he said with a shrug. "So, they had to go back and do it. They were debating, a little, about where the body was buried. Finally, they agreed on the spot."

Clausen seemed to buy it.

"Show him the photo," Susan said, and Eric presented the photo of the footprints and the chain saw indentation.

Clausen gazed upon it with grave interest. "Wait a sec. If they were going back to conceal their tracks, how come these marks are still there?"

That, she and Eric had not discussed. It was so obvious—how had they not caught such a large hole in their story?

After a pause, Eric said, "I honestly don't know. Come to think of it, one of them did get a call as they walked out of the bathroom, so maybe they got called away."

"Hmm, could be," Clausen said. He peered at Eric suspiciously. "You didn't get one of your—whatcha call 'em—*feelings*, like you did with those kids in California?"

Susan was taken aback. The man was sharp. And scarily accurate.

Stogg sighed loudly. He was having none of that.

Eric smiled pleasantly. "No, no, nothing like that. I can assure you that I'm not clairvoyant, or whatever it is that they've been saying."

"But everything you did—"

"Was just a series of really good hunches," Eric said and then gave the remaining details.

There had been a moment when Susan feared that he might slip up and mention the thug's bicep tattoo—he wouldn't have had a way of seeing it from the bathroom stall—but he omitted it. The whole story sounded pretty flimsy to her ears, but Clausen didn't seem to question it. They could have said that they'd been transported there on flying pigs and he probably would have believed it, he was so excited by their Death Farm affiliation.

Stogg questioned it enough for the both of them. "That's pretty lucky, isn't it? All those tree stumps out there, and you two just happened upon the right one—with footprints, no less." There was a string of mozzarella stuck to his chin.

"And a chain saw indentation," Clausen added. He seemed to be trying to wind up Stogg, and it was working. Susan suspected that he liked the sheriff about as much as they did.

Stogg shook his head. "And what does *that* prove? Everyone has a chain saw in these parts. You have one; I have one; every forester, logger, and fireman for fifty miles has one. Hell, my eighty-year-old granny Pearl has one—maybe she's got a couple bodies buried out in the forest too."

"Eat your sandwich, Stogg," Clausen said, quietly apologizing to Eric and Susan for the sheriff's behavior. "You know, you turn into a real pill when you're hungry." Stogg, Susan saw with a surreptitious glance, had already plowed through half a foot!

After he finished filling out a report, Clausen said, "Wondering if you two might want to accompany me into the forest to go have a look? I don't think I'll ever be able to find the right stump without you guys being there to point it out, despite this handy-dandy—and very detailed—map you've drawn me, Susan. You could have a second career as a cartographer, you know that?"

She laughed.

"Anyway, call it an occupational hazard, but if you've seen one stump, you've seen them all."

Eric and Susan exchanged a quick nod. "Sure, we don't have to be in Seattle until tomorrow afternoon," Eric said. "We marked the spot to turn off the trail with a pile of rocks, but I guess it'd be tricky to see if we weren't there to show you exactly where. What I'm worried about is *how* we're going to get the stump *up*. We tried to move it, and it was like trying to lift an elephant. There's no way just the three of us will get it to budge."

Clausen shook his head. "You're right; that won't work. You said the hole was deep, right? I'll just cut a wedge from the stump—at least that way we can look down inside to see if these two hoods in the bathroom were telling the truth about placing a body in the hole. For all we know, they might have realized that you were in the bathroom, and so they started messing with you."

Susan appreciated that Clausen's doubt rested on the two criminals and not on her and Eric. "So, you actually believe us?"

"I see no reason *not* to believe you, and I can't imagine what either of you two would have to gain by coming in here with this story. I don't know if we're going to actually *find* anything under this stump . . ." Clausen shrugged. "But, given your track record, I don't see what it could hurt. If it were *me* under there, I'd want somebody to come looking for me. But there's just one problem."

"What's that?" Eric asked.

Clausen tapped his watch. "It's already pretty late in the day to go trekking out into the forest. And it wouldn't be the safest thing, running a chain saw in the dark."

"That's the most sensible thing you've said all day," Stogg commented behind them. Susan didn't need to turn around to see that his mouth was full of the potato chips she'd heard him munching on.

Clausen made a sour face. "*Anyway*, you said you don't need to be in Seattle until tomorrow afternoon. Would you be able to meet me at Mugachopee in the morning? Is six thirty too early for you?"

It wasn't.

CHAPTER 7

Eric had told Susan that she was nuts for wanting to go to the gym after the day they'd had, but a hard workout was exactly what she needed to help put her agitated soul at ease. Plus, loving herself a good bargain, she didn't want to let the two free passes from Ben Harvey go to waste. That simply would have been criminal.

She'd taken Madison, a fellow gym junkie (despite her "occasional" cigarette), with her, as Eric had scoffed rather disagreeably when she'd asked him to come along—his exact words had actually been: *I'd rather stick my head in the toilet and give it a couple of flushes.* She was relieved when Madison headed straight for the cardio machines once they left the locker room, as she was eager to lift weights in silence and without the worry of having to make small talk. She liked Madison well enough, but she wanted to be alone with her thoughts, especially the negative ones she'd been keeping buried at the pit of her mind. It was time to dig them up and confront them so that they could be dealt with and purged—so that she could finally move on from the painful memories that had been haunting her, despite her pretending that she already had.

What had been weighing heaviest on her psyche was what had happened when she'd returned to the job after her ten-week sabbatical.

She hadn't gone into the station that day anticipating a banner, cake, balloons, and marching band to commemorate her return; she was not three years old, and truth be told, she found such attention a little embarrassing. Still, despite her desperation to return to business as usual, she'd felt that getting *something* would have been nice. A small gesture, if only the teensiest welcome. Because it had started to feel as if she had never left, as if nobody cared that she was back *at all*.

Then, she'd realized that wasn't entirely correct. A few of her coworkers *were* providing their own version of a special greeting: dirty looks, an incredulous shake of the head, snide remarks whispered under their breath. She kept a pleasant smile pasted to her lips, acting as if she wasn't noticing any of it, but internally she was seething. Though she had been mentally prepared for the hostility, no part of her had truly *expected* it. These men and women weren't merely her coworkers; they were also her friends.

At least they *had* been.

But that was before Death Farm.

Feeling herself going tense from the shameful memories, Susan began her warm-up. She stretched her tightly coiled muscles, taking pleasure in the pain that the exertion provided. It felt good to let loose inside her own mind, unhindered by the facade of happiness she so often felt she had to maintain in front of others, so as to not worry them.

So that they wouldn't worry about *her*.

Her mind drifted back to Perrick PD.

She felt that her brothers and sisters in blue had a right to know what had happened on that fateful night on the farm, but she'd been forbidden by higher-ups at Perrick PD from expanding on the specifics of the human casualties. Lives had been lost, yet she couldn't say how or why, which pissed off *a lot* of people— most everyone she knew, to be specific. She needed to keep mum, they'd said, to protect the integrity of the department's good name, as well as the reputations of all those involved.

Susan had kept her word about remaining tight lipped, which had not endeared her to her coworkers, who equated her silence with guilt.

These were not stupid people; they'd seen her blood-soaked uniform in evidence lockup, and they knew that *something* untoward had taken place on the farm. Given the smallness of the station, snippets of information had slipped through the cracks here and there, and when no information was provided, they'd found ways to fill in the gaps for themselves. Gossip had the tendency to spread like wildfire among police officers, a group whose bond was so tight it was almost incestuous.

Her commanders didn't seem to *care* that people around town—people who'd known her since she was a baby—now acted as if they hated her, that the press painted her as uncooperative, that her fellow officers didn't trust her. As long as their dirty little secrets were safe—that was the bottom line. And she'd gotten official accolades from the FBI, so why make a fuss?

After the hubbub had finally started to die down, they'd extended Susan the offer—"offer" being an indirect order that she'd been compelled to accept—of a leave of absence. To "clear her mind and reboot," they'd said, as if she were a computer on the fritz. They felt to do this would take approximately three months, a time length she'd initially balked at, but ultimately agreed to.

She'd completed just one month of her sabbatical before she started to go stir crazy. By month two, she was practically tearing her hair out. She toughed it out for two more weeks before throwing in the towel. After the way she'd been treated on the first and only day that she'd been back, she was starting to think that they'd been right in telling her to disappear.

It wasn't as if she missed being a cop, not really. She'd never be so indulgent as to use a term like *existential crisis*, but her excitement toward crime fighting *had* waned—probably something to do with the betrayal by the force she felt, never mind nearly being slain on the job. What had and continued to burn Susan was that, while her bosses were pretending to have her best interests in mind, the leave of absence she'd had forced upon her had less to do with her recuperation than it did with them saving face. Her presence at the station and around town as a representative of Perrick PD inspired the asking of questions, none of which they were keen to answer.

Now good and fired up, Susan left the warm-up area and went to the section with the free weights. She must've been wearing a hard expression, because Madison gave her a puzzled look when their gazes met. Susan flashed her a smile and a thumbs-up, though her mind was still back in Perrick.

Questions. How there'd been so many damn questions about the case. Questions sly acquaintances found ways to slither into idle chit-chat at the grocery store, the gas station, the post office: *Well, hello, Susan, almost didn't see you standing there! How are you—good, that's good. Say, far be it from me to bring up any bad memories, but I heard you were almost murdered by a serial killer? Oh, it's fine if you don't want to talk about* that, *but I'm also wondering if you might know what* really *happened to Police Chief Ed Bender—and why Perrick PD is working so gosh-darn hard to keep the details of his death quiet? Sure, sure—you can't discuss it, but can you at least tell me what it's like working with a psychic? Can't you tell me* anything *at all?*

Her own mother had been treating her as if she were a fragile porcelain doll, as if one word spoken in the severest of tones would shatter her spirit and send her spiraling down to the blackest depths of existence. Harsher individuals who'd lost their faith in her seemed to feel as if her calm demeanor was merely a front, that it was only a matter of time before she snapped and lost it on the first unlucky individual who happened to accidentally bump into her on the street.

So, she wondered resentfully, *Which is it: Am I delicate or dangerous?*

Delicate be damned, she snarled internally, and then she added more weight to her last set of bench presses. When she was finished, she racked her weights and went to check in with Madison, who was ambling to a stop on the treadmill.

"Perfect timing! Just finished my cooldown," she said, her voice still sounding scratchy from the show. Susan didn't know how the girl did it; she was such a tiny thing, but her voice could fill the Grand Canyon. They headed toward the locker room to collect their things.

On their way toward the exit at the front of the gym, Susan inadvertently knocked a mop out of the janitor's bucket as she threw her gym bag over her shoulder. It hit the floor with a clatter and spilled half the water out of the bucket, causing Madison, caught off guard, to let out a loud squeal. Susan blushed to the color of beetroot, since half the people in the place were now gawking in their direction.

A gigantic man who stood a full foot taller than Susan came out from a small supply closet hidden behind the front desk. He walked with a pronounced limp, and with speech that was slurred, he cried, "Oh no! Pardon me, please! Pardon me!"

"I'm so sorry," Susan apologized, making a move to clean up. She felt particularly bad, as she sensed that he might be mentally challenged.

"Pardon me!" the janitor repeated. His name tag read Big Ian. He shook his head hard when Susan seized the mop. "It's my job. I clean and I cook and I get money. I'm good at my job, and I don't need help."

Cook, Susan wondered, *at the gym?* Maybe he had two jobs. "No, of course you don't," Susan smiled and handed him the mop. "I'm sorry for making a mess for you, Big Ian—that's you name, is it, Big Ian?"

"Yep." The man nodded and brought his thumb to his chest. "That's me. I'm the janitor."

Right away, Susan was struck by the redness of the skin on his hands. He'd been burned badly, and very recently. "May I see your hands?" she asked.

Big Ian shrugged, set the mop aside, and held out his hands for Susan to examine. She nearly let out a cry when she saw the extent of the damage that had been done to them. Several dime- and quarter-size blisters covered his palms and fingers, and the skin on the back of his hands had been scorched down to the dermis. He flinched when she made a move to touch his wrist.

"Doesn't that *hurt*?" Madison asked, sounding on the verge of passing out. She fanned her face with a hand woozily. "I'm sorry . . . I'm not good around this . . . stuff."

Susan saw that she was not exaggerating, as her skin was the color of custard. "Go have a seat," she said gently, and Madison quickly made her way to a nearby bench. She turned her attention back to Big Ian. "This looks like a chemical burn. How did this happen?"

"I don't want to say." Big Ian looked around nervously, pulled his hands away. "I can't talk about it."

"I saw him go into the pool area earlier," Madison said, holding her face in her hands. "Could it have been the chemicals—chlorine or whatever they use?"

Susan asked, "Did you burn your hands on the pool chemicals? Is that why you don't want to talk about it—because you think you'll get into trouble? If it was an accident—"

"No!" he yelled. "I'm good at my gym job! Everyone says so."

"I'm sure you are." Sensing his agitation, she carefully reached out toward his hands, moving at a snail's pace, so as not to spook him. "I'm a police officer. I've been trained in first aid. If you want, I could clean and wrap your hands—"

"No police! No! Don't you touch me!" he screamed.

Susan recoiled. "Okay, okay. It's all right." Now they had the attention of the entire gym. People were stopping exercise bikes and setting down weights to get a better view of the show.

A middle-aged blonde woman came running out from an office near the front check-in area. Her name tag revealed only her title, not her name: General Manager. She glared at Susan. "What's going on here? What did you say to him? Ian, are you okay?"

The janitor wouldn't meet her eyes.

Susan, who'd been confronted by countless angry and irrational individuals while on the job, calmly explained, "I'm not trying to cause trouble, only help him. See? He has severe chemical burns on his hands, so I was offering to—"

"We can take care of our own here."

"Clearly not," Madison retorted from the bench, which did not help matters whatsoever.

Susan was about to say something constructive to hopefully diffuse the tension, when the woman screwed up her face and snapped, "I don't recall asking *you* to join this conversation, Ms. *La-di-da*."

Madison's mouth dropped open. Looking at Susan, she shook her head as if to say, *The nerve of this woman!*

"Is Ben Harvey aware that you treat people this way?" Susan asked.

This pulled her up short. "What do you know of Ben Harvey?" Her face was still indignant, yet underneath the anger, her voice was cautious.

Madison answered for her. "I know that he probably wouldn't want you speaking to his customers this way." Susan imagined that Madison was only speculating—actually, it was more like she was outright pretending to know the man more than she actually did, given that they'd met just the one time for the tour he'd given the band. But who was she to contradict her? "Especially as the general manager. What kind of place are you running here, anyway? Your employee is all burned up, yet you want to stand here, arguing with us, instead of getting him the help he clearly needs."

The woman looked over the gym, the rubberneckers quickly turning their attention elsewhere when she frowned at them. Quietly, she said, "Look, I'm sorry. You're right. It's been a stressful day and . . ." She shook her head, flapped a hand. "Ian, come with me. We'll get you fixed up." She put her arm around the janitor and began leading him toward her office. When she was nearly there, she looked over her shoulder and said to Susan and Madison, "If you don't mention this to Ben, I'd be grateful. I was having a bad day, and I shouldn't have taken it out on you. Again, I'm sorry."

Merrily, Madison said, "Our lips are sealed."

The woman glanced at the workout room, her expression fretful. She gave the pair a small ironic smile, as if to say: *Let's hope theirs are too.*

CHAPTER 8

The first time Eric got a sinking feeling in the pit of his chest was when Pete Clausen pulled into the parking lot of Mugachopee National Forest in his official ranger vehicle.

The problem wasn't the hour; Pete had been so considerate as to arrive at 6:25 a.m., five minutes earlier than their agreed-upon time, offering them two beeps of the horn and a jovial wave before he parked. It wasn't the weather, which was overcast but mild enough that it did not leave them chilled to the bone. It was the passenger frowning out at them from behind the windshield.

Their new skeptical friend—

"Sheriff Stogg," Susan said. "Wonderful."

"Why'd he bring him?" Eric asked, unable to disguise his displeasure. He didn't care if Stogg saw him frowning; he was merely returning the favor.

"Guess we're about to find out."

The two men got out of the vehicle, but it was only Clausen who stopped to greet Eric and Susan, carrying the chain saw he'd promised to bring. Stogg walked directly to the base of the trail, only turning around once he realized they weren't following. "The stump's this way, right?" he asked sullenly. *What's the holdup?* his tone implied. *Let's get this over with.* Maybe he had a sandwich waiting for him back at the office.

"That's right, Stogg," Clausen called cheerily, beckoning Eric and Susan forward. Quietly, he said to the couple, "Sorry about sourpuss up there. His wife left him, I hear, so he's been a little down in the dumps as of late. But I had to bring him along, professional courtesy and all. I'm sure you understand what that's like, Officer Marlan. Always got to be on the lookout for toes you want to avoid stepping on."

Susan smiled. "Don't I ever. And call me Susan. I'm not up here in any official capacity, which you know."

They set out on the trail, which looked vastly different from the last time they'd been there, even if it had only been the day before. It felt different too. The squishy earth made squelching sounds underneath their boots, the small puddles they tramped upon wetting pant legs. "Did it rain last night?" Eric asked.

"It *always* rains up here," Stogg answered. He was huffing and puffing, but he did not break stride. Too much pride, Eric thought. The man would rather keel over dead than admit to weakness. Unlike ultra-fit Clausen, whose body fat percentage was probably that of a slab of marble, Stogg could've stood to lose a few pounds. It was far too easy to imagine him holed up in the ICU with a heart attack within the next ten years, sooner if he was a heavy drinker, as the broken capillaries scattered around his nose suggested he was. "It stormed for a couple hours last night—a pretty big one too. Started in the middle of the night, around two. Took out some power lines; half the town's without electricity."

"Did you lose power at your hotel?" Clausen asked, and Eric and Susan said no.

Stogg glared back at them and grunted, as if they were spoiled brats, these *outsiders* living high on the hog with lights and heating while the locals had to suffer—visiting royals spitting down on the commoners from an ivory tower.

"I think the E-Z-Sleep Motel might have a backup generator," Eric said defensively, and Susan shot him a weird look.

Maybe he *was* hearing a tone that wasn't there only because he was quickly growing to dislike the man. It wasn't his dour attitude that irked him; it was that he was letting his personal problems affect his attitude *on the job*. Eric had always prided himself on keeping both separate— business from personal—as a way to manage his schizophrenia, and he didn't consider himself special in any way. So, if *he'd* been able to maintain his professionalism (for the most part) during a particularly nasty split from his wife, Stogg should be able to as well.

Eric also wasn't much of a morning person—some, like Susan, might even say he could be cranky—especially at this ungodly hour. Any time before 8:00 a.m., and he couldn't guarantee a sunny disposition, or even a halfway agreeable one. As consolation, he imagined that the band would be feeling worse than he did this morning; he'd noticed earlier that Madison's van was still gone when they'd left to meet Clausen. That must've been some night out on the town. He shuddered to think of the hangovers they had coming their way.

But you're not just tired and irritated by the sheriff, a voice spoke up inside his head. *There's something else upsetting you, isn't there?*

Is there? Eric wondered.

You know you're being watched. You can feel it.

But watched by whom—Clausen and Stogg? Susan?

They see everything, even when you think you're alone. They're always watching, watching. Eyes are everywhere.

Whose eyes?

He ground his jaw sideways and cleared his nose with a harsh snort. His hands twitched at his sides, fingertips drumming the tops of his thighs. His gaze darted to and fro.

He felt . . . anxious yet uncomprehendingly exhilarated. He never wanted the feeling to end—he wanted more, more.

You're high. That's what you are. Best feeling in the world, better than sex.

And then it was gone.

"You're under—*a lot* under. You been skimming?" a man said so close to his ear that he could feel panting on the back of his neck and smell the tobacco on his breath.

Enraged by the accusation, Eric wheeled around, his dukes up. *I didn't take any. It's all there,* he thought so clearly and loudly that, for a moment, he believed that he might have truly yelled it.

The confused expressions on his companions' faces showed him that he hadn't.

"Something the matter? You look like you're expecting a psycho in a hockey mask to come racing out of the trees," Clausen teased with an easy grin.

"No, sorry," Eric said, shaking his head. The group looked as if they were expecting further explanation, so he added lamely, "A raindrop fell down the back of my jacket. Felt like someone had tapped on my back." This seemed to satisfy them, though the edges of Susan's lovely features were blemished with distress. He could practically see the warning beacon flashing above her head: *Red alert! Your mentally unstable boyfriend is losing it! Evacuate while there's still a chance of escape!*

He commanded himself to get a grip. Now was not the time to start bugging out, when he was deep in the forest with two strangers—one of whom, Stogg, was already convinced that he was a fraud—and on their way to unearth the body of a murdered man.

"I think we're getting close," Susan said, blessedly taking the attention off him. Maybe she was trying to help out, sensing that he was—

What? the voice inside his skull demanded. *Partaking in a schizophrenic episode? Seeking attention? Having an adverse reaction to the new meds? Excuses, excuses. When will you stop playing games and accept what you are?*

Which is what? he wondered.

The sinking feeling returned to his chest when they stopped before the stack of rocks he and Susan had arranged in a pyramid the day before to mark where they needed to veer off the trail when they returned. "It looks like somebody kicked it over," he said, pointing at the splayed rocks, some of which were embedded deep in the mud, as if they'd been stomped on.

"You sure this is the right spot?" Clausen asked.

Susan said, "Positive. See there? We tied a shoelace—I always carry a spare set in my backpack—around the biggest rock."

"Probably the storm," Stogg said, sensibly enough.

Eric and Susan led Stogg and Clausen down the embankment to the stump Eric had headbutted. They knew when they reached it with certainty, as they'd marked it with the other matching half of the shoelace they'd tied around the rock. "Looks like the storm wiped out all the prints too," Eric commented after they moved aside several snapped tree branches that were scattered at the base of the stump.

Stogg looked at him as if he wanted to say: *If there were any to begin with.*

Eric glared back: *Go on, I dare you. Say it.*

Clausen powered up the chain saw and went to work cutting a wedge away from the stump. The ground around the roots was muddy and uneven, so he was taking his time and being cautious. Eric was glad for this; he'd feel bad if Clausen lost a hand over the ordeal.

Upon approaching the stump, Eric had started to worry about falling into another fugue state in front of the two officials. But, other than feeling tired and eager to go back to bed, he felt fine. Which concerned him. He'd been so certain about the presence of a body back when he was jacked up on fear and adrenaline that he felt equally uncertain that there might *not* be one, now that he wasn't spooked. He shot Susan a worried glance, but she was focused on Clausen's progress with the chain saw.

What if he was wrong? he wondered. What if he dragged them all out into the middle of the forest for no other reason than his overactive imagination? Would they think he'd gone crazy?

Was it possible that he'd grown cocky because he'd made a few lucky guesses in the past—maybe he only wanted to *believe* that he was special, gifted. Maybe he was just another garden-variety schizophrenic with an unnecessarily inflated ego. *I am the chosen one*—it sounded ridiculous when he ran through the words in his mind.

No, he decided. A body *had* to be there. The vision he'd had was far too real to be fabricated—he had a *name*, a vivid description of a tattoo. He'd seen the rifle, the chain saw, gleaming as bright as day—

"Help me with the wedge," Clausen said.

Even with the four of them, the hunk of the stump was hard to move, mostly because of its awkward shape. It was also wet and slightly slimy, which made maintaining a grip difficult. They cast it aside and Clausen extracted the flashlight from his utility belt. He made a move to shine the light down in the hole, and Stogg stopped him.

Stogg said, "I don't need to remind anyone present that, if there *is* a body down there, this is an active crime scene. But I'm going to anyway: We need to tread lightly, so as to not disturb any evidence. So, nobody go reaching down in there or anything, okay?"

Eric suspected that Stogg was delivering the warning for his benefit alone, since everyone else present would know not to disrupt evidence to the point of it being second nature. He appreciated not being called out, which warmed him to the man.

Slightly.

But then, a few moments later, Stogg peered down into the hole and said with a snort, "Yah, there's a body down here, all right. A dead *squirrel*."

And Eric went cold.

CHAPTER 9

No matter what Susan said, Eric was going to take it the wrong way. He hadn't said a word since the discovery of the squirrel in the hole, but she knew without even having to ask that he was mortified. She'd be, too, and in fact she was—for Eric and for herself, since she'd been the one to vouch for him as a law enforcement officer.

Still, she had to try. "You shouldn't feel bad, you know," she ventured. "They really didn't seem to mind too much." Well, *Clausen* didn't seem to mind—really, *he* seemed almost thrilled to be out there in the forest, away from the stuffy confines of the trailer—but Stogg looked as if he could commit murder.

Which, she suspected, was a by-product of his aggravation at having to make the hike. He was far from the outdoorsy type. By the time they returned to the parking lot, his face was the color of eggplant. She suspected that he might have tried to have it out with Eric had he not been so winded. The way he'd slammed the door of Clausen's ranger vehicle had communicated plenty, though.

"I think you and I both know that isn't true," Eric finally said.

"On the bright side, they don't seem to think we're crazy." Good—she'd said *we're* and not *you're*, which she'd nearly done. "They're blaming our made-up thugs. Seems they're dismissing it as a couple of criminals trying to show off for one another. They can't fault you for what you're saying you overheard. You were a Good Samaritan trying to do what you thought was the right thing."

"And what do *you* think?" he asked. "You know that there were no thugs—that our entire investigation was based on a vision I had. So, what's your take on *that*?"

Tread carefully, girl, she thought. "What do *you* think?" she evaded.

He glanced over at her with a wry expression. "I think that you're trying to avoid answering the question."

"I—and don't get mad at this—wonder if maybe your vision is a subconscious response to dealing with what happened to you."

"Interesting. In what way?"

Uh-oh. She detected a tone. "Don't you find it a little . . . coincidental? You were thrown in a hole on the farm, and now you're seeing a man in a hole?"

"I'm failing to see how one has anything to do with the other," he said, snappish. "I like pizza and so do some mass murderers, ergo anyone who likes pizza could become a mass murderer, right? Because that seems to be the sort of logic you're following."

"That's . . . what? That doesn't make any sense," she said, shaking her head. "All I'm saying is that it wouldn't be too far of a stretch to imagine that you might be experiencing some residual trauma after what happened to you. And nobody, including me, is going to fault you for that. You were almost *killed*, Eric."

"So were *you*," he pointed out. "And all *I'm* saying is that you're overlooking some very important details. If this really *was* about my near-death experience, why would I wait almost three months to have a freak-out, and why would I do it up here in Washington State and not back in Perrick, where, most days, I have to drive past the very place I was held captive?"

"Maybe being out of town has disrupted your routine?"

"My routine? You act like I'm some small-town bumpkin who's never strayed too far from the prairie, and now I'm just so overwhelmed by the bright lights of this big city we're in, Clancy. I moved to Perrick from *Philadelphia*, Susan."

Ouch, that one stung. "Is that what you think of *me*? That I'm just some sheltered bumpkin?" The back of her neck was sizzling. As far as a first fight as a couple went, this one was turning out to be a real doozy.

A look of horror crossed his face. She could practically hear the sound effect of him rewinding his last statement back in his head like an old cassette tape, reexamining it. *Rrrrrrrrrpt.* "Of course not! No! I could never think that about you. That's not what I meant." He reached over for her hand. Quieter, he said, "I don't want to fight."

She accepted his hand. "Me either."

"I just . . . I don't like that you're worrying about me." He raked his free hand through his hair in a gesture that was pure frustration. "It makes me feel like I'm less of a man because you think that you can't depend on me—or that *you* think I'm less of a man. I have to say, it's not the best feeling."

"That's ridiculous!" She slapped a hand down on the wheel. "If I thought anything of the sort, do you think I'd waste my time dating you? Do I *really* strike you as the sort of individual who'd stay in a relationship out of pity or because I'm too chicken to end things?"

She was relieved to see him smile. "Not when you put it like that."

"It's not that I'm worrying—okay, maybe I'm worrying *a little*. With these new meds that you're on . . ."

"It's not the meds," he interjected with a shake of his head. "This isn't my first rodeo. I've switched up meds countless times throughout my shining career as a schizophrenic. Trust me, I'd know if I was having an adverse reaction. It wouldn't only be mental symptoms but physical ones too. Do I look like I'm zonked out? Do I sound as if I'm on the verge of vomiting? Because that has always been the case in the past whenever my body and brain rejected a medication."

On that front, he did seem okay, she had to admit. "You haven't seemed fully like yourself since we've been here."

"I haven't been," he agreed. "This place—Clancy—it gives me the heebie-jeebies. I can't put my finger on it, but I don't *like* it. I feel like . . . it's not *safe* here."

It was strange, but she felt the same way. Even earlier, when they'd been out in the forest she'd initially found so pretty, she'd felt unwelcome. Like they were being stalked by a creature.

Eric continued, "Also, don't you think I'd be focusing more on children and not a middle-aged man named Miguel if this vision or whatever I had was rooted in unresolved Death Farm issues? And what about the whole praying-in-Spanish thing? Why would I do *that*? I don't know anyone named Miguel, and my Spanish is so bad that I can barely order at Taco Bell."

She chuckled lightly. "But how do you even know that you *were* speaking Spanish? For all you know, it could have been utter gibberish and only sounded like Spanish."

"So many questions!" he said, frustrated. "So many questions, my sweet Suzy, yet you keep failing to ask the right one."

"Which is?"

"How did that dead squirrel get down in the hole?"

She opened her mouth, closed it. She could think of absolutely no response. How *had* that squirrel gotten down there?

"You saw its body. It looked *fresh*—like it was still gooey. Like it had been run over by something big and then tumbled into the hole to die. But how could it have done that, if the stump was down like when we'd seen it yesterday? And you saw those rocks we'd used as markers. They weren't just blown over. They were squished into the ground, also like they'd been run over."

She couldn't dispute a single thing he'd said. On that front, he was accurate in every detail. "So, what are you saying?"

"I'm saying that I think somebody went up there—possibly with a tractor—and moved the body last night."

CHAPTER 10

Jake had paced the parking lot of the E-Z-Sleep Motel—in Clancy, there were no popular chain hotels with multiple floors and indoor room entrances like Hilton, Holiday Inn, or even the old standby, Motel 6—so many times that morning that he'd lost count. He was growing more panicky with each minute that passed, beginning to genuinely entertain ideas about being abandoned in Clancy, which he'd earlier dismissed as ridiculous. Where the hell *was* everybody?

He pulled out his phone, saw that he still had no messages, and let out a series of loud, frantic curses. The cantankerous old biddy who'd been staying in the motel room next to the one he and bassist John were sharing ceased shoehorning her rotund husband into the passenger seat of their ancient Honda and provided him a look that was far from tender. *"Excuse me?"*

"Sorry," he called, not just for the profanity but for all the noise he and John had made the night prior, which had undoubtedly kept them up. At least, that's what *she'd* claimed during the ten or so calls she'd placed to the front office, starting at 8:00 p.m. on the dot. The giddy girl working the desk had told them as much. Jake suspected she might have a crush on John, which would be a fruitless endeavor on her part, since John approached romance with so much apathy that he was practically asexual and personified the old joke: *What does a bassist use for birth control? His personality.*

"Up yours!" the biddy shouted at him with a shake of a fist. She snatched up the tatty hard-shell suitcase at her feet, skulked to the open trunk, and hurled it in. With a final glare at him over her shoulder, she slammed it shut. He imagined she wasn't all too upset to be heading off to their next location, wherever it was—though she probably wasn't too happy about it either. People like that rarely were about anything.

"Have a nice trip!" he smirked, and she huffed out a breath and gave him the finger. Sometimes he didn't know when to quit.

Jake let out a relieved "Thank God!" when Eric and Susan pulled into the parking lot a couple of minutes later. He was descending on their car before they even had a chance to open their doors. "Where have you guys *been*?" he demanded as soon as they got out.

He'd startled them with his urgency, he saw. Good, then they'd all be on the same page.

"Why, what's going on?" Eric asked.

"I've been trying to call you guys forever!"

Susan pulled out her phone and checked it. Eric did the same. "You have? When? I'm not seeing any missed calls." Eric wasn't either.

"I've been trying pretty much from the moment I got up to about an hour ago. I gave up after the zillionth time not being able to reach you. I got worried that you'd left," he said, sullen.

"Left? Like for Seattle? We wouldn't have done that without first talking to you guys," Susan said. "We've been out in the forest. The reception is *terrible* out there. Look, you can see for yourself, no missed calls."

Jake took in their hiking gear, flapped a hand. "It doesn't matter."

"What's going on?" Eric repeated.

"You aren't going to believe this, but I think Madison and Chuck are missing. I think something's happened to them. Like, they've gotten lost out in the wilderness or something." Jake's sentences were coming out as single breaths.

"We're not the only paying guests here," Susan said after a door opened and someone peeked out at their parking lot spectacle, annoyed. "Let's go inside so we don't get thrown out."

Eric said, "Good idea. I want to get out of these muddy clothes."

"Me too. I'm cold."

"What *were* you guys doing?" Jake asked.

"We'll tell you later. You go first," Susan said as she let Jake into her and Eric's room. "Where's John?"

Jake pulled a sour face. "Where else? In the room, sleeping. He sleeps like the dead once he's out. It's impossible to wake him. He's not getting up until *he's* ready."

"I'm guessing the coffee in these rooms is nothing to write home about, but I'll make some anyway. Oh, look, they've even got powdered creamer, yum-yum." Susan set about filling the carafe with water and unwrapping coffee cups from the plastic film only motels feel necessary to encase them in. Jake sat on one of the two full beds available, the one that was still made.

Returning from the bathroom in dry clothes, Eric said, "I saw the van was gone when we left this morning—around six. Did they go somewhere?" He sat down opposite Jake.

"Yah, last night," Jake said.

Susan sat next to Eric on the bed. She glanced at the time on her phone. "We've got to check out soon."

"And Madison and Chuck know that," Jake said. "So where the hell *are* they?"

Eric said, "Did they go to a party or something—maybe they're passed out on somebody's sofa? You said Madison has a friend here who you went to see—"

"No way they're *there*. I don't think you understand how badly that scene went down. Darla would probably rather face a firing squad than see Madison again. And they're not at a party. They know as many people in town as we do, and it's not like they made friends after the show the other night. You saw what the crowd was like. Not the friendliest people, am I right?"

"So, where do you think they are?" Susan asked.

"Last I talked to them—this was last night—they were going out into the forest to . . ."

"To what?" Eric asked.

Jake shifted his gaze to Susan. Things were about to get a little awkward. "I'm not sure if I should say, with Susan being a cop and all . . ."

Susan laughed throatily. "They went into the forest to get high—is that what you were going to say? Smoke a joint?"

Jake gave her a lopsided smile. "Maybe."

"Jake, I'm not on duty. I don't even have jurisdiction up here!" Now Eric was laughing too. "And, even if I did, I think marijuana might be legal in these parts. Unless they were out there doing something else?"

Jake shook his head. "No, no, it was just pot. Madison and Chuck aren't druggies—they don't take pills or shoot up heroin or anything crazy like that. I know a lot of musicians do, but those two just enjoy the occasional toke. We're in Washington, like you said, so when in Rome, I guess. I don't do the stuff—I heard it stunts your growth," he said with a wink, and Susan gave him a *hah!* "No, really, it makes me too foggy to play the violin. John doesn't do it either, which is why we stayed behind. And no freaking way you're going to find me tramping around in a dark forest sober with two high yahoos during a full moon. I've seen too many werewolf movies."

"Why don't you just tell us what happened?" Susan suggested to Jake.

"Sorry—sometimes I babble when I'm anxious. Okay, so last night around nine, Madison and Chuck got a wild hair up their butts to go out into the forest to smoke a joint. They actually wanted to go *because* it was a full moon—guess they've never seen *An American Werewolf in London*."

"I *love* that film," Eric said.

"Guys, focus!" Susan interrupted. And then quickly and quietly: "But I love that film too."

"They took the van and headed to the woods. That's the last I saw of them," Jake said with a shrug.

Eric got up and poured them all coffee. "Maybe they came back and then left again early in the morning, but you just don't know it because you were asleep. Did you guys get into a fight or anything? Maybe they went to Seattle without you, thought you guys would hitch a ride with us."

"Nope, no fighting. As a band, we have surprisingly little drama. We tease John for being lazy, but that's about it. And the girl at the front desk let me into their rooms—she said normally she wouldn't, but she's got a thing for John, I think, so . . . anyway, their beds haven't been slept in."

"Ugh, this swill's bad," Susan said, grimacing, after taking a sip of coffee. "Was their stuff still there?"

Jake nodded. "Everything. Their clothes, instruments . . . even their toothbrushes were in cups by the sink, dry." The hair on the back of his neck raised. He realized that he was deeply frightened for his friends. He had a bad, bad feeling that extended beyond them being lost in the forest, hungry and hypothermic. His mind began to scour the possibilities— bear attack, rock avalanche, drowning, crazed ax man—and he shook his head, cutting the thoughts short.

Eric said, "Okay, the most logical step is to go to the trail they went to. I'll drive us there. For all we know, they could've been so ditzy after their toke-a-thon that they decided to sleep in the van in the parking lot. They could still be asleep there now, so maybe we're panicking over nothing. Do you know where they went?"

"They told me, but I honestly can't remember," Jake said, mad at himself for not listening to his friends better. "It was a Native American– sounding name."

"Which is literally every trail in these parts," Susan said. "And there's *so many* trails here too."

Jake perked up. "They *did* say that they wanted to enjoy the view of the lake. How many trails around here have lake views, do you think?"

Susan said, "Let's get a map and find out."

CHAPTER 11

It turned out that there were three trails in the area that overlooked lakes: the Obapatchee, Anquikia, and Manatopikean. They elected to visit Obapatchee Trail first, simply because it was closest to their hotel.

Eric, Susan, and Jake knew instantly that Madison and Chuck had not visited there. The foot of the trail was marked off with several splintery sawhorses that were linked together with a thick, rusty chain. And, if potential hikers still didn't get the picture, there were various signs: **KEEP OUT, UNSTEADY GROUND, MUDSLIDE AREA**. A person would have to be suicidal to enter, and Madison and Chuck, according to Jake, were not.

Eric got an uneasy feeling in his chest as they pulled up to the second trail, Anquikia. Madison's white van was nowhere in sight, but he was *positive* that they'd been there; he knew it like he knew the nose on his face, or . . .

Like he knew the voice of a dead man named Miguel. "I think this is the one," he said.

Jake frowned. "Why? The van's not here."

"I can see that." There was, however, a dilapidated Winnebago at the far end of the parking lot, the only vehicle in sight. "Maybe they saw something."

The Winnebago looked as if it had seen half a million miles on as many bad roads. Its paint job on the side that faced out, created by what

could only be spray paint, was a pink-and-blue camouflage pattern—
ironic, since this thing could be seen coming from the next county over.
The hood was adorned with blurry peace signs, also spray-painted, in
every color of the rainbow. Attached to the front grille was a large sign
made from what looked like the lid of a metal garbage can. A dozen or
so troll dolls had been tacked down around its perimeter; these, like the
windshield, were crusted with insects. The sign read: PIPPI & PAPPI'S
LOVE WAGON.

"If Pippi and Pappi *did* see anything, it was probably aliens," Jake
muttered.

They walked around to the other side.

Eric had been expecting a crew of old fogy burnouts, but the boy and
girl they found lounging on crisp green canvas lawn chairs were in their
early twenties. The couple did not take notice of their approach, as they
both had their eyes glued to their gleaming smartphones and were com-
plaining that they couldn't get their Instagram photos to upload because
of bad cell reception. They wore copious amounts of beaded hemp jewelry and had obviously tried very hard to capture an air of vagrancy—torn
jeans with patches, natural fiber shirts, ratty dreadlocks—but their pricey
Ray-Ban sunglasses betrayed their look. At their feet sat two upturned
to-go coffee cups and a MacBook Air laptop that a French bulldog was
using as a bed. Leaning against the vehicle were two identical carbon road
bikes. Eric recognized the brand because a neighbor of his back in Philly
had bought one for a little over $3,000. Used. These looked as if they'd
never been ridden.

"Looks like we got ourselves a couple trustafarians," Jake said under
his breath, and Susan snickered.

Eric couldn't bring himself to laugh because the bad feeling in his
gut was intensifying, twisting his bowels like a tumor spreading with
impossible swiftness. He tasted fear on his tongue, hot and acidic, his
back slicked with sweat. Something bad had gone down here, something

so bad that he wanted to spin around on his heels and run back to the car, shrieking with his arms flailing above his head.

"Hey, guys, what's up?" the girl asked in a sing-song voice.

Jake jumped right in. "We're looking for our friends, who we think might have gotten lost in the woods last night. We're thinking they might've come here. Have you seen anyone?"

The couple nodded. The boy said, "A few people have trickled through here. Not too many, though, with tourist season being over. Can you be more specific? What do they look like?" They seemed eager to help, which would make things easier.

Jake pulled his phone from his pocket and showed the pair several photos of Madison and Chuck. Their faces remained blank, lacking any signs of recognition. "You sure you haven't seen them? They wouldn't have been dressed like hikers, but in regular clothes. They wouldn't have had backpacks or anything either. It was a spur-of-the-moment trip." They shook their heads. Jake kept scrolling, determined.

Eric peered away from them to look at the forest, noticing a twinkle of light from the corner of his eye. It lasted less than two seconds. "Did you see that?" he asked Susan.

"See what?"

"Wait!" the girl said. "There! Can I see your phone?" She accepted the phone from Jake and tapped the screen to enlarge it. "That van—I *did* see that van here."

"Are you *sure*?" Jake asked.

"I'm sure."

"Was it *this* white van or *a* white van?" Susan asked. She'd told Eric once that she was always wary of witnesses who answered too quickly, because it showed that they hadn't thought too much about the question before speaking. Ditto if they claimed to be 100 percent certain about anything. He suspected that this was what she was thinking now.

Something flickered in the girl's eyes. Now, she wasn't so sure. Everyone saw it, including her boyfriend, who said, "I don't remember seeing a van."

"Well, *I* did," the girl retorted with unmasked annoyance. "And maybe you didn't *notice* it, but that's different than not *seeing* it."

"True," Susan agreed.

The girl said, "I can't swear that it was *this* van specifically, but there was definitely a white van here."

"What time?" Jake asked, sounding hopeful.

"Last night, it was around midnight or so—at least, that's when I noticed it. I don't know what time it arrived. I remember because I wanted to step outside and have a smoke, but there was the van out there, and—no offense to your friends—it looks like something a kidnapper would drive. I didn't want to step out alone, so I asked Oscar to come with me, but then this dude started up the van and drove away." She paused, tilted her head to one side. "Oh, I guess I forgot that part too. Sorry, I just remembered."

Eric asked the guy he assumed was Oscar, "Did you see the van?"

"No, but I do remember her asking me to go outside."

"And you're sure he—this guy—was alone? There was no girl with him?" Jake asked. "And did he look like my friend that I showed you? Did you get the license plate?"

"It was dark, so I couldn't tell you what the guy looked like, other than the fact that he was average height and build—oh, and also wearing a baseball cap. But there was definitely no girl. He was alone. And it was too dark to get the plate, but I got the feeling that the van was from out of state."

Jake asked, "Why, do you think?"

"I don't know—it's just a sense that I'm getting, like the van felt like it wasn't from around here. Neither are we, so maybe it takes one to know one?"

Susan asked the girl, "What was his demeanor like? I know you didn't get a good look at him, but what about his posture? Did it seem like he was in a hurry or running to or from something? Did he look around suspiciously?"

The girl shrugged. "I . . . I don't think so. I mean, I wasn't staring out the window watching him or anything. He might have glanced over his shoulder once or twice, but that also could've been because he saw *our* Winnie in the lot. I'd be afraid if I saw this thing," she said and laughed.

"Maybe it wasn't even them, then," Jake said. "What now?"

Eric was not getting a good feeling about any of it. "We could walk along the trail a little bit, see if we notice anything. Call out their names?"

"It's closed," the couple said in unison.

Susan asked, "What is, the trail?"

Oscar nodded. "It must've closed recently too. It was open when we went to get coffee earlier—they don't like people camping in the parking lot, so we leave from time to time so it doesn't look like we're hanging out here—but there was a sign up when we got back. No explanation either. Just 'Trail closed.' We were going to go for a hike, but now we're biking instead."

Eric, Susan, and Jake thanked the couple for their time. They returned to their vehicle and headed to the third trail. Eric still felt anxious enough to vomit, though the feeling was fading with every mile he put between them and the Anquikia Trail. He couldn't shake the feeling that there was something he was missing.

Susan asked, "So, what do you guys think? Think they're on the up-and-up?"

Jake said, "They may be spoiled trust fund kids pretending to be broke—why anyone would *want* to slum it when they didn't have to is beyond me; I'd take the cash and a mansion any day—but I don't think they were lying, do you?"

Both Eric and Susan shook their heads. "Still, there's something off here, you think?" Eric asked. He was fishing more than anything else. If Jake and Susan had gotten any bad feelings from the place, they'd made no indication of it.

Jake said, "I think this whole place is off. I've been dying to see this area for years because of those Kincaid films, but, now that I'm here, I hate to say it, but . . . Clancy *sucks*. The whole town's run down, the locals are creepy, and now my friends have disappeared. I can honestly say that this is one of the worst places I've ever been to."

Eric was taken aback by the outburst. Jake sounded deeply incensed, which was unlike his usual jovial behavior. Maybe it was the air in Clancy that made people guarded, hopeless.

"That's weird about the van, though," Eric said. "That there was only a man driving it?"

"Not that weird," Susan said. "I drive alone all the time."

"That's a coincidence, though: another *white* van." Eric was reaching, he knew.

"People come here from all over to camp and hike," Jake pointed out. "I bet vans are a dime a dozen. And most of those cargo vans like Madison's come in white, so it might just be a coincidence by default. Now, if her van was hot pink, that'd be another thi—"

"Wait! Stop!" Susan said. "Look, there's a white van parked right over there."

The van was parked at the foot of a trail, the Mitchatepi, which wasn't on their list. Eric might have missed it, had Susan not pointed it out; he'd been so deep in his thoughts about the evil he felt. He pulled into the lot, and they quickly scrambled out.

Susan asked, "Is that Madison's? Do you recognize the license plate number?"

"I don't even know the numbers on my own license plate," Jake said. "But this looks like it could be hers."

Eric examined the large areal map at the base of the trail. "Why would they come here if they wanted to look out at the lake? This is just a straight climb to the top and then back down again—it doesn't even loop around. It's no novice climb either, from the look of it; it zigzags straight uphill. It's showing a round-trip time of about five hours. This doesn't make any sense." He also wasn't getting any strange feelings here the way he had at the other trail. Something wasn't adding up. Then again, maybe it wasn't her van, and he was getting fired up over nothing.

Squelching Eric's hope, Jake looked into the van's window and let out a whoop. "Look there—that's my hoodie! And there's our crushed Red Bull cans from the drive up, and shells of those nasty sunflower seeds Chuck is always popping in his teeth. This is Madison's van." He tried the doors and found them locked.

"But no sign of them," Susan commented, letting her eyes move along the trail to the highest part of the mountain. She sighed. "If we're going to hike in after them, we're going to need some more water. Food too."

"We're also going to have to call the motel and extend our check-out," Jake said. "And if they don't turn up soon, I'm going to have to call the club in Seattle and cancel our show."

"And if *you* don't start pulling your weight, *I'm* going to drop this bitch," Eric snarled. "Come on, grab her feet."

Jake and Susan gaped at him. "Eric, what the hell was *that*?" Jake asked, bewildered.

Susan placed a hand on his shoulder. "Are you feeling all right?"

"Did I just say something weird—because I feel like I might have just said something weird."

"Did you see something—a vision or whatever you have. Who is *her*? Was it Madison?" Jake asked, looking utterly frightened.

"I have no idea. It's like . . ." Eric shook his head, thought for a moment. "Okay, have you ever taken a long drive and then arrived wherever it was that you were going, but when you look back, you have no idea how you got there? It's like that. I was aware that I was talking, that I was engaged in a conversation, but what I said . . ." He shrugged. "I have no idea."

"Are you saying that somebody else was 'driving' you?" Jake asked.

"Sure, but I have no idea who."

CHAPTER 12

It was as they neared the peak of the Mitchatepi that Susan began to truly suspect that Chuck and Madison might be in real danger. They'd hiked the entire trail from bottom to top, yet they'd seen no indication that the two had ever been there. They'd also run across three other clusters of hikers, all of whom claimed they hadn't seen anyone matching Chuck's and Madison's descriptions.

"How cold was it last night?" she asked, trying her hardest to keep the concern from her voice.

"I was just thinking the same thing. It was damn cold—I know that. And Madison and Chuck were only wearing light jackets," Jake said miserably. "And I doubt they would have been carrying more than a bottle of water and a candy bar each. Probably not even that. They aren't exactly the planning types. I bet they weren't even halfway up this trail when Chuck started bitching about being hungry . . ."

Jake stared out at the horizon forlornly, and Susan saw for the first time how scared he'd become. She turned to Eric, who looked just as worried as his eyes scanned the various cliffs around them. Nobody wanted to say it, but the same thought was on everyone's minds: Chuck and Madison could be dead if they'd taken a few steps in the wrong direction.

"Whatever were they *thinking* by hiking up this trail in the dark? High as kites, even!" Jake said, sounding angry. "How irresponsible could two people—*adults*—be? They didn't even have flashlights, I don't think. They must've been using the ones on their cell phones. Look around! Ledges everywhere—how stupid! And there's got to be all *kinds* of wild animals up here—what's up this way? Mountain lions?"

Bears, mainly, Susan thought, and lots of them. But she wasn't going to share this with Jake. "Maybe they stepped into the woods and got turned around," she said, desperate to change the subject. Getting hysterical wasn't going to help anyone. She lifted her chin toward the forest that nestled up against the trail. "Look how thick that is. If they didn't have real flashlights, they easily could have walked into the trees and gotten lost. There's no cell reception up here, and if their phones died, they would've been in total darkness. They would've had to wait until daylight before they could even make a move."

"Okay, so where are they now, then?" Eric asked. "It's nearly three in the afternoon."

"They could still be lost wandering around in the woods," Jake said, sounding as if he really wanted to believe it.

"I think we should head back down and talk to Pete," Susan said.

"Oh, I'm sure they're going to be thrilled to see us again." Eric scowled. "Stogg, especially."

"Who're Pete and Stogg?"

Susan and Eric exchanged a look that said: *Might as well tell him.*

"Come on," Eric said with a beckoning wave as he started back down the trail. "We'll tell you all about it on the way down."

It took some time to reach the bottom of the trail, but it wasn't as late as Susan would have expected.

"It's always faster on the way down," Eric explained, and she trusted him on that. He was unquestionably the keener hiker of the two, always going for pleasure hikes around Perrick—he actually found *joy* in the act, which Susan couldn't fully understand. While she also enjoyed the occasional foray around the craggy coastline they were lucky enough to have so close to their homes, she would never describe herself as a hiking enthusiast. She was too much of a multitasker, and with most cliffside hikes, like the Mitchatepi, you had to pay attention or *splat!*

Once they reached the car and pulled onto the highway, Jake made a suggestion. "I'm wondering if maybe it wouldn't be better if you stayed behind at the hotel, Eric. If you're saying that this Stogg guy has it out for you, it might aggravate him seeing you again—with it being just this morning that it happened."

"It feels like a week ago," Eric said. "I don't know about you guys, but I'm bushed after all this hiking."

"Me too," Jake said and then continued. "It's just that we're going to need their cooperation on this, and I'm wondering how generous this guy's going to feel after . . . you know, everything that's happened. I'd say that you should stay back, too, Susan, because the guy doesn't sound too fond of you either. But since you've got the whole background in law enforcement . . ."

They'd told Jake the unfiltered truth, which included every detail of Eric's vision, plus the part where they'd found nothing but a dead squirrel that appeared as if it had been killed recently. He'd listened quietly and without judgment, and he had very little to say once they'd finished. Had it been a different circumstance, Susan imagined the questions would have come firing out his mouth like a bazooka going off. Who wouldn't demand more details? As it was, Jake had his mind on the more pressing task of getting a search party organized for Chuck and Madison.

Eric said, "I certainly wouldn't mind staying behind, if you guys don't mind? I don't really see what good I could do being there. And I think Jake is right; it'd only put Stogg in a sour mood."

Susan snorted. "I think you mean *sourer*."

CHAPTER 13

Though Jake was adamant that Madison and Chuck would not be there, Susan still thought that dropping in on Darla on the way to the authorities would be smart.

"She's been living here for some time, right?" she said to Jake. "So, at the very least, she might offer some clues on where to look, being a local. And she knows Madison, so she could also have an idea about the sort of places she would like to go—places that we might not even think of, because we wouldn't even know about them, not being from around here."

"Maybe," he said. "Although it doesn't seem that Darla has much of a life here. She complained about not having enough money to go and see us play at our show the other night, so I don't think she's a woman-about-town."

"That seems to be an issue for a lot of people around here, doesn't it—not having enough money. What do these people do for income, I wonder?"

"I have no idea," Jake said with a shake of his head. "And I know what you mean. When we went on our Kincaid tour, we saw that every other business in town was shut down."

"Or, if they weren't shut down, they were close to it. A lot of the places Eric and I saw had 'Going out of business, everything must go' sale signs. I bet you could take a nap in the middle of the street downtown and not be hit by a car. It's like a ghost town."

"Right. It was kind of sad. But, you can understand it, can't you?" Susan glanced over at Jake. "What do you mean?"

"It seems kind of dumb, doesn't it, that these people would base their livelihood on something temporary? Did they think that Dylan Kincaid would be around forever? They must've known that people would lose interest over time. It's not like the books and films will have some lasting historical significance. I mean, it would be a different story if we were talking about classics. Like, if Clancy was the setting for *The Catcher in the Rye*, or maybe a few Alfred Hitchcock films. But, in ten or fifteen years, people won't even know or care who Dylan Kincaid is."

"Good point," Susan agreed. "Eric and I were also wondering if there had been some kind of gold rush here when the books and films came out, or if local businesses shifted to accommodate the needs of tourists."

"Gold rush?"

"I'm guessing that the real estate here is pretty cheap—or at least a hell of a lot cheaper than in California."

Jake chuckled. "Almost everywhere is cheaper than California."

"True," Susan said with a grim smile. "But even Seattle or Portland is probably ten times as expensive as Clancy, even when Clancy was at its peak."

"Probably even more than that, I bet."

"Right. So, what we were wondering is if people in surrounding areas moved here—because of how cheap it was—to open up a Dylan Kincaid business. Then, when the tourist money started to dry up, they jumped ship and went back to wherever they came from. It would make sense, wouldn't it, given how many houses are vacant here?"

"It's weird, right?" Jake said. "We noticed it too. It's like the damn *Mary Celeste* here. People just *vanished*."

"And it looks like they did it quickly, too, right? Like they took only what they could carry and skipped town. There's so many streets here with abandoned cars just sitting there, rotting."

"That's funny that you said that about the cars, because John and I were talking about the same thing last night. John's a big conspiracy theorist–type guy, and he has a whole theory about this town."

Susan arched an eyebrow. "Do tell."

"What he noticed was that on the majority of the abandoned cars we saw, the registration tags on the license plates expired in staggered years."

"What do you mean by *staggered*?"

"They're not all abandoned in the same year. What John pointed out is that there are two types of cars you see parked around town: those with current tags, which people are obviously driving now, and then the tags on the abandoned cars. The interesting thing is that the earliest abandoned cars have registration stickers dating back exactly four years, but there are other abandoned cars with stickers from each of the years since then. Seven cars in total all had the earliest date, and those were just the ones we saw—I'm sure there's probably more. We kind of made a game of it, searching for the dates."

Susan was impressed. "Good eye. John should've worked in law enforcement."

"Hah! Yah, right! Not unless he could nap on the job. You'd find his squad car parked down some alley, and he'd be inside sleeping while a bank was being robbed around the corner," Jake said with a snort.

Susan said, "What's weirder is that they've allowed those cars to sit on the street for four years. You'd think a tow truck would take them away or something, though maybe all the tow truck businesses in town have gone under."

"Wouldn't surprise me. And no tow truck driver is going to drive fifty miles down from Port Alden just to make a few bucks on an abandoned car that nobody will ever come to claim."

Susan's interest was piqued, but the conversation was making the hairs on the back of her neck stand up. The more she discovered about Clancy and its people, the more it gave her the heebie-jeebies. Never in her life had she had such a visceral reaction to a place, not even when she'd gone on a walking ghost tour of Gettysburg, Pennsylvania, and she'd sworn that an unseen figure had reached out from the shadows and run its fingers through her hair. Clancy was a different kind of haunted—the kind of haunted that hinted at a very real and physical threat. "Tell me more about the abandoned cars."

"There's not much more to tell. Like I said, the first ones date back four years. But then there are others peppered about town that span the years." He paused. "So, I guess it's not *really* like the *Mary Celeste*, because it's believed that they all vanished at once from the ship. Here, it's like people have been consistently vanishing throughout the years. Creepy as hell, right?"

"I'd say so," she agreed. "So, what's John's theory?"

"He doesn't really have one; he just thinks something hinky is going on."

"Okay, what's your theory? You big into conspiracies too?"

Jake shook his head. "Nah. What I think is that the town's major industries have gone under. During our Darkest Thrills tour, our guide Ben—"

"We met him too," Susan interjected. "Kind of an odd guy. Sorry, I interrupted."

"No problem, and yah, he's way weird. He kept trying to flirt with Madison. Man, was he barking up the wrong tree. It was *so obvious* that she wasn't interested—it was embarrassing. She even started to insinuate that she was Chuck's girlfriend, so that he'd back off. I think he finally took the hint, though, because he got a little sulky toward the end of our tour."

"Ick. She could practically be his daughter." A very quiet alarm bell went off inside her head, and she made a mental note to check up on a couple of facts later.

"Right! Anyway, creepiness aside, Ben knows everything about this town. He mentioned that there used to be some major businesses here—a lot of industrial-type stuff—that went under a few years back. Apparently, there was a paper mill that employed like half the town, and some kind of big electrical company headquarters that shut down after they were absorbed by the Seattle branch. My guess is that people lost their jobs and were unable to pay their bills—car payments, insurance, et cetera. So, they just left their cars behind, probably with the hope of coming back to retrieve them."

"But why didn't they ever come back?"

Jake shrugged. "No idea. Maybe they didn't make enough at their new jobs."

"But *where* did they go?"

"That's the big question, isn't it? Because if you're so broke that you have to abandon everything you own, how are you affording to travel to someplace new?"

"It shall remain a mystery for the time being." Susan slowed as they pulled into Darla's neighborhood. "Is this it?"

He made a face. "Unfortunately, yes. We can go up there, but I'm telling you, don't be surprised if she slams the door in our faces."

"But why is she so hostile, do you think? Is it possible that she might have had something to do with them disappearing?"

Jake peered over at her. "I don't think she's *that* crazy, no. I got the feeling that maybe she was more . . . hmm. Maybe embarrassed or angry about the state of her life. I mean, look at this place. If you lived here, and if your boyfriend skipped out on you and took all your money, would you be happy?"

She gave Jake a wry look. As they got out of the car, she said, "Do I even need to answer that?"

Darla was waiting for them on the front porch; she must have been watching their movement since they pulled up. Susan saw that she was peering up and down the street skittishly as they approached, as if anticipating an attack. Odd behavior. She couldn't help thinking that the girl could be a potential drug user, probably methamphetamines. She had the classic telltale signs: rail thin, dirty hair, sallow skin, bad teeth. The dark circles under her eyes gave her the appearance of a raccoon—or the ghost of a raccoon.

It was difficult to imagine health nut, go-getter Madison associating with such a person, as the two women likely had very little in common. Although Jake had mentioned that their friendship had diminished over the years. Looking at Darla, it was easy to understand why. Susan wondered if it had been the loser boyfriend who'd gotten her into drugs. It often was.

When they got close enough, Darla said to Jake, "Why did you come back? And who's this? I thought I told you the last time you were here—"

"Madison has gone missing," Jake said. "And we're wondering if you might know where she could be."

"She's . . . gone?" The devastated expression Darla wore told Susan everything she needed to know about her potential guilt. There's no way this scared-looking girl hurt her friend in any way.

Susan did, however, get the feeling that she might have an idea about what could have happened to her.

Susan extended a hand to Darla and introduced herself. Darla looked down at her hand as if it was a foreign object. It had been a long time since anyone had wanted to touch this girl, or even extended the smallest act of respect to her, Susan imagined. Jake had said that Darla was a loathsome individual, but what she felt toward her was pity. Maybe because she'd encountered endless women like this back in Perrick as a cop—women who'd come from nice homes and had once shown potential, but then they'd gotten mixed up with the wrong guy or the wrong situation, and everything fell apart. They lost their sense of worth, just as it sounded like Darla had, and they got stuck in a rut with no idea how to dig themselves out. So, they just stayed where they were, stagnant, and used drugs to dull the splintery edges of their hopeless lives.

When Darla didn't take her hand, Susan moved it up to her shoulder. Susan turned the girl toward the door and guided her inside the house, without making it obvious that she was the one doing the leading. It was a sneaky move that she'd executed countless times on the job, but it worked almost every time, as it did now.

Once the three of them were inside, Susan shut the door behind them, making a conscious effort not to let shock show on her face. She'd been in some real ratholes in her day, but Darla's took the cake. It wasn't so much about what she had, but rather what she *didn't* have.

She was using folding lawn chairs as furniture, and the long "coffee table" in the center of the room was an old splintery door that she'd propped up on two cinder blocks. Socks and underwear sat in messy piles on the floor. No dresser, then, either. As far as she could tell, there was no television or any other electronics in the place—which would be pointless, anyway, as there also didn't seem to be any electricity. With the curtains drawn, it was dim to the point of it being difficult to see, yet she had no lamps lit; their cords, she saw, had been pulled from the walls. Susan listened and heard no hum of the refrigerator, which would explain the presence of the two large ice chests in the living room, though it didn't seem that Darla was doing much eating these days. On top of one of them was an old oil lamp and a set of matches.

Susan also saw empty dime bags scattered about, their insides coated in a thin dusting of powder—so she'd been right about the drugs. She pretended not to see them. Lecturing Darla about the evils of whatever it was she'd been sniffing or shooting up would only make her shut down and throw them out. Their first priority was locating Madison and Chuck.

Darla, who did not offer them a seat or a drink, launched right into it. "When did she go missing?"

Jake said, "It's actually *two* members of our band who are missing. Remember the guy who waved at you the other day? That was Chuck. He's gone also."

"Oh," Darla said, fidgeting. She seemed to be debating with herself about speaking further. "Where did they disappear from?"

Jake told her the circumstances while she listened quietly. Her face was a mask of guilt, the frown lines across her forehead deepening as he spoke.

"You don't seem too surprised," Susan said, keeping her voice neutral. It was her cop voice. "Do people go missing around here often?"

"I tried to tell her," Darla said quietly. To Jake, she said angrily, "I told you to leave town, didn't I? So why didn't you guys just go?"

"Do you know what happened to Madison and Chuck?" Jake demanded. "Did you do something to them?"

"No! Of course not! I'd never hurt her! And I don't even know that other guy."

"So, what is it, then?" Susan asked gently.

"Look, for my own safety, I can't tell you anything. My boyfriend ran his mouth, and look what happened to him . . ." Darla broke off sharply, realizing her slip of the tongue.

"I thought he left you," Jake said, suspicious.

"Please! I can't say anymore! I shouldn't even be seen talking to you!"

"But you're not being seen," Susan said. "We're inside your house."

"They're watching all the time!"

Jake was obviously getting angry. "Who are *they*? Enough of this horseshit! What happened to Madison and Chuck? Where are my friends?"

Darla recoiled from his shouts.

"There's no need for that, Jake," Susan said soothingly. At some point during their conversation, she and Jake had fallen into a good cop, bad cop routine. "I'm sure Darla wants to help us find her friend—isn't that right?"

Darla's breath hitched, and she sniveled. "I want to help, but I don't know anything!" She swiped a fat tear from underneath her eye with the back of her hand. "All I can tell you is that there are some seriously evil fucking people running this town, okay? People you don't want to cross. My boyfriend took some things from them that he shouldn't have, and he . . . he . . ."

"He what, Darla?" Susan prompted.

She caught her breath, swept a hand out in front of her. "Look at how they're making me live. I have to live like an animal because of what *he* did! *I* have to pay off his debts, even though *I* took nothing! Do you think I want to live in this godforsaken shithole? I want to leave, but I can't—they'll find you wherever you go! But you guys *can leave*, so I suggest you get the fuck out of town before they get you too."

Susan's pulse was thudding in her ears. The right question just might make Darla spill her guts completely. "I can't help feeling that you want to let us help you, but maybe you're afraid. We can help you. What aren't you telling us, Darla?"

"And she's good about sensing when people are lying, too, because she's a cop," Jake interjected. "So spare us the bullshit."

Susan squeezed her eyes shut. She really wished Jake hadn't revealed that detail.

Darla reacted exactly how Susan expected her to. "You're a *cop*?" she sneered. "Oh, no, you need to go. *Now.*"

And then they were out on their butts, standing like fools on the porch.

"Sorry," Jake said. "My temper got the better of me." He shook his head angrily. "I know she *knows* something, but she's more concerned with saving her own ass."

"You're understandably upset. It's okay," Susan said, though it wasn't. She couldn't help thinking that they had been on the brink of uncovering something monumental—that, had they been allowed just a minute or two longer with Darla, they might have unlocked the mystery of their friends' disappearances.

CHAPTER 14

Jake could already guess how their visit was going to go by the way Stogg greeted him and Susan, which was to say not at all. They stood looming near the door in anticipation of the sheriff—the only official present in the trailer because of the late-afternoon hour, or else they would have gone to someone else, preferably Clausen—getting off his apathetic ass to do his job, but clearly they'd expected too much. (Surely the man didn't believe he was such a charmer that Susan had returned for the sole purpose of gazing upon him from afar.)

When it became evident that Stogg had every intention of staying put, Jake whispered to Susan a fierce and monstrously paraphrased "If the mountain won't come to Muhammad, we go to the asshole's desk" and made his way across the room in a hurry. Susan followed. Stogg watched them both blandly, the way one would a golf tournament on the television.

At Stogg's desk, Jake stated their business quickly and efficiently. "I'd like to file a missing person's report."

Stogg's eyes shifted to Susan. "Not this Miguel business again—"

"No, someone else. Two people, actually," Jake said.

"Wow, you guys have got people disappearing all around you left and right, don't you? Maybe I should handcuff myself to this desk, so I don't go missing too." Stogg pulled a pack of gum from his desk, extracted two sticks, and popped them both into his mouth. He placed the pack back in the drawer without offering them any.

Jake detected Susan tensing beside him; he could practically feel the heat of her anger radiating from her body. She opened her mouth to speak, but he cut her off before she had a chance to lay into Stogg. Not yet, not yet. They wouldn't play the nasty card until they needed to.

Jake quickly described the details of Chuck and Madison's disappearance, outlining the basics.

Stogg smacked his lips disinterestedly. "It's not a crime in this country for people to go missing," he finally said.

Jake's hackles were rising fiercely. It was like trying to reason with a tar baby. "Which is why I'm not here to report a *crime*, but a *missing person's report*." *You absolute dullard.* "Two people who are out lost in the forest *right now*, probably suffering from hypothermia and God knows what else! They could *die* out there—what don't you understand?"

"Let me ask you something, son—"

"It's *Jake*. As far as me being *son*, I'm guessing that I'm only a few years younger than you. So, unless you believe you became a father in kindergarten, I suggest you start addressing me by my first name. That, or you can call me Mr. Bergman, or even *sir* if you forget entirely. I'll leave the choice up to you."

Susan placed a hand on his shoulder and gave it a gentle squeeze. Probably trying to calm him. They'd warned him that the guy was a total waste of space, but still he was appalled. Didn't sheriffs have to be elected? Who thought that putting this dipshit in charge was a good idea?

Stogg did not acknowledge the clarification, nor did he apologize for his disrespect. He also made no move to pick up the phone or write down any details in a report. "Let me ask you something," he repeated, this time wisely omitting *son*. "Did you see anything on that trail that indicated your friends had been there? Anything at all: footprints from their specific brand of shoes, a piece of clothing, or maybe even a butt of one of their cigarettes?"

"No, but—"

"So, there *is* a possibility that they could have just parked there and gone off someplace else, hitched a ride? It *is* possible that they never stepped a single foot onto the trail."

"Okay, sure, I guess, but why would—"

"And have these friends of yours committed any crimes to your knowledge?"

"No."

"Are they in possession of any of your property? This van you say they drove—is it yours?"

Jake could see where Stogg was going, and he did not like it. "No."

"Have they been missing for at least twenty-four hours?"

"No . . ." Jake folded his arms across his chest.

Stogg shrugged. "What do you want me to do? They could've left town, for all you know."

"I want you to organize a search party, is what I want! And, no, they didn't *leave town* because, as I already told you, *the van sitting abandoned at that trail is Madison's,* so they'd have no *reason* to hitchhike. And they didn't leave bread crumbs lying around like Hansel and Gretel because they probably weren't anticipating getting lost. Our band had a show scheduled for tonight that I had to cancel—a show that was pretty big money for us. Their beds are untouched at our hotel. Madison's journal is still sitting on the nightstand, along with the necklace her dead mother gave her. She never would have left without those things, and they never would have left with a show booked for tonight. In all the years I've known them, not *once* have they flaked on a show or disappeared without a word."

Now, finally, Stogg seemed to be paying attention. "You and your friends are musicians?"

"Yes. What does that have—"

"They involved in drugs?"

Jake felt as if he was losing his mind. He turned to Susan. "Oh my God, are you hearing this? What else do I need to say—what are the magic words to get this guy to spring to action? I'm at the end of my rope."

Susan said, "Look, Sheriff, I know that this morning didn't have the outcome we were expecting—"

He snorted. "What *you* were expecting, maybe—I always knew it was a wild goose chase. It's a shame Clausen didn't, too; could've saved us some time and a pointless hike in the mountains."

Ignoring him, Susan said, "My point is that these two events are entirely unrelated. Madison and Chuck have nothing to do with the other, Miguel, disappearance. Please don't punish them for what happened this morning with us."

Apropos of nothing, Stogg asked, "What's the name of this band?"

"Ours?"

"You're the only one here who's a musician, aren't you?"

This was the first time in his life that Jake fully comprehended the physical meaning behind the phrase *bite your tongue*. "Augustine Grifters."

Stogg flapped a dismissive hand. "Never heard of you."

"I'm okay with that; we've never heard of *you* either." Jake was done playing around with the idiot, who he suspected might have thrown a few back before his shift—maybe even *during* his shift. He grew very, very still. "But, unfortunately for you, Sheriff, there are over half a million followers on our Instagram, Twitter, and Facebook accounts who *have* heard of us. And, if you continue stonewalling us, I can promise you that every single one of them is going to hear about how you sat on your ass doing nothing while two members of their beloved band were lost in the forest, freezing to death."

"Now, wait just a minute—"

"Then, I'm going to call up Madison's brother, who is a big-time advertising executive with media connections you can't even *imagine*. Once he learns of your behavior, he'll probably do a little advertising of his own, broadcasting to every news station from here to Timbuktu how you're doing absolutely nothing to find his baby sister. Then, I'm going to call our business manager and tell him to do the same. Then, our agent. From what I understand, you people up here hate publicity; your own mayor told me as much."

"The mayor? When did you talk—"

"By the time I'm through with you, you're going to have so many goddamn reporters up your—"

Stogg put his hands up, palms facing outward. "All right, all right. I understand." He brought his hands down flat on his desk, as if to steady himself.

It had probably been a long time since he'd been threatened so savagely—and that's what it was, Jake realized with zero remorse, a threat that was blackmail in disguise. It gave him a perverse sort of joy to know that he'd upset the man on such a deep level that he had him over a barrel. "Good," he said. "That will save us from wasting anymore time."

CHAPTER 15

While Jake and Susan were dealing with the sheriff, Eric was going to have himself a nice little nap.

That had been the plan, anyway, but shortly after he closed his eyes, there came a persistent knocking at the door. He jolted from bed, telling himself not to get too excited. It could be Chuck and Madison, or even housekeeping with the ratty, off-white rags that they had the audacity to call "fresh towels."

He flung the door open and discovered a small group of adults and a couple of teenagers gaping back at him. A few months back, their appearance would have made him scream in terror. Now, it caused him little more than a mild jolt of surprise.

They were all dead.

He knew this unequivocally because of their state of decomposition—rotting flesh, missing eyes, dried blood encircling wounds. That, and they were opaque. Some were naked, and some were cloaked in clothing that had long ago eroded into rags. He sighed.

At least, he thought, *there are no children. Not like last time.*

He decided that he could either continue deluding himself into thinking that he was merely imagining things—that he was overworked, or depressed, or experiencing side effects of his meds, or it was his schizophrenia, or one of a million other reasons he provided to avoid facing facts—or he could confront the issue head on. As he'd discovered with the haunting little boy Lenny Lincoln, ignoring the dead does not make them go away. It only makes them try harder to be seen.

"What is it?" he asked, despondent. He was sick of being haunted, sick of the weird sounds and smells that nobody other than him detected, sick of losing sleep and being possessed. Why couldn't the dead communicate with him in a more reasonable fashion—when he was awake and alert, and with clear statements that had discernable messages?

A man at the center of the group seemed as if he was going to speak up, but when he opened his blood-smeared mouth, Eric saw that a few of his front teeth were missing, and he had no tongue. It had been cut out, and only a jagged nub remained. The man turned so that he was standing sideways, and the rest of the group followed suit and parted so that they were standing on either side of him. He slowly brought up a hand and gestured to the forest in the distance.

Eric found himself being pulled forward, not exactly *against* his will, but not willfully either. As much as he'd been commanding himself to go with the flow, the sense of being controlled and manipulated frightened him. They encircled him as they drifted. "Where are we going?"

The man with no tongue tilted his head toward the trees. A naked woman to his right with spidery tree roots growing through her breasts, neck, and face shushed him. She linked an arm through his and pulled him along.

"Is that where you're buried, in the forest?"

Shhhhhhhh. Not just the woman this time, but several members of the group.

"Who did this to you? Can you give me a name?"

A skinny, bald man whose skull was partially visible wheeled around and seized Eric by the shoulders. His mouth dropped open above a jaggedly slashed throat, and he screamed. But what came out was unlike any sound Eric had ever heard a human make. It was the sound of a chain saw.

Eric let a scream of his own out and covered his ears, but it was no use. Attempting to tune out the sound only seemed to make it increase in volume. The man began shaking him, shaking him—shaking him so hard that it felt like his head might pop right off his shoulders.

"Eric! Oh my God!"

Susan, calling him from back in the hotel room, her voice faint against the roar of the chain saw. He craned his neck so he could look at their room over his shoulder. She was shouting into the room from the doorway, then she disappeared inside.

"Snap out of it! Hey!"

Eric blinked his eyes open, finding Susan hovering above him. He wiped the sleep from his eyes and sat up in bed . . . no, make that on the floor. "Why am I on the ground?" he asked sleepily.

She seemed to be relieved that he was speaking. "I was going to ask you the same thing. Another nightmare?"

"Eh," he said. "Nothing worth mentioning." More like: nothing he wanted to mention to *her*. She looked plenty stressed out as it was, and what was he going to say, anyway—that he saw more dead people? "Guess I rolled out of bed."

"I guess." She quickly outlined how the meeting went with Stogg and Jake.

"Is there something else that's bothering you?" he asked. "Because you seem a little down."

She sighed heavily and flopped down on their bed, her expression dark. She looked at her phone disgustedly and then shoved it down deep into the pocket of her jeans.

"Care to talk about it?"

"No." She groaned. "But I will in a minute. Just let me calm down first."

"Sure, take your time."

"It was my dad."

Susan didn't often talk about her father, but when she did, she rarely had anything nice to say. He hadn't abused her in her adolescence, at least not in the physical sense, but the indifference he had and continued to exhibit toward his only child was still plenty infuriating. Eric considered Susan to be one of the most wonderful human beings he'd ever met, probably *the* most wonderful. It shocked him that anyone could treat such a kind, decent person as something so insignificant, let alone her own father, who called just a couple of times a year out of obligation—which Eric knew, because she'd told him as much. He pretended to be flustered. "Calvin? Oh no! Did I forget your birthday today? Did somebody die?"

She let out a snort. "My dad calling today should tell you that it *isn't* my birthday. He can never get the date right. Last year, he called a week late and asked how it felt to be in my thirties. I told him that I wouldn't know, since I'm only twenty-nine."

"Ouch, I bet that was awkward."

"My dad doesn't do awkward. He only said that the present he'd gotten me would be wrong, then, and that he'd have to return it and get me something else." Her expression was bitter. "As if he'd gotten me a diamond pendant with a three-zero on it or something. Oh, *sure*."

"What did he get you instead?"

"The same thing he's gotten me every year." She brought her index finger to her thumb so that it made a nice round zero shape, and then whistled.

"What a guy."

"You aren't going to believe this. He's been talking."

"About Death Farm?"

"Yep."

"To the press? That son of a . . ." Eric bit his lip. Jerk or not, he *was* still her father. Wasn't there an ancient rule etched in stone somewhere that stated couples aren't allowed to verbally attack their mate's parents before marriage? (After, it was all bets off.) "You think he's the one leaking info—saying that I'm psychic? Giving away details of the case?"

She shook her head. "No, nothing like that. At least, I don't think so, and not because I'm under the impression that he'd never sink so low. I have no doubt that he would for the right price, or even just for sheer bragging rights, but he doesn't know *anything* because I haven't told him *anything*. I have no idea who he's been talking to, but, I tell you what, there's going to be a major ass kicking when I find out."

"And I'll be more than happy to help. So, what did your dad want, then?"

"Apparently, this editor—Todd somebody—at some big-time publishing house out of New York wants to write a tacky tell-all book about Death Farm. He promised to cut my dad in on the deal if he can convince me to talk. Guess they're willing to pay big bucks for the story, on account of how quiet we've been keeping everything."

Eric huffed out a breath. "Wonderful. What did you tell him?"

"I told him to sign me right up, obviously!" She blew a raspberry to show that she was kidding. "What do you think I said? I told him no way in hell would I do that—that, not only do I have no desire to rehash the worst experience of my life, but I also don't want to face legal repercussions, which I almost certainly would; as a law enforcement officer, you just can't go around discussing details of cases, even closed ones. Then, my dad got angry, because he's been running his mouth and promising things to this Todd guy that he can't deliver. I hung up on him after he asked why I was being so selfish, only thinking about *my* needs."

"Family can sure suck sometimes." Which he, having a brother who'd stolen his wife, would know firsthand. He went to the bed and began kneading her shoulders. "Sounds like you won't be getting that diamond pendant for your birthday this year."

"Or any year," she said with a scowl.

CHAPTER 16

Susan disconnected with Mayor Moulden, satisfied that she was onboard with their search for Madison and Chuck.

She'd promised Susan that she'd be available to them, day or night, should she need them. Susan believed that she would, too, but she didn't buy the mayor's alleged "devastation" over the event, which she'd made a point to reiterate numerous times throughout their conversation. What Susan thought was more likely was that Moulden was trying to do a little spin control after the way they'd been treated by Sheriff Stogg—that, and she wanted assurances that the story wouldn't be leaked to the press, because, golly, wouldn't the locals just hate *that*. Phoniness aside, the mayor had promised to extend the town's resources for the search, which, at the end of the day, was all that Susan really cared about.

Susan took a moment to prep herself for the next call that she needed to make, which was to the FBI. She had not spoken to Special Agent in Charge Denton Howell for a few weeks, so she was feeling anxious about making the call to his office. There was that, plus the man's cool-as-ice demeanor, which had often left her feeling as if she should reach over and check his pulse during the few conversations they'd had immediately following the events at Death Farm.

Howell, who'd stayed on in Perrick to help out for a couple of weeks while the case was coming to a close, had made several off-the-cuff statements to Susan in regard to her quitting her dead-end job at "Podunk Perrick PD"—an establishment he made absolutely no effort to hide his disdain for, not after the way they'd mishandled everything so royally—and putting her skills to better use at the FBI in San Francisco. It was his version of "What's a girl like you doing in a place like this?"

Though, technically, no job had *officially* been extended outright, he'd made it clear that he could pull some strings and get her where she needed to be. She was wasted talent in her current position, he'd said, and they could use her keen insight in his department. The problem was that she hadn't been feeling keen about crime fighting as of late, not after the way she'd been treated by the force. She was, for want of a better term, in a funk. She'd told Howell that she'd think about his offer, that that was the best she could do.

After providing her a much-needed pep talk, Eric left her in the motel room to make the call. Stalling, she made coffee, which she drank now as she sat on the bed, unaware of her hand wringing. How could she, she wondered, phrase her inquiry without sounding like she'd developed an obsession? She had no basis to back what she was beginning to suspect, but between Eric's insistence that something *really bad* had happened to Chuck and Madison—something that was not rooted in Mother Nature getting the better of them—and the hostility some of the locals had displayed, she had to wonder if Chuck and Madison had been attacked by a fellow human. Of course, this could be a jump she was making because of the horror she'd seen in Perrick.

Susan frowned as she argued against herself inside her head. Perrick didn't have the only serial killers on the entire planet. Was it so implausible that there could be one operating out of Clancy? And though she did not want to conceive of something so awful, she also had to consider the possibility of a sex crime. Had some unsavory creep—and she even had one in mind—stumbled upon the pair in the dark and then killed Chuck to rape Madison, and then killed her too? It sounded far fetched, especially in a town as small as Clancy, but, as she knew, stranger and worse things had happened in less convenient circumstances. And Madison and Chuck had gone into the woods on their own, inebriated, late at night. She doubted they'd been carrying any weapons. They would've been easy pickings for a predator, had they encountered one.

She also didn't foresee Stogg breaking his back to find Chuck and Madison. He'd kept his word about contacting the mayor to organize a search party for the following morning, but he'd clearly done it only to placate Jake and keep Clancy out of the media. What she questioned was Stogg's level of competency. Clausen had attributed his lackadaisical attitude to marital problems, which, from what Eric had told her about his own, was an unpleasant affair at the best of times. Still, regardless of the reason, Stogg was a man distracted by his personal affairs, which meant that he wasn't giving himself entirely to the job.

There was also Stogg's pickled appearance to consider—the glassy eyes, marred with red veins, the gin blossoms on his nose—as well as his smell. His breath had been so boozy during the encounter with her and Jake at the station that she was surprised it hadn't melted the flesh right off their faces. It was no secret that law enforcement officials had a propensity toward drinking, but if Stogg was boozing on the job, he'd crossed the line from heavy drinker to full-blown alcoholic.

Of course, Clausen was always there to assist, but she questioned his capability to handle a missing person's case, being a forest ranger in a small town. It was unfair of her to be so quick to judge when she herself was a small-town cop, she knew, but fairness wasn't her objective—finding Chuck and Madison was. Given Stogg's problems at home and blatant alcoholism, as well as Clausen's unknown proficiency, Susan figured it wouldn't hurt to get a little help from an outsider. Especially when the particular outsider was a high-ranking member of the FBI. Susan snapped up her phone before she had a chance to change her mind, hitting the speed dial button for Howell's direct line that she'd programmed in her phone what now seemed like forever ago.

She had a whole introduction plotted out, one that involved catching him up on her life since they'd parted, as well as her reason for calling. But then he went and spoiled her plans by throwing her off her game with an unusual greeting. "When can you start?" he asked in his smooth, no-nonsense tone.

Susan pulled the phone away from her ear to make sure she'd dialed correctly. Though she couldn't imagine anyone else who would greet her that way either. It was Howell, all right. "Start?"

"Here," he said, as if it was obvious. "I assume that's why you're calling."

"Not exactly."

"Oh?"

Susan quickly summarized the trip she'd taken to Clancy, along with the details of Madison and Chuck's disappearance. Howell was so quiet on the other line while she was speaking that she stopped a couple of times and asked if he was still there, until he started to sound annoyed. Though she was loath to, for the sake of full disclosure, she also mentioned the initial trip she'd taken with Eric to see Stogg and Clausen about the man named Miguel. In the long run, it would have been far worse—and embarrassing for everyone involved—if he'd called Stogg and was blindsided with the information.

"I'm not sure I'm buying this business about Eric overhearing the exchange in the bathroom," he said dryly.

Susan felt her cheeks go hot. Howell was sharp, which was probably why he held the position he did at the FBI. You don't get to the top by staying quiet and accepting ridiculous statements at face value. "But," he added, "I'm guessing this Miguel thing is not why you're calling."

"It's not," she said, relieved that he'd elected not to press her. Howell was curt and intimidating, but he was also no time waster. She went on. "We've had no issues with Clausen, who we'd been hoping to deal with again, but he was out of the office when we—Jake and I—went in. Now, we're stuck with Sheriff Stogg, who may not be entirely competent. I don't trust him."

"You think he's dirty?"

Susan didn't have to think long before she answered. "I honestly don't know, but I don't think so. He seems like a big drinker, and from what I understand, he's having some issues at home, so he could just be distracted. He's working closely with the mayor of Clancy to get a search party organized for tomorrow. So, hopefully, we'll find something."

"But you don't think you will," Howell deduced.

"I don't. It's just a feeling I have. I don't know why, and I could be wrong—"

"Your feelings were right about those missing kids, and you saved lives. Don't discount your intuition, Susan. You're good at what you do."

Susan didn't need to look in the mirror to see that she was blushing. Howell was a man she respected highly, so it made his compliment all the more meaningful. "Thank you, I won't," she said awkwardly, uncomfortable with the kind of flattery she hadn't received much of during her time on the job at Perrick PD.

"So, why, exactly, *are* you calling? Do you need help up there?"

"No, not exactly *help*. What I need is more like advice. Maybe I'm thinking this because of what happened on the farm, and I could be entirely off—"

"You're doing it again, Marlan. Don't apologize for having a hunch when that hunch could be right," Howell said. "If you're going to be working in my department, you'll need to start showing the sort of self-confidence that borders on arrogance."

Did I say that I wanted to work for you? she almost asked, but then it hit her: she *did*. She really, *truly* did. Working for Howell would be scary and challenging, and she'd probably spend most days feeling as if she was in over her head, but it would also be exhilarating. Just speaking with him had renewed her interest in law enforcement, which, she couldn't deny, had dropped to the point of nonexistent and had even started to make her feel a little sick after the disheartening first day she'd had back on the job at Perrick PD.

"I'll just tell you what's on my mind, then," she said. "I'm wondering if you might know of any killers who might be operating out of the Pacific Northwest? Clancy, specifically. Or someone who the FBI might be watching up this way?" She scrunched her eyes shut in anticipation of him saying something along the lines of: *Ha-ha, you've encountered one serial killer in your life, and now you're seeing them around every corner! Silly, silly girl!*

He, of course, didn't. "You believe your friends might have been murdered?" He didn't sound unbelieving, so that was promising.

"I think it's a possibility. The way the locals behave here is really strange. It's as if they hate—or maybe *distrust* would be a better word—outsiders collectively. We've received several veiled warnings about how it isn't safe for outsiders. Which is very odd for a small town, don't you think? I could understand if this was San Francisco, but not a town with a few thousand people in the Middle-of-Nowhere, Washington."

"Right," he agreed.

"And the way Madison and Chuck disappeared is very odd. We talked to some witnesses who saw a man drive off from a trail in a white van around the same time Madison and Chuck were allegedly out on a hike. Initially, I'd dismissed it, because it was at an entirely different trail than where we ultimately found the van. But now I'm wondering if the tip might have some merit—that maybe a man hurt them and then moved the van to throw us off. Which brings me to something I'm hesitant to bring up."

Susan waited for Howell to invite her to speak up, which he didn't. He'd already warned her twice about second-guessing herself, which was apparently his limit. It was probably not wise to keep testing his patience, not if she wanted to keep him interested in hiring her.

She said, "Jake mentioned that a tour operator here in town had taken a romantic interest in Madison but that she'd rebuffed his advances. From what Jake said, he was coming on strong enough that Madison started to pretend that Chuck was her boyfriend, which he isn't. It's a stretch, but I'm wondering if he might have followed them into the woods and attacked them."

"Doesn't sound like too much of a stretch to me," Howell commented.

"I only say that because I met the man and he didn't strike me as the predatory type. But I guess the true predators never do. He was nothing but respectful toward me, but I had gone into his store with Eric, and maybe I'm not his type."

"His store? I thought you said he was a tour operator."

"He is, but he also has a store here in town, Clancy Fancy, as well as a gym, Clancy Fitness. This seems to be par for the course here, people doing side jobs to make ends meet. The economy is not doing well, and a lot of people are behaving as if they've got nothing to lose, which is also concerning. Anyway, looking into the guy could possibly turn up a lead. His name is Ben Harvey."

Susan paused to give Howell time to write down the information.

She said, "I hate to say it, but I don't think we're going to find anything during the search party tomorrow. Eric feels the same way. Something about this town feels wrong . . . I have a feeling Chuck and Madison might be dead."

Howell said, "There are no killers operating out of Clancy—at least none that we are watching or are aware of—but there might be something else. When you first said the name, it rang a bell because a contact of mine in the DEA has mentioned it before. Can you hang on a second?"

"Sure. Of course." The DEA? Drugs hadn't even crossed her mind, beyond thinking that some of the locals—like Darla—might be on them.

But it would make sense. They were in the right area for it—at least she *thought* they might be. She'd heard of Murder Mountain in

Humboldt, California, which was only about six or seven hundred miles south of Clancy. There, where millions of dollars of cannabis was grown in the mountains illegally each year, endless people had vanished without a trace, hence the forbidding nickname.

Could that be what had happened to Chuck and Madison—was it possible that they'd stumbled upon someone's pot farm and were murdered for their mistake? Or, would they have been foolish enough to *seek out* a pot farm—had they heard one was off the trail? Had the whole "smoke a joint by the lake" story been a cover for a sneaky scavenger hunt they'd embarked on late at night—a search for a few poached marijuana plants that had gotten them killed? Was that why the van was found in an area that contradicted what they'd told Jake before leaving?

She'd gotten so wrapped up in her thoughts that she jumped when Howell got back on the line and began speaking.

"I gave my contact, Mark Kinger, a call over at the DEA. He confirmed: Clancy is along the main drug trafficking highway they've been watching for a little over three years."

Susan's bad feelings were sinking deeper. It had iced her blood, and now it was chilling her bones. "Three years? That's a long time. Marijuana?"

"No. It's a new street drug called Pop C. It's cheaper to produce than cocaine, but its effects are similar, except that it has the lasting power and addiction capabilities of methamphetamines. It's not too complicated to produce either, if you know what you're doing. But, if you don't, the drug becomes lethal. There's been some instances where it's rotted flesh straight to the muscle after frequent injections. I've seen the photos, nasty stuff. They've had several reported deaths in Arizona, Texas, California, and Washington. Canada too."

Susan picked up the E-Z-Sleep Motel logoed pen that was sitting across a pad on the nightstand. She pinched it in her lips, pulled off the cap, and then jotted down a few quick notes—she had to be quick with

Howell, because he was a busy man who spoke fast. "Canada? How are they getting it across the border?"

"That's why Clancy is a particular area of interest for the DEA. Have you heard of Port Alden?"

"Yes. It's up the road from us on the highway. Right on the water, just across the way from Victoria . . ." She paused. "Of course. A port town a stone's throw from Canada."

"That's how they're getting it across, on boats. The majority of ocean smugglers are getting nabbed, but it takes only a few to slide under the radar," Howell said. "According to Mark, the smugglers operate with loss in mind. They've already got backups in place long before any of their product is seized."

"Hmm. I haven't heard anything about it up here. Of course, being from California, nobody tells us anything. I have encountered a few strung-out-looking locals, but I'd assumed it was alcohol or maybe meth. You think this ties in with Chuck and Madison's disappearance?"

"I don't know," Howell said. "But it's one more possibility for you to consider."

"I'll keep you posted."

"Yes, please do. I'll look into this Harvey guy. And good luck on the search party tomorrow."

Luck? Susan thought. *What we need is a miracle.*

Chapter 17

Eric had not been expecting such a turnout for the search party at Mitchatepi Trail. He was downright shocked, actually, by the sheer size of the crowd that had turned up. Stogg had really pulled through for them.

Or so he'd thought.

But, then, Mayor Julia Moulden approached Eric, Susan, and Jake shortly after their arrival and wasted no time stating that it had been *she* who had come through, not the sheriff. "I'm rather disappointed in Stogg's handling of things. Had I heard about your friends' disappearances earlier, I would have jumped in immediately to offer my assistance."

She could've saved herself the breath, Eric thought, and just said: *I take credit for the whole thing. It was all me, nobody else.*

It was a sad, pathetically veiled attempt to throw the sheriff under the bus, should Jake ever decide to make good on his threats of going to the media. "I had to scramble to get the search organized. With it being so cold, every second counts." In a quieter voice, and as if confiding in them, she added with a nauseating wink, "He may be good at upholding the law, but he's certainly no organizer. From now on, I want you to forget Stogg and come directly to me."

"Thank you; we really appreciate that," Susan said, then quickly caught Eric's eye. No, she wasn't buying the mayor's line of BS either. Or was she? Susan, being a police officer, would know all the right things to say to keep the peace with the powers that be. "And we appreciate you putting the search party together so quickly."

The mayor's demeanor was steady and appraising. She was like a robot-monster invading from another planet in the disguise of an attractive, capable woman, as if she'd been designed with deception in mind. *Hello, Township of Clancy, take me to your leader.* And now here she was, running their town. Soon, the rest of the pod people would arrive, if a few weren't already there. Pod people might even be more normal than the locals.

Eric imagined that the mayor cared about the disappearance of Chuck and Madison about as much as she cared about the trash that miraculously disappeared from the front of her house on pickup days. "Yes, we really do appreciate it," he repeated weakly, only so that he could contribute. He was dying to get the show on the road. It was *freezing* out.

"And where is your bassist?" the mayor turned to Jake and asked brightly. The insinuation being: *We, a town full of utter strangers are here, but your own band member couldn't be bothered to show? For shame!*

"John's mother has been really sick—she has dementia. His father called yesterday afternoon and suggested that he come home immediately. It doesn't sound good."

"That's too bad. I'll keep her in my prayers."

Oh, I bet you will, Eric thought and had to focus hard to keep himself from snorting.

Lightly, as if it had only just occurred to her, the mayor asked, "Speaking of heading home, when are you guys hitting the road?"

The trio exchanged stealthy, if not incredulous, glances. Could she have picked a less appropriate time to ask such a question than at a search party for their missing friends?

"We'd like to find our friends first," Jake said slowly.

"Of course," she said with a thin smile.

"I don't see Darla," Jake said to the group. "Can't say I'm surprised."

"Darla?" the mayor asked.

"Oh, Darla Manns. She's Madison's friend—moved here from California a while back," Jake said.

The mayor nodded, shook her head. "Don't know her, I'm afraid."

"Trust me, you're not missing much," Jake muttered sourly.

Eric said, "I don't see Ben Harvey here, do you?"

Jake and Susan looked around, shook their heads.

"Oh, you won't see *him* here," the mayor said in a prickly tone. "He's not big on community."

A personal grudge? Eric wondered. He was going to quiz her further—he found small-town gossip beguiling at the best of times, having come from a metropolis like Philly—but Sheriff Stogg was starting to organize the party into groups at the base of the trail. Clausen was there, too, though he was handing out coffee in white Styrofoam cups. Good, keep the crowd caffeinated. Stogg, wearing his usual frown, was all-business. Probably hungover.

Clausen, not surprisingly, seemed to have a far better rapport with the crowd, who he chatted with jovially. Had he not known better, Eric might have assumed that this was because of the coffee—because, hey, who wouldn't like that?—and not because of their personality differences. Eric raised a hand and gave them both a quick wave. Clausen waved back. Stogg did not.

Shocker.

It was the sort of damp, miserable morning that made one's breath come out in little white puffs. The locals, no strangers to the unrelenting rain of the Pacific Northwest, had dressed in anticipation of it. Most everyone present, including the mayor, wore heavy hiking boots and waterproof jackets, which Eric, Jake, and Susan did not have, as they had not anticipated having to attend a search party for their two missing friends when they had packed for the trip.

They'd done the best with what they had—layering several shirts under sweaters and their dressier city jackets—which made them look all the more out of place. Many of the locals hadn't bothered to disguise their sideways glances at their attire, which they delivered with an unspoken *Where do you people think you are, Seattle?*

Hah. Didn't they *wish*.

The search was fairly straightforward. They were to assemble in a straight line across the trail horizontally, with a searcher placed "every few feet"—because of the unevenness of the trail (and, what was more likely, because they were so inexperienced with organizing search parties), precision was not stressed as much as alertness. There would also be other groups of four to five who broke off from the main group and searched the woods in clusters. Jake and Eric separated and joined the clusters of locals to search the forest, and Susan joined the long line that spread across the trail. The three of them figured that they might have a better time finding something of significance—assuming there *was* something to find—if they split up, since they'd know specifically what to look for. They also suspected the locals might do a better job with the search if they knew they were being watched.

While he hoped that his feelings had been incorrect, Eric couldn't help sensing that they were looking in the wrong place. The dead who'd come knocking had directed him toward the forest, but he wished they'd specified which one, because this one just didn't feel right.

Much to his surprise, Susan had begun to echo his opinions. She'd also told him what Howell had said during their phone call, which had only added to their sense of foreboding. They'd decided to keep Jake in the dark about such matters, at least for the time being, lest he give up hope. Or, what was more likely, post angry social media rants about Clancy, which would make working with the local authorities all the more difficult.

Eric had been expecting the locals in his group to treat him with indifference, so when they did, he let it roll right off his back. What he did find strange was their behavior as they searched—or, rather, *didn't* search—the woods. He watched the men and women as they walked, paying close attention to their disinterested expressions. While they did scan the ground and the horizon, it was apparent that they weren't really *looking*. They were merely going through the motions. As if they didn't anticipate finding Chuck and Madison alive. If at all.

Eric, unfortunately, was beginning to share their outlook.

A shout in the distance, the loud blaring of a whistle. "Hey! Over here! I've got something!"

Eric took off running. Not surprisingly, his counterparts did not seem to feel the same urgency. They chugged along about as slow as vehicles in a parade; the only thing they were missing was candy.

Jake and a couple of men from his cluster of searchers were already at the spot by the time Eric arrived. They were gathered around some debris scattered on the ground at the base of a tree. Jake did not appear as enthusiastic about the find as Eric would expect him to be. Strangely, he seemed fairly incredulous, which, he supposed, was a good thing. Had the bodies of Chuck and Madison been found, Jake would have been a lot more torn up.

Still, his friend looked pale and drawn. The strain the disappearance of Chuck and Madison was putting on him was evident on his features: dark circles under his eyes, mouth downturned, slumped shoulders. The light inside him was not extinguished, but it was certainly dimmed.

Sheriff Stogg arrived shortly thereafter, followed by numerous members of the search party—almost half by Eric's estimate—including Pete Clausen. The sheriff had a quick look around and then leaned toward Jake and said something that Jake obviously didn't like, as he began aggressively shaking his head. The two men seemed to be arguing. Eric threaded through the crowd toward them, so that he could listen better.

In a fashion that sounded rhetorical, Jake said to Stogg, "It seems like a big coincidence, doesn't it? Just yesterday you suggested that Chuck and Madison left town, and now here we find this? If you ask me, this seems like it was staged." A folded piece of paper flapped in his hand as he gestured.

"Staged?" Clausen asked, as if Jake might be pulling their legs. He glanced at Stogg and Jake with what seemed like frank confusion. "Why would anyone want to do *that*?"

"If someone had hurt them, then obviously . . ." Jake, it seemed, couldn't bear to finish the statement.

"I'm sorry, son—*Jake*," the sheriff quickly corrected. "But it looks like your friends are gone." Eric found the compassion in Stogg's voice startling—and confusing, with his use of "gone." Were Chuck and Madison dead after all?

He stepped around a rotund man in overalls and a puffy coat to get a better understanding of what was happening. He pointed to what looked like trash on the ground. "Jake, what is this?"

"I understand that this is upsetting," Stogg interrupted, but not unkindly. How bad must the situation be if the prickliest lawman of Clancy was feeling pity for Jake instead of anger over being dragged out into the forest for what was beginning to sound like nothing for the second time in the matter of a few days? And not only him this time, but practically the whole town.

Then again, the sheriff could have been only feigning sympathy and grandstanding for the audience—Mayor Moulden in particular, who was hardly his biggest fan and wasn't shy about expressing her disappointment in his job performance. The man didn't seem to be the most stable emotionally, but raging alcoholics rarely were.

Stogg said, "The evidence here suggests—"

"This is *not* evidence," Jake said, having none of that.

Eric moved closer, so that he could get a look at the so-called clues for himself: a cigarette butt with a smudge of lipstick on the end and a smattering of sunflower seeds. But what was most perplexing—yet probably irrefutable evidence in the eyes of Clausen and Stogg—was the *C+M* carved into the tree trunk.

"Do you know if that's the brand of cigarettes Madison smokes?" Clausen asked. "And those sunflower seeds?"

"This stuff could've been taken from the van, which was probably planted here too!" Jake shouted explosively at the poor ranger, who was only trying to be helpful. A few people in the crowd flinched. "There's at least a dozen of her cigarette butts in the ashtray, and Chuck's seeds are all over the floor. An orangutan could've figured out how to stage this scene."

Clausen kept his cool. "It's theirs then?"

"They did *not* skip town! *Look* at this stuff—it's been put here with such obviousness that there might as well be a neon sign nailed to the tree here marked 'clues.' I mean, this is straight out of *Scooby-Doo*. You can't actually be buying this!"

Jake was right; it was like a spoof of a crime scene. Too convenient and conspicuous, particularly because he was in agreement with Jake that his friends would never skip town. "What are you holding?" Eric asked his friend.

Jake handed him what turned out to be a trail map, which explained the skipping-town theory. The map covered miles of a single trail that jutted off from the one they were currently on. Bright X-shaped marks had been made along the trail, which ultimately dead-ended into a major highway that was several miles north of Clancy. The mileage from their current location to the final stop on the highway had been calculated next to each *X*. The entire hike would have taken approximately half a day.

"This whole thing is illogical," Jake said. He paused to calm himself, and when he spoke again, his tone was rational, albeit sarcastic. "Okay, so let's just say that this stuff did come from Chuck and Madison— that they just happened to hike into the forest one night and suddenly decided that they wanted to run off together, despite us having a high-paying gig scheduled in Seattle for the following day. Let's just say that two of the kindest and most decent people I have ever known suddenly stopped caring about the unnecessary worry they'd cause their family and friends, when all it would take was a ten-second phone call to let even one person know that they were okay. Let's say we all buy that. Why on earth, then, would they leave behind the map they needed to get to the highway? And why would they even *need* to hike miles and miles to thumb a ride, when Madison's van is parked just down the way in the parking lot?"

"Sometimes, people just lose it," Stogg said, reasonably enough. Eric could hardly argue with him on that one, given that he'd lost it plenty in his lifetime.

Clausen endorsed the idea with a nod and his soft Southern twang. "It does happen from time to time up this way. City folks come to Clancy with the intent of recharging, but then, after a couple days of taking in all this unadulterated nature, they decide, you know what, maybe they don't need material *things* anymore. Maybe life would be a whole helluva lot simpler if they turned their backs on it all—the noise, the bills, the pollution, the sheer responsibility of *living* in a metropolis . . ." He shrugged, offered Jake a kind smile. "And they just walk off. Can't say that I haven't thought of doing the same things myself, from time to time. Maybe that's what happened with your friends. Being artistic sorts—and I mean no disrespect with this—perhaps they're naturally more inclined toward flights of fancy. Especially if they're earthy types who drive old VWs, like your friend."

Clausen was so good at setting the scene that Eric was nearly inclined to agree with him. Nearly. While it was a nice narrative, it just didn't add up—at least not for Chuck and Madison.

"Don't let Madison's old van fool you," Jake said with a heavy shake of the head. "You know those goofy key chains people have, *My other car is a Porsche*? Well, Madison actually *has* a Porsche—some rich guy she was dating bought it for her as a present a while back, believe it or not. That, and a mound of designer handbags that could cover some kid's college tuition for all four years with change leftover, if she ever sold them. She's a lovely person, but she's about as materialistic as you can get, despite her hippy-dippy ways. Chuck's just about as bad. If you knew them, you'd understand how ridiculous the notion of them running off together to live off the land is.

"Furthermore, Chuck and Madison aren't even a couple," Jake said. "And, before you ask, they never have been. They're like brother and sister. So, whoever did this obviously didn't know them, because if they did, they'd know that they weren't a couple."

"Maybe they were dating behind your back?" Stogg suggested.

Jake gave the sheriff a hard stare. "Trust me; I'd know. Also, Madison was a staunch environmentalist. She never, ever would have left cigarette butts out in the forest, let alone carved her initials into a tree trunk. Same goes for Chuck. It's just . . . *ridiculous*."

And it *was* ridiculous. Still, it caused Eric pause. If the debris was, indeed, Chuck and Madison's, then who had put it there and why? Was this somebody's idea of a cruel joke against outsiders, or was there something more sinister at play, a cover-up of a bigger and deadlier crime? If someone had planted evidence (and, in Eric's mind, they most likely had), then it would mean that they'd had access to the inside of Madison's van—which would also mean that they'd had her keys. And how had they acquired those? The bigger questions: Where *were* Chuck and Madison, and why would anyone want to suggest in such a clumsy manner that they'd left Clancy?

CHAPTER 18

Jake was going stir crazy in the motel room by himself. He'd never thought he'd see the day that he'd miss the presence of John so desperately, but even hanging with the sullen bassist would be volumes better than the agitated lonesomeness he was feeling now.

When it got to the point that he could no longer take it—when he began to suspect he might implode if he didn't get out of the room and get some human contact—he pocketed his wallet and room key and headed down the walkway.

"That was fast," Jake said after Eric answered before he had a chance to knock.

"I was by the window and saw you coming up."

"Sure you did, psychic." Jake winked. It tickled him to joke with Eric about such things, mainly because he wasn't entirely sure that the nickname was inaccurate. He'd met some interesting individuals in the years he'd served as a musician, but Eric was the first (maybe) psychic who he'd known.

"What's up?" Eric stepped aside so Jake could enter.

Once inside, Jake let out a startled gasp and quickly threw a hand over his eyes. "Whoa, sorry, Suze!"

Susan let out a throaty laugh and then threw the bedcovers off herself, which she'd had tucked up under her chin. "No worries, fully clothed—see!"

Jake dropped his hand from his eyes and placed it over his heart. Susan was dressed from her neck right down to her socks, much to his immense relief. "Thought maybe I'd walked in on something. *Awkward.*"

"Would I have answered the door if that was the case?" Eric grinned.

"Guess not. So, listen; I'm wondering if you guys are up for a beer? Was thinking that Clancy Grill place up the way, the one with all the taxidermy. They've got chow there, too, if you're hungry. But I don't mind if you want to go somewhere else—I don't care where we go, I just need to get out. I'm bouncing off the walls over there by myself. I feel like I should be doing *something* for Chuck and Madison, but I don't know what."

"You up for a beer?" Eric asked Susan.

Susan shook her head, glancing down at her phone as she fired off a quick text. "That was the mayor. She's agreed to meet me for dinner."

Eric made a sour face. "Ugh. Why?"

"I know you guys don't like her—"

"It's not that we don't like her, per se," Jake said. "She's just . . ."

"A smarmy politician," Eric finished for him.

"Exactly," Jake said. "During our tour, that Ben Harvey guy and I got to talking about her—guess he's not too fond of her either. They've got some kind of beef going, I think. Anyway, he said she's never off— that she's always 'politicking.' That was the way he put it."

"What does that mean?" Eric asked.

"Ben said she's got 'national aspirations,' which I think means that she wants the hell out of Clancy. Can't say I blame her for that one," Jake said. "But the way he made it sound is that she's impersonal because she's always maneuvering."

"That's the vibe I get," Eric said.

"Nobody around here really trusts her because she never lets her guard down." To Eric, he said, "You know what moving to a small town is like, how you're treated as a newbie. You've got to work extrahard to prove yourself. You have to be willing to give in a little to people's nosiness."

"Totally true. If people don't know your business down to your hair follicles, it's like they don't know you at all," Susan said, and Eric and Jake chuckled.

Jake said, "So, while she puts her face time in around town as a mayor, nobody really *knows* her on a personal level. She never reveals much about herself beyond the basics, and she interacts on the surface. Of course, this is all according to Ben. If he has a grudge against her, he's not going to have too many nice things to say."

Eric said, "Seems pretty spot on, from what I've seen."

Susan frowned. "Okay, she *is* annoying, but you can't begrudge the poor woman having goals. And I bet if she were a man doing the same thing, people wouldn't find her half as suspicious, and you know I'm right. People do that same thing to me in Perrick and I hate it—and I'm from those parts. They can't understand why I'm not married with a couple kids by now, or why a 'nice girl like me' wants to carry a gun and interact with the dregs of society. You're telling me they'd be saying that crap to either of you if you were in the same position?"

"Not the most progressive of individuals in Perrick," Jake said and then grew serious. "I'm not going to lie, you guys; I really wasn't expecting to find anything during the search this morning, were you?"

Eric and Susan exchanged a look, and then Susan said, "No, sorry, Jake. We weren't either."

"That's about what I thought," Jake said with a sad nod. "And what the hell was up with those 'clues'?"

"Probably a prank," Susan said. "There's some sick individuals out there who'd find that sort of thing funny."

"It is strange, though, that they'd know to put sunflower seeds and cigarette butts there," Eric said. "They'd have to be familiar with Chuck and Madison enough to know that those things were specific to them—otherwise they might have planted, I don't know, a granola bar wrapper and ChapStick."

"I've been thinking about that," Jake said. "We're pretty open on social media. Anyone who follows us and has scrolled through our photos would know about Madison's smoking and Chuck's sunflower seed habit. That, or if they've seen us live. And people have been speculating for years about Chuck and Madison secretly having a thing for one another."

"But what would someone get out of doing that?" Eric asked. "Why go through all the trouble?"

"What do people get out of doing any of the cruel, twisted things they do to strangers—trolls on the internet spreading hate and writing ugly things, people leaving shitty reviews just because they can, kids sharing videos of homeless people beating each other up for money because they think it's funny? We live in a culture where strangers hurt one another for entertainment."

"So you think someone planted those things to get a rise out of you?" Susan asked.

"Maybe," Jake said with a shrug. "But maybe, on the other hand, someone really has done something to Chuck and Madison, and they're doing whatever they can to prevent us from searching. Maybe they're hoping that, if we think they've left town, we'll leave town too."

Eric nodded. "Could be."

Jake said, "I've been thinking, and the way we found Madison's van is also fishy, almost like somebody had parked it right along the highway so we'd find it. The way it was parked at the farthest end of the lot wasn't Madison's style."

Susan sat up in bed. "What do you mean, not her style?"

"Madison is notoriously lazy. Which is crazy, right, since she's always running all those marathons? I've known her since we were yea high," Jake said, bringing a hand down to his knee, "and when she's not running or lifting weights or punishing her body in some other insane way, she's a complete sloth. She'd rather take eighty laps around the Target parking lot looking for a space up front than walk a few extra yards from the back—I've seen her do this hundreds of times over the years, easily, and she always tells me to shut it whenever I call her out for it. And, whenever she comes to hang at my place, she'll park in my driveway like a *millimeter* from my garage door—even though I always tell her not to—so she won't have to walk as far to my front door. It's almost like a point of pride for her, seeing how close she can get. Anyway, you saw how far the van was from the trail entrance; if it was any farther away, it would've been on the damn highway. So, tell me, why would Madison have felt the need to park at the very back?"

Eric said, "It *is* weird, but maybe they had to park that way because the lot was full."

"I thought of that too," Jake said, shaking his head. "But that wouldn't have been the case when they were there at ten at night."

Susan said, "Right. I bet they would've been the only ones there, especially because it's not a very popular trail. Not like the one with the trust fund hippies, or whatever you called them."

"Trustafarians."

"Right. That trail."

"It may be a long shot, but I'm thinking that maybe it wouldn't hurt for us to go up there tomorrow and have a look around."

Eric said, "Sure, couldn't hurt."

"Isn't it closed?" Susan asked. "The trail? That's what that couple said anyway."

Jake gave Susan a sly smile. "From what I understand, Suze, you've been known to be a bit of a rule breaker."

"I may have bent the rules from time to time," she said, nonchalant.

He laughed. "Okay, then! And if anyone catches us, we'll just say we didn't see the sign or something. Worst they'll do is call us idiots and kick us out."

"Unless it's Stogg who catches us," Eric said. "Then we'd probably get the death penalty."

Jake let out his breath and scratched the back of his neck. Internally, he was psyching himself up for the subject he'd been hesitant to approach. He'd avoided it long enough, and it had gotten to the point where he'd run out of time and needed to speak up. He cleared his throat. "And . . . while I'm on the topic of Chuck and Madison, I'm wondering how much longer you guys are planning on staying around?"

"Why, do you want us gone, *Mayor*?" Eric asked teasingly, and Jake snorted.

"I think you guys are being a little harsh on the mayor," Susan said. "I know she's—"

"Smarmy," Eric repeated.

"No, I was going to say *politically driven*," Susan corrected. "But imagine what it must be like for her, trying to bring this dying town out of the Stone Age when half the locals resent change. And, as prickly as she is, you have to admit that it was still decent of her to show up and help out with the search. At least she walks the walk; she could've just sent an assistant or somebody, but she was out there with the rest of us, slogging through the mud."

"Careful, it sounds like you're starting to drink the Kool-Aid," Eric said.

"All I'm trying to say is that we don't have too many people on our side in this town, so let's try to not alienate the few who *do* have our backs—even if the only reason she does have our backs is because she's trying to get ahead politically. She can exploit our tragedy all she wants, as long as it helps us locate Chuck and Madison."

"Fair enough," Jake said and then paused before changing the subject back to the original topic. "I was only asking about your plans because I know this can't be fun, and it's not really your responsibility to stay behind and search for my friends. So, if you want to leave Clancy, I totally understand. Trust me—I'm dying to get out of this godawful place, too, but I wouldn't feel right leaving with Madison and Chuck still missing."

"Have you called their families?" Susan asked.

"Not yet. I don't want to do it until we have a chance to search around some more. I keep hoping that they'll come walking through the door with some cockamamie story to explain where they've been, but that's just wishful thinking. I'll do it tomorrow if we don't find anything at the other trail. They both live on their own, so it'll take some searching to locate their families' numbers. But John also said he'd make some calls too."

"Why don't you just . . ." Eric broke off and shook his head. "Never mind. I was going to say, why don't you just look in their phones, but—"

"Yep, those are missing too," Jake finished for him.

Susan said, "I don't suppose they'd have an address book or—"

"When was the last time either of you had an address book?" Jake said, but not unkindly. "That you traveled with."

"Good point." Susan smiled.

"I don't think I've *ever* had one," Eric said. "Back before cell phones, I'd usually just write numbers down on whatever scraps of paper I found."

Susan rolled her eyes and said teasingly, "Why doesn't that surprise me?"

Eric gently tossed a throw pillow at her. "Anyway, as far as how long we're staying up here, we're really in no hurry to head back."

"Really?" Jake asked, feeling the utmost relief. He was overwhelmed as it was, and maybe even feeling a little guilty because he was still safe and sound while his friends had vanished like ghosts in the night. He didn't know how he'd cope if he lost the support of Eric and Susan.

Susan added, "Honestly, we don't mind. We've talked it over, and we have no need to be back, not when we're both off work." Eric nodded enthusiastically to second the motion.

"Even if *you* don't mind, I really appreciate it," Jake said, thankful that he had these two wonderful souls in his life.

CHAPTER 19

If the numbers Eric had obtained from his cursory glance around the bar were correct, the ratio of dead animals to humans inside Clancy Grill was about three to one. There were so many beasts mounted behind the bar that it made the wall appear as if it was wearing an enormous fur coat with eyes.

On the wall opposite, where the entrance was, there were stuffed things that had once dwelled near water: crocodiles, a half dozen or so varieties of fish, and a nightmarish hybrid creature that had the head of a turtle, the body of an otter, and the wings of a seagull.

Rustic hand-painted signs were also scattered about:

BEER SERVED AS COLD AS YOUR EX
BEWARE: PICKPOCKETS & LOOSE WOMEN
ALCOHOL MAY NOT SOLVE YOUR PROBLEMS, BUT
NEITHER WILL WATER

And, behind the bartender: **I TAKE CASH, GRASS, OR ASS. NOBODY DRINKS FOR FREE**

"I'm guessing they don't get too many vegans in here," Jake said from the side of his mouth and laughed uncomfortably.

The carcasses on the wall were the most pleasant thing about the place, Eric thought, and that assessment included the locals. "Or outsiders. Notice how everyone here is staring at us?"

"Yep."

The "everyone" had not been an exaggeration on Eric's part. The sizing up they were receiving was not limited to only the patrons, a couple of whom had a lip curled up in one corner to demonstrate exactly how they felt about Eric and Jake's kind coming in to drink at *their* local establishment. The bartender, three waitresses, and the line cook were getting in on the action, their curiosity masked marginally better than that of the individuals who weren't getting paid to be there.

"And here I thought I was paranoid. I don't think we should order any food. No telling what they'd do to it."

"I second the motion," Eric agreed with a nod. "We can have a beer, at least—and I do mean *a* beer, because every minute we stay in here, our chances of getting our asses kicked increase tenfold."

Jake laughed. "No doubt. But let's sit at the bar so we can watch the bartender pour."

They took two corner stools at the bar and ordered beers once the bartender glowered at them. He made no attempt to make idle chit-chat as he worked, which must've defied every bartender cliché conceived since the dawn of man. The only words he spoke to them during the entire transaction were numbers, when he delivered the total. He frowned when they left a tip on the bar, but he took their money anyway. The locals had their pride, but evidently that pride stopped short of refusing cash from outsiders.

"Chatty," Eric said under his breath.

"I'm waiting for his cronies to show with torches and pitchforks." Jake took a hefty swig of his beer. "I mean, Jesus, have you ever been treated worse anywhere else in your entire life? And I say this as a *dwarf.*"

"I can't even begin to imagine the things you've had to put up with," Eric commented. "In bars, especially."

"Oh, you mean like the complete strangers who ask me all sorts of crazy shit that's none of their business, like if my penis is 'normal size' or if I drive a special tiny car? Then there was the bachelorette party who pretended to flirt with me only so their friends could take pictures when they thought I wasn't looking. The best, though, was the crew of drunken frat boys who tried to pick me up and throw me across the room—because, apparently, it's okay to do that to a *human*, yet people would lose their freaking minds if it was done to a *dog*."

Eric glanced over at his friend, who was taking a bitter swig of beer. "I hate people," he commiserated. "The ones who suck, anyway."

Jake placed his beer atop the bar and tilted his head toward where the majority of patrons sat drinking at tables. "I think a few of these sucky people hate *us*—that's for sure."

Thankfully, most of the drinkers had gone back to their business, but there were still a few at tables who occasionally glanced their way. It made them uneasy, that feeling that these strangers might be plotting an attack. Eric said, "I think we're the only ones in here without beards. Ditto on not wearing a flannel shirt."

Jake gestured at the bartender for another beer.

"What happened to just one drink?"

"Eh, why not live a little? It's been a stressful couple of days."

Eric shrugged and ordered another beer too.

Jake said, "I'm trying to understand the vibe of this place. Are they hipsters, you think, or actual lumberjacks?"

"I'm going with lumberjacks," Eric said. "I'm seeing a couple of people who were at the search this morning, are you? There's one at that table kind of in front of us but a little off to the right—don't look now; I'll tell you when—with those five dudes. Okay, look."

"The blond kid, right?"

Eric nodded. "That's the one. He was one of the few who actually seemed nice and genuinely concerned for Chuck and Madison."

"Wonder what he's doing with *that* group of yahoos? He's the only one not mad dogging us . . . uh-oh, don't look. I think he's coming over here . . ." Jake pretended to be deeply engrossed in his beer.

Moments later, the blond kid was standing at the bar next to them, holding his hand out for them to shake. He had deep-blue eyes and a baby face that gave him the appearance of a teenager, yet Eric figured he was at least twenty-one, being in a bar. He introduced himself as Miles, offered to buy them a round, which they accepted, and then took a seat. Eric caught Jake's eye while the kid was paying for the drinks and gave him a quick *I don't know* expression.

Miles distributed the beers and then began chatting away, behaving as if he'd never been more excited to see two individuals in his entire life. "I just moved here from Idaho, like a couple weeks ago," he said after a long slurp of beer. He used the back of his hand to wipe his mouth. "I feel like everyone has known each other since birth, so I cannot tell you how nice it is to see other out-of-towners. This hasn't been the easiest place to make friends."

"Aren't those your buddies over there?" Jake asked.

Miles brought his hand up and moved it side to side. "*Kind of.* I work with them indirectly—I'm a forester. A couple of those guys are foresters, too, but there's also a couple loggers. I just happened to be there today after work when they were talking about going out, so I was lumped in with the invite."

"How're you liking it here so far?" Eric asked, fishing.

"It's different." Miles puffed air out of his cheeks, further dodging the question. "I'm still getting used to it."

Eric and Jake exchanged a look, and then Jake asked, "They like to keep to themselves here, don't they?"

Miles gave them a relieved look. "*Thank you.* I've been feeling like I'm losing my mind! I can't say that it'd be any better back home—I moved here because I broke up with my fiancée, which my family is still pissed about—but at least there I'm not treated like a complete leper."

"Why do they act that way here, you think?" Eric asked. He saw that the kid was hitting the drinks pretty hard—he was nearly finished with his beer, and he and Jake had had only a few sips of theirs—so he was hoping that he'd be nice and loose lipped.

Miles did not disappoint. He flapped a hand. "Small towns come with small minds, like the saying goes. Some people here just don't like change, you know? And you should *hear* how they talk about the Kincaid tourists."

"I can imagine," Jake said dryly.

Eric slyly placed a hand on Jake's arm. *Let him talk,* his eyes said. Anything the kid had to say was likely of no consequence, but he figured it couldn't hurt.

Miles continued, "Then there's people who don't like you just because you're from out of state. It's like you have to jump through a bunch of hoops proving yourself before you're let in."

"Let in to what?" Eric asked lightly. "You make it sound as if they're operating a secret society. You think they've got something to hide?"

Miles's gaze flickered to the table where his coworkers sat. "I never said anything about anyone hiding anything," he said. He added in a near whisper, "But I've heard"—fingers raised in quotation marks—"'rumors.'"

Eric and Jake leaned in close in a classic *do tell* gesture.

"For starters, you don't want to get on the bad side of anyone around here who's got any power over you. From what I hear, the cops and judges are just criminals under a different name—an old boy network on steroids. But if they're not dirty?" He took a sip of beer, shrugged. "I'm sure you heard about those government buildings going up in flames, right?"

"Arson?" Jake deduced.

"I'm afraid I can neither confirm nor deny," Miles said and then went to take a swig of his beer. "Oh, I'm empty."

Eric ordered him another beer and quickly paid.

"Also, let's just say that your friends weren't the first people in Clancy to go missing, and I'd bet my next paycheck that they won't be the last."

"Under what circumstances?"

Maybe it was the drinks that led Miles to believe that he was being sneaky when he glanced at his coworkers, but he couldn't have been more obvious if he was setting off fireworks. One of the men at the table elbowed the guy sitting next to him, and they began watching the bar closely. Eric didn't like it.

Miles took a leisurely sip of beer. "It's the forest, man; it takes people. I'm creeped out half the time I'm working out there—I'm alone most of the day, as a forester. I'm not looking forward to when it starts getting dark early." When he saw Eric pull out his phone, he said, "Don't bother googling it. The disappearances are never reported. It's always locals, and they're usually the kind of people everyone's a little glad to see gone, anyway—know what I'm sayin'? So I've heard—don't take any of my gossip as gospel. People talk, you know, and I'm always quick to listen. Your friends are the first tourists I've heard of who've gone missing."

"People disappear on hikes or . . . ?" Jake frowned. "Wait, you don't mean monsters, like werewolves. Or that the *trees* eat people . . ." Jake's gaze flitted between the kid and Eric. "What?"

Miles barked out a laugh. "Naw, man, nothing like that! Maybe I'm not saying it right, I've had a few. People don't *necessarily*"—slurred drunkenly as *ness-airly*—"go *missing* in the forest, but that's where they get put to *stay gone*. That's what everyone says but doesn't say, if you catch my drift." He turned and raised his glass at his table of coworkers, grinning. He did not wait for them to raise their glasses in return before he turned back around, which was a good thing, since they didn't.

"How?" Eric asked, keeping one eye on Miles's associates, who were looking pretty riled. Three of them were starting to get out of their chairs.

"The trees! You step outa line, and that's where you're going—"

"You making friends, Miles? Whatcha talkin' about?" asked a man the size of a gorilla—at least he seemed that big to Eric. He had to tilt his head all the way back from his seated position just to meet the guy's eyes. He made the ginormous bouncer at the bar where Jake had played look like a gnat. The man's hair was oily black and slicked back off his face. On his neck was a poorly executed tattoo that was meant to look like lipstick marks left by a pair of women's lips but actually looked like two slugs. He was grinning down at them like an alligator watching wounded prey. He was missing a tooth, and Eric suspected that he wouldn't mind losing another for the sake of a good barroom brawl.

The other two men kept quiet, but their aggressive stances suggested they were ready to rumble. Eric didn't dare look at Jake, because then the jig would be up, and they'd know they'd succeeded at intimidating them. Then, they'd be forced to make a move. And, considering that they were so heavily outnumbered, whatever move they did make would be a bad one.

"Oh, you know, just making our two visitors here feel welcome," Miles said jovially. He was either in complete denial or drunk out of his gourd, because he did not seem fazed by their evident attempt to shut him up.

"Perhaps your friends would feel more welcome outside," the man said. "I bet we could all use some fresh air?"

"We're good here," Jake said. Eric quickly glanced over at his friend and saw that, despite his casual tone, he was frightened. And for good reason; the gorilla-man could squish him under his foot as easily as he could a beetle.

The man's leer stretched to an alarming proportion. "Naw, but *we're* not. Let's go outsi—"

"Don't you be starting shit in *my* bar," said a threatening voice near them.

It was their strange new buddy, Ben Harvey. Unlike the day Eric and Susan had met him in his shop, he wore no delicate wire-rimmed glasses and baggy sweatshirt. Tonight, his eyes were as clear and menacing as two sharpened knives, and his well-honed muscles were pumped and ready for action beneath the flimsy T-shirt he sported. He did not take his gaze off the troublemakers, but his hand fell to his hip, as if he might be packing.

Eric had never wanted to kiss a man so much in his entire life.

"It's cool," the grinning fool said, raising his hands up.

"I think it's time you two boys got on home," Ben said to Eric and Jake.

They did not argue.

CHAPTER 20

On their way back to the hotel, Jake said, "Mind taking a detour?"

"Not at all. Where to?"

Jake began directing Eric to Darla's house.

"I thought you and Susan talked to her and she threw you out?"

"She did. But that was after she found out that Suze was a cop, and Suze's not with us now."

"And you think she's going to be nicer now? I doubt it," Eric said.

"Here's the thing: both times that I've gone to Darla's house, she was afraid that someone—her nosy-ass neighbors in particular—was going to see us talking to her."

"That's weird, but weird behavior seems the norm in Clancy. They haven't exactly welcomed us with open arms in any of the places we've gone."

"Right, I don't think we've made anyone's Christmas card list since we've been here," Jake said darkly and then directed Eric to park once they entered Darla's neighborhood. "It's this one on the right."

Eric turned to Jake. "Okay, so then why are we here?"

"I was hoping that you might get one of your *feelings*, or whatever, about Darla."

"It doesn't really work that way, Jake," Eric explained with a sigh. "I can't control when these . . . insights come. I'm not psychic. And, as you saw on the trail, sometimes they hit me when I least expect it, and for no reason."

"Sure, sure, I understand that." Jake hoped that he hadn't offended his friend. "But I figure that it never hurts to try. Come on, man, I'm desperate. Even if there's the slightest chance . . ."

Eric nodded. "Okay, but I don't want you to get your hopes up."

The two men made their way up to the porch, but even from the lawn they could sense that the house was vacant. They used their cell phones as flashlights, seeing that the curtains were missing from the windows. What was left in the living room were things that had obviously been abandoned. The ice chests were gone, but wire hangers were scattered here and there, as if they'd been dropped and forgotten. A busted ceramic lamp that looked as if it'd gotten kicked over during the move sat upturned in the center of the room.

"Looks like she left in a hurry," Jake commented.

"Is it me, or does it look like this place has been ransacked?"

"It's hard to tell, because it was a dump even before she skipped out."

"What the hell is going on in this town?" Eric said with a slow shake of the head.

"First Chuck and Madison disappear and now this broad."

"Wait! There's someone inside!" Eric whispered. "He just walked into the back room, see?"

"I see him. You think he saw us—our lights?" Jake and Eric quickly turned off their cell phones.

"I don't think so. I also don't think our guest had been invited."

Unaware of Eric and Jake watching him, the prowler skulked from room to room, as if searching for something specific. With only streetlights shining in, it was difficult to make out his features, but he moved with the air of a man who was up to no good.

Jake walked inside.

"Jake!" Eric hissed, yet he followed.

The two men stood silent and motionless in the front room, listening as the man was rooting through the few things Darla had left behind. It sounded as if he was sifting through paper and dumping things onto the ground. A moment later came a curse, followed by the sound of an object being hurled against the wall.

"Hey!" Jake called.

The man came scrambling out from the back room, his eyes wide. In the blink of an eye, he was bolting down the hallway toward the back door of the house.

"What do we do?" Eric asked excitedly. "Should we go after him?" And then he did just that before Jake had a chance to answer.

Luckily, Eric was quite the runner, and he effortlessly caught up with the guy and grabbed him by the scruff. The man, who Eric could now see was a couple of decades older than him, didn't put up much of a fight. Actually, he didn't put up any.

"Easy, tough guy. Cool your jets," he said with a scowl. "I ain't going to run." He shook Eric's hand off his shoulder, reached into his pocket, and pulled out a small canister of chewing tobacco. He uncapped it and offered a pinch to Jake and Eric, who both declined. "Smart move. You guys don't want to start up on this stuff. It's disgusting." He had a cleft lip, gruff voice, and gruff demeanor to match.

"Why'd you run?" Jake asked.

The man shrugged. "Dunno. Why'd you chase me."

"Dunno," Eric said, and both the man and Jake had to laugh.

"Glad we got that settled," the man said. "One of you her new boyfriend?"

"Please. Do I look like the sort of person who'd go out with her?" Jake said, and the man snorted.

What an odd exchange, Eric thought. And here he'd been preparing for a confrontation. "No, we're just looking for her. Why are you here?"

The man was surprisingly candid. "She owes my boss money. I came to collect."

"I hate to break it to you, friend, but I don't think she's got much money to spare," Jake said.

"I know. They never do." The man sighed. "Do you know where she is?"

"No idea," Jake answered. "Do you know where *my* friends are?"

"Dunno. Who are your friends?"

"Their names are Chuck and Madison. They disappeared up here."

"Oh, yah. Heard about that. Sorry, can't help you."

"Can't or won't?" Eric said. Because, if he wasn't imagining things, something on the man's face had changed—there had been . . . a flicker of recognition in his eyes, maybe? But he knew a fruitless task when he saw it. This guy wasn't going to give anything away. And, though he was playing it calmly, Jake was under no illusion that the man wouldn't turn to violence, should it be required. He was undoubtedly armed in some fashion, as he'd heard men in these parts so often were.

Without another word, the man walked off. They didn't try to stop him.

"Should we call someone—the cops or . . . ?" Eric said after a long stretch of silence.

"For what reason? To report a break-in while we're doing a break-in?"

"Good point."

"Anyway, it would probably be Sheriff Stogg. You fancy seeing him again? With our luck, he'd just end up arresting us."

"Let's go back to the hotel. This place gives me the creeps."

CHAPTER 21

The only thing Susan had really learned from having dinner with Mayor Moulden was that she appreciated punctuality. As Susan had slid down in the seat opposite, the mayor pointedly glanced at her watch and gave her a smile that seemed genuine. Susan then allowed herself to relax, thinking that maybe the meeting might yield some ripe fruits after all.

But then had come the showboating: her plans for national expansion—the mayor hadn't laughed when Susan asked her if she wanted to one day be president—her constant struggle to bring the town into the modern age, her veiled criticism of locals who did not share her vision . . . and on and on. It was nothing she hadn't heard during their previous conversations, which made her wonder if the mayor was only capable of discussing politics.

Not once had she asked Susan anything about herself, other than her inadvertent questioning about when she, Eric, and Jake were planning on leaving town. Driving toward Ben Harvey's health club for an impromptu visit, Susan silently chastised herself for being surprised. She shook her head and laughed. What had she expected, for the mayor to reveal a softer side of herself and for them to become bosom buddies? Maybe she was optimistic to a fault, like her mother, always digging around the personalities of others in search of better qualities they believed could be unearthed with the right amount of prodding.

Susan tried not to take the bad treatment personally. Some people, like Mayor Moulden, simply don't want to be excavated. She doubted that she treated anyone else in Clancy any better.

Susan didn't believe that the mayor's aloofness was rooted in some kind of petty female rivalry, or that it had anything to do with her being a lowly cop and the mayor being, well, mayor. It was more like she didn't let *anyone* in. Case in point: everyone in the diner had insisted on calling the woman Mayor; not a single soul had once addressed her as Julia, which was telling if not a little odd. Did nobody in the tiny town she called home know her on an intimate level? Did she have *any* friends? She was like a pretty rug hiding a splintery floor; look underneath, and no telling what ugliness would be found.

Another odd thing that had happened was the so-called eyewitnesses who'd come forward. Their waitress had mentioned that three separate parties she'd waited on had claimed to have seen Chuck and Madison hitchhiking their way out of town. While Mayor Moulden had seemed to (smugly) accept the claims at face value—as proof, even, that the pair weren't really missing—Susan was dubious. Oftentimes, in high-profile investigations, people linked unrelated events. Maybe there actually had been a pair of hitchhikers who'd been spotted, but were they truly Chuck and Madison? There was no way to confirm or deny, so it did nothing but muddle the investigation.

In the parking lot of Clancy Fitness, Susan provided herself a quick reminder to not let her guard down and inadvertently reveal her suspicions of Harvey. She would stick to her story about the off-the-cuff visit, stating that she might have left a pair of earrings in the locker room during her last visit. And, hey, while she was there, why not ask the staff a few questions about the owner?

Despite her prepping, she was taken aback when she walked in and found the man himself sitting at the front desk. This, she had not expected, yet he acted as if he couldn't be happier to see her. As if he had nothing to hide.

"Sunflower seeds," she said, commenting on the shells scattered around the desk. A coincidence, or was he so arrogant and convinced that he couldn't be linked to Chuck and Madison's disappearance that he could blatantly consume one of the few "clues" that had been found at the site of the last place in Clancy that they'd allegedly visited?

"Yep, want some?" He smiled, popping a few into his mouth and then offering her the bag. "I never leave home without 'em! My one vice."

Your one vice, she wondered, *in addition to murder?*

CHAPTER 22

The young hippy couple was long gone from Anquikia Trail, but the closed notice was still present. There was just one, a flimsy plastic sign attached to a knee-high rope with a thin thread of wire: **TRAIL CLOSED**. As if that would stop anyone determined enough to trespass.

And Susan was.

"Sign? What sign?" she said after she liberated it from the wire and rope with just a few twists of her fingers. She hid it behind a large rock at the base of the trail. "This way, if anyone catches us, we can say that we didn't see any sign."

"So diabolical," Jake smirked.

"That's my girl," Eric added with a fair amount of admiration in his voice, "the rebel."

Susan rolled her eyes at them. "Let's go, you fools."

They'd made sure to park so that their car was concealed as much as possible, yet still in a sanctioned area of the parking lot—with the trail being closed, they were the only ones there—so as to avoid looking like they were up to the no good that they were. They were angled in such a way that the overhanging trees obscured much of their car from the road, yet they were far from invisible. So, if anyone *did* ask, they could still deny guilt. Diabolical, indeed.

They marched on.

For a closed trail, Anquikia was well kept. There had been no rock- or mudslides, at least from what they could tell, and the path was clearly marked. There were also no signs that the area had been potentially damaged by a storm. In fact, it looked as if it had been recently cleared by machine.

"Kind of strange they've closed this down, don't you think?" Eric commented.

Jake said, "My only concern is that they've closed it down because of animals."

"You mean like a rabies outbreak?" Susan asked, and then she gave Eric a dark look when he laughed, presumably at her. "What? Don't make fun. Bats live in caves up here, and bats *do* carry rabies. So, if there was an attack on a hiker, they'd likely shut the trail down. We do the same thing in Perrick if there's a mountain lion sighting—well, *I* don't, personally, but I know the rangers do near the coast."

Suddenly, Eric didn't seem so smug. "Bats, great." He tugged his jacket up over his neck, and now it was Susan who was doing the laughing.

Susan pulled her jacket tighter, too, zipping it all the way up under her throat, but only because it was cold out. *Really* cold. Strands of flyaway hair clung to her face like wet spiderwebs, and her fingers were so chilled that she could hardly bend them. She'd brought a small thermos of coffee with her, and she sipped it to warm her bones.

"I was actually thinking more of bears," Jake said. He glanced at Susan. "Think they'd shut the trail down because of a bear sighting?"

"Sure. But I can't imagine why they'd leave it closed for so long. If there was an immediate danger, they would have specifically noted on the sign I removed that there had been a bear sighted—at least that's what they do with mountain lions back home. People ignore *keep out*— obviously—but they see *dangerous animal* and they stay away."

"Maybe someone took that sign down and hid it too," Eric said dryly.

She winked at him. "It's a good thing you're such an avid jogger, then, isn't it?"

The trail wasn't too steep, but it appeared to stretch for infinite miles, curving sharply here and there. It was a pretty view, though she couldn't imagine that Chuck and Madison would've been able to appreciate it in the dark. A view of the lake either, but maybe they had plans to hike right down to the shore. Stoner thinking.

"How long should we hike for?" Jake asked. He seemed to be struggling somewhat to keep up.

Susan did not call attention to it, so as to spare him any potential embarrassment. A naturally fast walker, she made an effort to slow her stride. "I was just wondering that. I'm thinking we should go at least to the lake, and then maybe a little beyond."

"That sounds good," Eric said. "Because I can't imagine that they would've hiked beyond that. They . . ." He broke off, rubbed his chest.

"What is it?" she asked.

Eric shifted his eyes to Jake meaningfully, which she interpreted as his way of stating that he did not want to say anything upsetting in front of him. He'd mentioned to her before that he'd gotten a horrible, panicky feeling the last time they'd come to the trail, so perhaps he was feeling something unpleasant now. "I'm just a little short of breath. Nothing to worry about," he said and left it at that.

She did not press. Still, she didn't like the way he was rubbing his chest and then pulling his hand down to examine it, as if he was expecting to see blood.

"I'm good," he assured her with the vaguest of smiles. And then: "Actually, if you guys wouldn't mind, I could use a quick rest."

"Hey, fine by me," Jake said, heading off the trail. "Nature calls."

"Actually, I have to pee too. Been holding it in for a while. You sure you're okay?" She desperately wanted to ask Eric more, yet her concern that Jake might still be within earshot made her bite her tongue.

Eric nodded and then set his pack down on a rock. "I'm sure. Just need a quick rest and some water. And," he added with a guilty smile, "maybe some of that M&M trail mix."

"Humph. I think you mean you're going to pick the M&M'S *out* of the trail mix," she said, and he guffawed.

"Guilty as charged." Still, he continued rubbing the back of his head perplexedly. Whether he was aware of it or not.

Susan journeyed off the opposite side of the trail, dreading having to drop trou in such chilly weather—and she didn't want to *think* about what sort of insects might be scuttling around in the dirt, eager to jump up and sting her on the butt. She shivered, conjuring an unlovely image of a puddle of urine steaming up from the ground between her feet as she raced to drain her bladder. She knew she'd get stage fright if she didn't go deeper into the woods than necessary—she'd always been that way, freezing up even in public restrooms if somebody else walked in. Something about knowing that people could *hear* her. Ridiculous, of course, but that's who she was.

Deep in the woods, she squatted behind a thick, mossy tree that was so tall that she couldn't see where its top met the sky. She went about her business, cognizant of living creatures that might try to buzz up into places where she didn't want buzzing. As she stood and zipped up her pants, a flicker of something shiny and metal caught her eyes through the trees. Though she had no reason to be creeped out—well, maybe she had *some* reason, given their search for their missing friends—her hand instinctively flew to her hip, where, had she been on the job, she would have had her gun.

"Guys! Over here!" she called, and then she realized how senseless she'd been in her shouting, as they'd now lost the advantage of being undetected. She blamed the gaffe on her extended absence from the force. She wondered what Howell would have to say about that.

She must've sounded worked up, because they were at her side within seconds.

Jake's face was all eyes. "Did you find something?"

She realized, then, that she'd made a bigger mistake by getting his hopes up. "No, sorry—not along the lines of Chuck and Madison. But, guys, look over there. Do you see that? It looks like a shed, maybe."

Eric squinted in the direction Susan was pointing. "What *is* that? Seems kind of weird that a metal shed would be way in the middle of the forest on federal land."

"Jake! Wait!" Eric and Susan called as Jake took off running toward the structure. When he didn't stop, they sprinted after him.

And then he disappeared through the trees.

They found him standing at the edge of a long patch of flattened dirt, where vegetation had been removed. In its center was what looked like a metal shipping container, though it had been modified greatly. "What the hell *is* this thing?" he muttered.

The container was sitting atop a squat platform on wheels. Its sides had been cut away and replaced by Plexiglas; along its top were several vents. It had a single door at one end, secured with several locked dead bolts.

Susan performed a quick sweep of the perimeter. "Looks like nobody's here."

"No, but somebody could come back any minute," Eric said, looking spooked. "I can't help thinking about those urban legends that forester kid told us last night about people going missing out here. I'm guessing whoever owns this thing isn't going to take kindly to us snooping around—you don't put four dead bolts on your door because you want people to feel welcome."

Jake said, "I agree. This place gives me the damn willies."

Susan thought back to her conversation with Howell. It certainly fit. She stepped up onto the platform and peered into the Plexiglas windows.

"Careful, Suze," Jake warned. "Who knows what kind of hillbilly booby trap they've got rigged out here."

It was just as she'd expected. "It's a mobile drug lab," she said, and Jake and Eric scrambled onto the platform to have a look for themselves. "I've made a few arrests at some labs in *houses*, but this is the first one on wheels I've seen in person. It's commonly known in law enforcement, though, that criminals set up meth labs on wheels. They use RVs, U-Hauls, that sort of thing—even cars. They can stay on the move, so they're harder to catch, plus it keeps their criminal activity away from their residence. So, if the going gets tough—*whoomp!*—they set the whole thing on fire. Better than torching your house, I suppose."

"I'd hate to see that happen out here," Eric said. "Probably burn down half the forest."

They craned their necks to get a better view. The container was lined with several shelves that held the sort of hazardous-looking chemicals that would probably melt one's flesh off if ignited. A scary thought, given that a few feet away sat a fold-up table with several Bunsen burners on top of it. There were also buckets; glass jars coated in a white, murky film; and several sacks of a powdery substance.

"I think they might be making that drug here that Powell was talking about," Susan said. "Pop C."

Eric tapped the Plexiglas. "See that over there—a damn pizza box! You wouldn't leave that sitting out here for days, so I'm thinking that we should get out of Dodge before someone comes back to finish their lunch."

"There's a key chain over there too—see it?" Susan said, indicating the neon-green dinosaur key chain sitting atop the table. "Maybe someone's car keys. And, if that's the case, they *could* be coming back soon. I wish I would've brought my piece." She stepped down off the platform, noticing an electric-blue fleck in the dirt. "What's this . . . ?" But she knew as soon as she picked it up. "Oh my God. We need to get out of here. Immediately. Jake, Eric—grab your stuff."

"What's going on?" Jake asked, craning his head over his shoulder so that he could look at her. He jumped off the platform and came running once he saw what she was holding.

"Jake, is this—"

He took the object from her, holding it up so he could examine it in the ray of light that sliced through the trees. He looked like he was going to be sick. "It's Madison's fingernail. She was wearing this color the night they left for their hike—she always wears this color for our shows. There's . . . oh my God. There's skin . . ." He thrust the fingernail at Susan and then ran to the edge of the clearing, where he bent at the waist and dry heaved.

Susan directed Eric to dump the trail mix and then turned the baggie inside out and used it to preserve the nail as much as possible—it had been exposed to the elements, so she hoped there was something left. Her hands shook badly. She was frightened, probably the most terrified she'd been on the job, barring her experience with Death Farm. These people meant business, and without her firearm, she felt naked. Maybe it was the police officer in her, but she felt responsible for the safety of Eric and Jake as much as her own. They needed to get out of there before they were confronted by a crew of armed gunmen, which typically accompanied meth labs the way french fries did ketchup.

"What do you think happened?" Eric asked.

"I think it's pretty close to what *we* just did. It was dark when they were hiking, so they probably saw a light and came looking—why, I don't know. Maybe it was sheer nosiness; maybe they heard noise and thought a party was happening; maybe they were scoping the place out and were ambushed . . . We can only speculate, but"—a little quieter now—"I don't think they made it out of here alive. If they weren't murdered, then what? You think they're being held captive somewhere up here?" She shook her head, as if to argue against herself. "I doubt it—there's been no demand for ransom, and what would be the point? My guess is that they saw something they weren't supposed to see—this lab and probably the people who were running it—and they were murdered because of it. It makes sense, with what Howell said and what you heard from that kid at the bar."

Eric nodded. "I think they were shot, but not here. Don't ask me how I know, but I *do*. I . . . I'm tasting blood—I've been tasting it since my chest started to hurt. I think one of them was hit in the face—the jaw. I'd bet my life on it."

They asked Jake, still bent at the waist, if he was okay. He gave them a thumbs-up and told them just a few more seconds.

To Eric, Susan quietly said, "If this is Madison's nail—and, at this point, we have to assume that it is, because what a coincidence *that* would be if it wasn't, given its bright-blue polish—then it looks like she put up a hell of a fight. There's some attached skin hanging from the nail—hers—but there's also some other skin caught underneath. I think it might belong to the attacker, and I'm hoping there's DNA. It's been out here for a couple days now, though, so . . . I just don't know."

"I also can't help thinking about what that girl with the Winnebago said about that van, that she'd seen a man drive off in it. I wonder if he was the—"

Bang!

Bang!

"Get down!" Susan shouted, and then she pulled Eric down to the ground underneath herself. Jake wasted no time dropping down flat on his belly too.

Bang! Bang! Bang! Bang!

The forest was eerily quiet after the gunfire ceased. "Where did it come from—you don't think it's them?" Eric whispered from underneath her.

"Sorry," Susan said, embarrassed, getting to her feet. She held a hand out to Eric, hoisted him up. "That may have been a bit of an overreaction. Sounds pretty far away. Hunters, probably. Sounded like a rifle."

"Let's take that as the universe trying to tell us something," Jake said. "And get out of here before somebody hunts us down."

They hiked back faster than they'd come in, frequently looking over their shoulders. When they reached the Jeep, Eric's breath came out in a soft little hiss. "My car." The back and side windows had been shot out. Bullet holes pocked the door and side panels.

Susan and Jake looked around worriedly—Susan searched around for brass bullet casings, finding none. Hastily, they unlocked the doors, swept the glass from the seats, and got in. She checked her bag for the fingernail, handling it with extreme care, formulating the demands she was going to make of Stogg. "No more bullshit," she said as they sped off.

CHAPTER 23

"Man, I'm going out of my mind here," Jake said, receiving no response from Eric once again. "I *said*—"

"I heard you." Eric flapped a hand alongside his temple, as if hoping to sweep dust from his mind. "Sorry, I'm just worried about Susan."

"I wouldn't worry too much—she could kick all our asses blindfolded."

Eric frowned. "It's not that, it's . . . I'm just wondering if maybe we shouldn't have gone with her to see Stogg. Offer backup."

Jake shook his head. "I don't think he likes us—he definitely thinks *you're* full of it because of the psychic stuff. What good would we do being there, crowding his desk? *My* only hope is that he hasn't been hitting the sauce today and actually does some—"

"Want to get out of here?" Eric asked abruptly. "I'm going to lose my mind, waiting."

"Sure."

"There's a gas station about a block away, if you don't mind that kind of coffee. Not fancy, but it'll get the job done. It's that or hoof it down to that drive-up coffee stand."

"Gas station it is. It's too cold to be out joy walking." Jake pocketed his room key and pulled on his wooly jacket. He eyed Eric's flimsy sweatshirt. "You going to be good in that?"

They set out once Eric returned from his and Susan's room. "It must be forty damn degrees out; I can't feel my feet," Eric said, his teeth clattering loudly.

"Your feet? I can't feel my *balls*! They're straight up in my guts," Jake said, and Eric barked out a sharp cackle, which he cut off with a *brrrrrrrrrrrrr!* sound.

At the Quick Stop gas station, they got their coffee, which was surprisingly decadent, with several strengths and creamer flavors offered. There was also a deli, which sold baked goods that appeared to be homemade. Eric picked up a couple of cinnamon rolls for Susan and himself and Jake bought a blueberry muffin. It was on the pricey side—$3.50 for a muffin was highway robbery, as far as Jake was concerned—but the taste justified the cost.

"Good call on the gas station cuisine," Jake said, his mouth full of blueberries. Eric's response was peculiar, a worried grimace. "What? Is there muffin on my face?"

"Isn't that the kid from the bar the other night? Miles?" Eric tilted his head slyly in the direction of a truck at the pump. "That *is* him—Christ, it looks like he's been put through a meat grinder."

"You think we should go talk—" he began to ask, but Eric was already on his way.

Miles's truck was packed to the gills with what looked like all his worldly possessions: mattress, boxes, mountain bike, desk, and a few cheap floor lamps, shades askew, which stuck out sharply like tentacles. Not one for organization, Miles. Over the top of it all were a few sheets of clear plastic that had been duct-taped together haphazardly. His eyes darted here and there as he pumped gas.

"Hey, Miles, what happened to you?" Jake asked as they approached.

The kid, nearly jumping out of his skin, turned to face them. Eric gasped. The damage was even worse up close: lip split, left eye sealed shut, nose swollen double its normal size. His posture indicated bodily harm as well; he stood stooped, his free hand hovering over his stomach, as if to stifle its ache. Broken ribs, Jake suspected.

"I can't talk to you guys." Miles's gaze bounced all over the lot, as if a million eyes were upon him. He squeezed the gas pump handle harder, as if that would expedite the process.

Eric placed a hand on the back of his truck. "You leaving town? Thought you just moved here."

The kid ignored the question.

"Who did this to you?" Jake asked.

Miles flapped a hand. "It's nothing. Just . . . rolled my four-wheeler at work."

"Right," Eric said. "A four-wheeler did that to your face? Was this because of the other night at the bar? Did those guys do this—your coworkers?"

The kid sighed, resigned. "I'm leaving town. And you should, too, if you don't want to end up . . ."

"End up like *what*?" Jake pressed.

The pump clicked, and Miles hurriedly slammed the nozzle back in its holder. He sidestepped the two men and made a move to get into his truck. "I gotta go."

Jake opened the passenger-side door of Miles's truck and then scrambled into the seat. "Not so fast. Do you know what happened to my friends?"

"No." Miles shook his head. "I don't know. I have to go!"

Eric took a step forward, and the kid jumped back skittishly. He placed his hands up coaxingly. "We're not trying to hold you up, Miles, all right? We're just trying to find out what happened to our friends."

"I don't know what happened to them. Honest to God, I don't." He paused. "But I've heard things . . . this place, it isn't good—that's all I'm willing to say, all right? I've been warned about talking to you guys, and I'm not keen on getting my ass kicked a second time. Will you *please* get out of my truck?"

Jake got out. "What sort of things have you heard?"

Miles pressed his lips together, folded his arms across his chest. "I can't—"

"Please," Jake pleaded. "*Please.* I need to know."

"Look, just don't . . . don't trust *anyone* in this town." He looked around fearfully. Quietly, he finally said, "I've heard *conspiracy-shit* kind of stuff, okay? Usually I dismiss small-town rumors, but I've heard this one so many times that I have to believe that there's some truth to it. Like, there's a story going around about a mill owner—I've heard this from at least three or four people. This new operation moved into town, and they wanted to use the mill to launder money."

"What kind of operation?" Eric asked.

"Drugs, from what I heard. Anyway, the owner, he was this real old-school guy; he built the business from the ground up, used his own name, and no way was he going to let *his* mill be used for illegal activity, right? So, what do they do? About a week or so after he tells this cartel to go to hell, his daughter is killed in an 'accident.' It was a car crash, but everyone in town knows it was them. It was as much of a punishment as it was a message. This town, it has a way of making people disappear. Like people who talk too much. Which is why I'm gonna bounce before it's too late. I suggest you do too."

"But who is *them*?" Jake asked.

"Nobody really knows," Miles said with a shrug.

"But—"

"I gotta go. I'm not saying anymore."

"But—"

"I'm sorry—and I'm sorry about your friends." Miles gazed at Jake and Eric hard, swept a hand over his body. "But, look at what happened to me—and this was done to me as a *favor, for my own good*, they said, because the alternative would have been them killing me. In case you guys haven't noticed, you're hardly welcome around these parts—your cop friend especially. People have it out for you."

Jake asked, "What people?"

"Assume everyone you meet here. So, if I were you, I'd get out of town—today. Because nobody's going to give you an ass-kicking warning. You'll be as gone as your two friends."

"But—"

Without another word, Miles got into his truck, slammed the door, and left them standing in the parking lot staring after him as he sped away.

Chapter 24

"So, let me get this straight. You're telling me that it was hunters who did that to Eric's car?" Susan said, wanting to bang her head against the wall in frustration. "You honestly *believe* that?"

Sheriff Stogg sat back in his chair, his expression aggravatingly impassive. "It's hunting season," he said with a shrug. "Who else would it be?"

"You can't be serious. One or two strays, I could maybe understand. But the entire side of his car was *shot up*. There were far too many bullet holes for it to be coincidental."

"And why would somebody want to shoot up his car?" Stogg asked. "You're not even from around these parts, so why would he—or any of you—have enemies?"

Susan had to focus hard to keep her voice even, a shout boiling up deep in the pit of her stomach. "Come on—I don't really need to spell it out for you, do I?" She sighed hard, noting the sheriff's bored expression. "Okay, maybe I *do*. You saw how the locals treated us at the search party. And let's not forget our two friends who've gone missing under suspicious circumstances."

"*You* think it's suspicious."

"Oh my God! It's like you're going out of your way to be obtuse!" Susan cried, her hands flinging up at her sides.

The sheriff leaned forward in his seat, his face darkening. "You'd better mind your tone, *Miss Marlan*. You might be the town darling where *you* come from, but around here you're still a civilian."

He was right, of course. "I'm sorry; I mean no disrespect," she said hastily, though she absolutely did not mean it. She could, however, face a serious reprimanding back in Perrick if Stogg took it upon himself to call her superiors. "This has all been so frustrating, with our friends missing . . . look, if you'd rather I deal directly with Clausen, I'd happily do so." And she'd wanted to, but once again, Clausen was nowhere to be found.

Stogg flapped a hand. "Clausen is off arresting teenagers for letting off fireworks in campgrounds or some damn thing." *Some damn thing* a euphemism for *some trivial task*.

Oh, because you're *doing a lot of good sitting on your lazy ass, you arrogant joker,* she wanted to say. *At least Clausen is doing* something.

"I'm the sheriff here, so you can deal with me. I have just as much authority as he does." His tone indicated that he believed his authority stretched beyond "just as much."

"All righty. Have a look at this, then," she said, producing the fingernail. He made a move to seize the bag, but she pulled it out of his reach. She trusted the man no farther than she could throw him—his competency not to lose the evidence in particular. He'd probably get drunk and throw it out along with his empty booze bottles.

"Am I supposed to know what that is?" he asked.

"This is a fingernail we found in a clearing off the trail. It's the same color nail polish Madison was wearing when she disappeared." She paused for effect. "We found it next to a mobile drug lab when we were out looking for her and Chuck."

His reaction was not as she'd anticipated, though she shouldn't have been surprised. "Oh, so now there's a drug lab out there too? Isn't that a coincidence—you didn't manage to find your friends, but you found *that*? Anything else? Amelia Earhart's airplane?"

Susan could have joyfully wrapped her hands around Stogg's throat and squeezed until she burst all the gin blossoms around his nose. "We were *just* there, less than an hour ago! Why on earth would I make such a thing up? I'll take you right to it, if you're determined not to believe me—which it seems you are."

"Oh, like how you and your boyfriend led me to the dead body under the tree stump?" he said with a vicious snort. "Only thing I'm determined not to do is waste time."

Susan clutched her hands into fists on her lap. "Are you going to help me or not?"

Stogg shook his head in a manner that was almost pitying. "Look, you wanted to search for your friends, and we did—even organized a whole party that most of the town showed up for. Volunteers, not getting paid. We searched nearly every inch of the woods, which you witnessed with your own two eyes, and didn't find them. And now . . ." He spread his hands out on his desk in a gesture that she could not interpret.

"And now *what*? What does that have to do with a drug lab being out there—*with* Madison's fingernail next to it?"

"I suspect this whole drug lab *narrative* is your way of getting us to search a new area. That nail could be yours, for all I know. And the fact that you were on Anquikia Trail when we found Madison's car at Mitchatepi shows how much you're grasping at straws. Want to know what I think? I think your *musician friends"—musician friends* uttered like *scumbag delinquents*—"did one too many hits of acid, and then they took off on you. You just don't want to face facts. My suggestion to you is for you and your friends to pack your things and go home. Because I can't waste public funds for the sake of your denial."

"That's ridiculous!" she shouted.

Stogg was not fazed by the outburst in the slightest. He probably galled quite a few individuals on any given day and was accustomed to being hollered at.

He lazily held out a hand. "Okay, then why don't you hand over that fingernail, and I'll have it tested? If it turns out to be Madison's, I'll look anywhere you want for the rest of the month. Hell, I'll even organize the search parties myself."

Susan placed a protective hand over the baggie. "No way."

Stogg raised his eyebrows. "No way?"

Susan exhaled hard through flared nostrils, feeling her heart thumping underneath her breast. "From day one, you have made it infinitely clear that you are unwilling to perform the bare minimum of your job requirements. It's a sad time in law enforcement when a *forest ranger* has to step up and do the job of the sheriff."

Stogg rolled his eyes. "Here we are on *Clausen* again. You want to go to him with this nonsense, go ahead. He might even entertain you. But, like I told you, he's out busting those *kids*—"

"No, we're beyond that now," Susan spat with an aggressive shake of the head. "I will be sending this nail out to the FBI in the morning, as I no longer have confidence in Clancy authorities to do a thorough and competent job. And I'm sure they'll be interested in hearing *all about* your unwillingness to help a fellow law enforcement official, *Sheriff.*"

Stogg sat up straight in his chair, his droopy jowls aquiver. "Now, hang on just a minute! I never said I wasn't going to help you."

"No, but you made it pretty clear," she said, quickly getting to her feet.

"Wait—"

"No, I'm *done* waiting." It was time to start getting results.

CHAPTER 25

Eric and Jake arrived back at the hotel at the same time as Susan. While they all wore miserable expressions, Susan's was more of the outraged variety. Her meeting at the sheriff's department had gone as well as they'd expected, which was not well at all.

"Man, Suze, you look like you're about to face a firing squad for a crime you didn't commit," Jake commented.

"Don't even get me started," she said grimly. "Let's get inside; I'm freezing."

Susan walked toward their room in front of Eric, so when she let out a horrified exhale, he initially didn't know why and for a moment he believed that an intruder was waiting for them with a gun.

But then he saw.

The door to their room had been kicked in, and the place had been ransacked. Their clothes were strewn about, many ripped into shreds. Feathers were scattered all over the bed, the floor, the air, as their pillows had been hacked apart. The mirror above their dresser was smashed, leaving shards of glass *everywhere*, as if it had exploded. Eric's laptop was sitting open, its screen shattered. LEAVE TOWN was written across the wall in Susan's lipstick.

"Why . . ." Susan looked to Eric, bewildered. "How long were you guys gone for?"

"I don't understand it," Eric said. "We weren't even gone that long. We only walked to the gas station to get some coffee. They must've been waiting for us to leave."

"Let's go check on Jake," she said, and they bolted.

The devastation in his room was far worse than theirs. They found him sitting on the bed, his eyes brimming with tears. He clutched a mangled object in his hands. "They smashed my violin," he said. "How could anyone do this to something so beautiful? It was an antique, irreplaceable. There will never be another one of these made again, ever. It was handed down to me by my great-grandfather, and it was the only one in existence. It was one of the few things he'd taken with him when he immigrated to this country from Norway, and they came in here and smashed it like it was nothing. It would have been better if they'd just stolen it. It was priceless."

And they hadn't only smashed the violin. Jake had been storing the band's equipment in his room, and all of it had been destroyed: guitar splintered into dozens of bits, drums kicked in, amps busted. How had they—whoever they were—been able to do this in the middle of the day without anyone noticing? On Jake's wall was a message written in the same shade of lipstick as the one in his and Susan's room: WE'RE WATCHING YOU.

The image of their friend's pain was so moving that Susan began to weep. She crossed to the bed and put an arm around Jake, muttering apologies. It hurt Eric's soul to watch, and he probably would have wept, too, had he not started feeling so strange.

His skull was throbbing as if his head had been smashed in as badly as the drum set. Woozy, he pinched the bridge of his nose, which did nothing to help. He took a step forward, fell to his knees.

"Eric!" he heard Susan and Jake shout from what sounded like the far end of a long tunnel. Jake set the violin aside and ran to his aid, placing a hand on his shoulder. Eric looked up into his face and shrieked.

Jake was dead—or he looked as if he might be dying. Blood poured down the side of his face, and his skin was ghostly white. Eric could feel every one of his injuries, which extended all the way down to his organs and bones. "Jake . . . no . . ." He could hear the screams of the other injured around him, smell the tang of fuel mixed with blood. And he was fading, fading, his consciousness drifting up from his body—

Jake pulled his hand away, and poof, the image was gone. So was the pain. Eric blinked, looked up, and saw the fright on Susan's and Jake's faces.

"What's the matter?" Susan asked, her face still wet with tears.

"I saw . . ." His gaze drifted to Jake, who had endured enough mental agony in the last ten minutes to last for the year. He wasn't keen to add to it by revealing what he'd just seen, particularly since Jake was a great believer in his psychic powers. He shook his head and got to his feet. "I don't remember, but I feel fine now. And, before you ask if I'm sure, I'm positive." He provided them a smile he hoped looked genuine.

"If you're sure you're feeling okay, then," Susan said, "I think we should go to the front desk and see how the hell this happened to our rooms."

"Let's go get to the bottom of it," Eric said, happy when they didn't press.

The three of them stomped down toward the office, their anger mounting with each step. When they reached the office, Susan yanked the door open, and the three of them fanned out. As they approached the front desk, Susan cleared her throat loudly, ready for battle, but it was Jake who beat her to it.

"Listen!" he yelled. "Somebody broke into our rooms and smashed apart all our things. I want to know how this happened in the middle of the day, with you sitting down here . . ."

The girl glared at them from behind the desk. Her face was red and puffy, her eyes bloodshot and brimming with tears. "You!" she screamed, jabbing a shaky finger at Susan. "You stupid bitch!"

The trio stood silent, the words shocked right from their tongues. "My brother Ian is dead!"

Susan looked confused for a moment, but then her face changed with understanding. "Big Ian from the gym?"

The girl swiped a stream of snot away from underneath her nose. "They found him in the pool," the girl sobbed, "with the cover pulled over him. He drowned. They're saying it's an accident, but we all know it wasn't!"

Susan hesitated. "I . . . ," she finally managed.

"You should've kept your nose out of things, you stupid, stupid bitch! You and your friend. Everyone here knows you're a cop—and you made Ian *talk* to you? *In front of everyone?*"

"What . . . but . . . I don't understand—"

"His blood is on your hands!" the girl shrieked. "You're going to pay for this! I hope you never find your friends!"

A man came quickly running out from the back office. He said a few quiet words to the girl, put an arm around her, and helped her into the back office. A few moments later, he returned.

"What can I help you with?" he asked with a polite smile, as if the interaction had never taken place.

Chapter 26

"I don't want to go home, do you?" Susan asked Eric and Jake back in their rooms. Jake and Eric had since apprised her of their interaction with Miles at the gas station, just as she had told them of her futile exchange with the sheriff. Now, they paced Jake's room uneasily, cleaning up debris as they went.

"Hell no, I don't want to go home. Okay, I *want* to go home, but I'll be damned if I do it without Chuck and Madison . . . or, at least until we find out what happened to them," Jake said stubbornly, folding his arms across his chest. "But I'd be lying if I said I wasn't scared. These people up here are maniacs. I mean, look at my room. And you should have *seen* that guy's face at the gas station, Suze. He looked like he'd gone a few rounds with a Louisville Slugger."

She looked to Eric, seeking confirmation. She didn't think Jake was an outright liar, but he did occasionally have a flair for the dramatic. "It was pretty bad," Eric agreed solemnly. "It makes me sick to think that they did that to that poor kid because of us."

"It makes me sicker to think that that would have *been* us had that Ben guy not intervened at the bar," Jake said.

Susan shivered, realizing how close the two had come to being jumped and beaten by a crew of vindictive drunkards. Or, worse, killed. After, would they have vanished into thin air the way Chuck and Madison had? What would she have done then? Jake was quickly turning into a close friend, but Eric had become such a welcome and uplifting fixture in her life that she couldn't imagine living without him in it. It hurt her deeply, thinking of harm befalling them.

"Even if we *did* leave town, like every damn person we meet keeps telling us to do," Eric said, "we'd only drive ourselves crazy."

"And we've faced worse," Susan said, not needing to clarify to Eric what she meant. "We're no cowards."

Jake asked, "What now, then?"

"I'm going to head over to our room and call Howell," Susan said and then shook her head. "I don't know why I didn't just do that in the first place—maybe it was wishful thinking that Clausen would be the one to help us after being shot at near the lab, but then I, of course, got stuck with Stogg."

"Think the FBI will actually assist on this one?" Eric asked.

Susan shrugged. "No idea. Probably not if it was just Chuck and Madison. But, with the drug lab and all the things we keep hearing about all these mysterious murders happening, they might take an interest. Howell mentioned that the DEA have been monitoring this area, too, so all these things might catch their attention. I won't know until I talk to him, but it doesn't hurt to make a call."

Fifteen minutes later, Susan was finishing outlining the previous days' events for Howell. He'd listened silently in his typical fashion, though she'd heard the scribble of pen against paper on his end of the line. She finished speaking, but he still said nothing, as if he was waiting for her to say more.

"And . . . that's all," she said awkwardly and with a weak chuckle once the silence got to be too much. She felt like an idiot immediately. Her desire to do right in Howell's eyes was so strong that it was almost pathological. She wanted, she realized, to work for the FBI so very, very much. And, once the mess in Clancy had been sorted out, she planned on taking Howell up on his job offer. Her mind was finally and absolutely made up on the matter.

"I'll call you back in a few," he said and hung up.

"A few" turned out to be an hour, but it seemed Howell had been busy. "I've contacted Kinger over at the DEA. He and I will be flying into Seattle tomorrow—"

"Tomorrow?" she blurted. "Just like that? I thought . . ."

"You thought what?" He sounded amused.

"It's . . . no, I'm grateful for the help! I'd only figured that it would take some time to get things organized."

"Normally, it would. And I don't typically work so closely with the DEA," Howell said and then paused. "This trip, however, will be strictly off the record. And, of course, I am the boss, so I have certain leeway at the FBI. Kinger and I will be traveling to Clancy strictly as tourists, understand? I need to know that I can trust you with privileged information?"

He phrased it like a question, so she figured she'd better answer. "Yes, of course."

"Kinger, as I may have mentioned before, works on a task force that has been monitoring the drug highway that runs through Clancy. I told him about your discovery of the mobile lab, as well as the other information you provided about your friends and other locals disappearing. I've only done so because I trust your judgment."

Susan's cheeks grew warm. "Thank you, sir." *Sir*, like he was already her boss at the FBI.

"Kinger has been building a case against a drug cartel that has been operating out of Clancy; it's only one of many, but a big one. It's been slow going because of jurisdictional restrictions. Additionally—and this is strictly confidential—Kinger suspects that there might be some corruption in the Seattle offices that is slowing things up. He wants to personally head to Clancy to assess the situation, and he has asked me to accompany him. He feels that if he can compile enough evidence, he might at last be able to make some moves."

Susan didn't know what to say. She had a flash of paranoia, questioning if she might have blown the entire situation out of proportion—that the two agents were flying up to Clancy for nothing. She pushed the thought away, remembering that she'd seen the lab herself. And Eric's shot-up car. And then there was the detail of Chuck and Madison going missing.

"There's one more thing," he said. "I ran a full background on Benjamin Harvey."

"Oh?"

"He had some trouble with the law a few years back, but it was a nonviolent misdemeanor. Things had gotten heated at an antilogging protest he'd attended."

"But nothing that would indicate that he would harm Madison or commit murder."

Howell said, "Not based on what I found, but that doesn't mean that he isn't capable. There's a first time for everything, and if things are as desperate up there as you say, he could've snapped."

"Perhaps. Thank you for looking into him, but . . . hmm."

"Is there something else?"

"Now that I think about it, there are *a few* things that have happened that link back to Harvey. The coincidences are big enough that it would be worth mentioning."

Susan paused to take a sip of water and Howell urged her to continue.

"I told you about the incident that just took place in the office, right? Well, the gym where Ian died, Clancy Fitness, is owned by Ben Harvey. There's also the interaction Harvey and Madison had on the tour—where he made passes at her, despite her apparent lack of interest—which you already know about. So that's two things. The third relates to something Ben told us—Eric and me—when we were in his shop. He said that his business started failing around the time the author of those Kincaid books died, which was four years ago. If the DEA has been looking into Clancy for *three* years because of Pop C manufacturing, isn't it possible that Ben Harvey could be behind the operation?"

"You mean because of his failing business?" Howell's tone was mildly skeptical. Or maybe it wasn't; it was difficult to tell with the man.

"Right. It's a leap, but there does seem to be a lot of hinky activity surrounding the guy. So, to break it down: Harvey hits on Madison, and she spurns him. He's probably feeling a little humiliated, even if he brought it on himself."

"But if he's delusional enough, he won't see it that way," Howell commented. "He'll blame her for the humiliation and for leading him on."

"Exactly. Then, Madison disappears during a remote hike with her so-called boyfriend, Chuck, who she used as a means to reject Harvey. Harvey owns an outdoor store, and he's so familiar with the trails out here that he could probably navigate them blindfolded. It'd probably take no effort at all for him to ambush Chuck and Madison in the dark, especially if they were inebriated.

"Then there's the fact that Ben Harvey's business begins to fail around the time that an illicit drug business starts up with such success that the DEA takes notice—assuming that it would take Harvey a year or so to get things up and running. He obviously knows how to operate a business, since he's got a bunch already.

"Finally, the janitor, Ian, is killed at the gym Harvey owns after he's seen talking to me, a police officer, about the chemical burns on his hands. And perhaps those burns weren't from the pool chemicals but were instead from the compounds they put in Pop C? Back in Perrick, I worked on a few meth lab busts, and some of the burns I've seen on the manufacturers were similar to what Ian had. Also—and I remember thinking it was strange when he said it, because we were at a gym—Ian told me that he got money from cleaning *and cooking*. I didn't make the connection at the time, because I was associating Ian with janitorial duties, and I'd just assumed that he had another job at a restaurant. But what if he meant cooking Pop C?"

"Hmm, could be."

"Ian was developmentally disabled, so perhaps Harvey was worried that he'd slip up and say something to me about the Pop C business. The general manager got disproportionally angry when I tried to help. Madison even got in a mild altercation with her, come to think of it."

"If Harvey was concerned about you being a police officer, wouldn't he think twice about harming Chuck and Madison?"

Susan shook her head, though Howell obviously couldn't see her. "Barring the couple of locals who were familiar with Death Farm, nobody around Clancy knew I was a cop until after Chuck and Madison disappeared. Harvey didn't seem to know when Eric and I were in his shop, asking about trails. At least, if he did know, he didn't let on."

Howell asked, "What does your gut tell you?"

"My gut doesn't know what to think. Ben Harvey is definitely off, but that's not saying much around these parts. Everyone we've met in Clancy has been odd in one way or another. So, on the one hand, there's all the connections I've just outlined, which suggests guilt."

"But on the other?"

"On the other hand, having grown up in a small town, I know that in a place like Clancy, *everyone* is connected in one way or another. These incidents with Harvey might just be coincidental, and I bet a couple dozen people in town might have similar connections. I suppose the best solution would be to keep him in our scope."

They finished going over the details of Howell and Kinger's arrival, and then Susan went to tell Eric and Jake the news. Finally, they were getting somewhere. Maybe.

Hopefully.

CHAPTER 27

"Man-oh-man, did Stogg catch hell from the mayor," a voice on the other line said as soon as Susan answered.

"Who is this—what time is it?" she asked groggily. She groped for the lamp on the nightstand and turned on the light. Eric mumbled sleepily next to her and rolled over to face the opposite direction.

"It's Pete Clausen," the voice said cheerily on the other line. "And it's just past seven. Sorry to call at this hour, but I wanted to catch you early."

"Okay . . . ," she said wearily. She placed a fist against her mouth and stifled a yawn. "Sorry—I'm not quite awake. What's this about Stogg?"

"Stogg told Mayor Moulden about your visit yesterday, and was she *ever* pissed when she heard that he turned you away. Seems he called her seeking commiseration after you stormed out and told him that you were going to the FBI—though I suspect he was just trying to cover his own ass—and his plan backfired. I came back to the office just as she was at the end of her reaming, and I swear there was steam coming out her ears, she was so mad. Something tells me you're going to be getting a personal apology from the sheriff, and would I *love* to see the look on his face when he does *that!*" Clausen cackled.

"Um, that's great . . . I guess. But couldn't this have waited until later?"

"I haven't gotten to the other part yet. The mayor has asked me, personally—and, unfortunately, Stogg—to escort you three out into the forest, so that you can show us exactly where this lab was that you saw. It's her way of offering an apology, though of course *she* won't be there." His tone indicated that the mayor would never lower herself to such a pedestrian task.

Susan sat up in bed. She gave Eric a little shake, and he groaned, never one to be accused of being a morning person. "Great. When?"

"As soon as you're available. I was directed to be at your beck and call."

"Thank you, Pete. We appreciate that. Let me rally the troops, and let's meet at the base of that trail at, say, nine?"

After they disengaged, Susan gave Howell a call. It went straight to voice mail, as she'd suspected it would, since they were probably en route to Seattle. She hadn't mentioned their upcoming arrival to Clausen, nor did she intend to. While she liked the ranger, she valued Howell's discretion more. Still, it would be prudent to maintain a cordial relationship with the local authorities, should Howell and Kinger decide to make their presence known.

Once she succeeded at the arduous task of getting Eric out of bed, she went over to Jake's room, surprised to find him already up. He was having trouble sleeping, he explained, which she could understand. He'd lost not only his best friends but also his band. She wondered if it had dawned on him yet that, with the lead singer and drummer gone, Augustine Grifters was no more—and on the brink of major success, no less. It was a pity, because Jake adored the band almost as much as he would a lover. It was such a big part of his life; what would he do now?

"I was up late making these," he said, producing a stack of **MISSING** flyers that featured Chuck's and Madison's photos. "The motel manager let me use the printer in the office."

Susan smiled encouragingly, though her heart ached for her friend. She suspected that some part of him knew that Chuck and Madison would never be coming back—he'd practically said as much—yet the optimistic side of him had to keep trying to locate them, if only for peace of mind. "Those are great, Jake."

He shrugged. "It's the least I can do."

She told him about Clausen's call and invited him along, relieved when he declined. Out of the three of them, she imagined Stogg liked Jake least of all, though, after yesterday, she might be in the lead. It was going to be uncomfortable enough with her, Eric, and Stogg, though she was thrilled to have Clausen there as a buffer.

"As you might have noticed, Suze, I'm not much of a hiker. I feel like I'd only slow you down. Also, I want to hang these flyers up around town—I'll do that while you're gone. I actually would have already started, but I had to wait for that office supply store over in that strip mall to open so that I can buy an industrial stapler and tape: stapler for wood, tape for metal. See, I've thought of everything." He provided her a sad smile, as if understanding the futility of his mission. "There isn't going to be a bare telephone pole in this whole town by the time I'm finished."

"That's great," she said, only to say something. Everything, she thought, was far from it.

Stogg and Clausen arrived on time and in full uniform, firearms and all. The uniforms she suspected had been the mayor's idea, but their carrying of guns gave her hope. Perhaps they believed her, then, about the drug lab. As inept as Clancy authorities appeared to be, even they knew better than to roll up without weapons on a drug lab, where they could potentially face armed gunmen.

She, too, was packing, though she was not going to mention this to the two men. As Stogg had so graciously pointed out, in Washington State she was merely a civilian. Although, as a law enforcement officer, she was within her federal right to carry out of state, she was loath to step on more toes than she already had. She'd been lucky thus far in the sense that Stogg hadn't contacted her superiors back home. She wasn't keen to press her luck.

She might not have thought to mention it to Eric either, but he'd questioned why her pack was so heavy when he'd handed it to her. Carrying a gun had become second nature to her, and on an occasion such as this—when she could potentially be walking into danger—she'd feel naked without it.

Stogg did not offer Susan the apology Clausen had promised, only a sullen look. His scowl deepened when he noted that it was just her and Eric. "Where is your little friend?" he demanded, not allowing the two of them the time to finish getting out of the Jeep. He gave Clausen a hard look, which Clausen seemed not to notice.

Eric snapped, "Does it matter where *Jake* is?"

"Yah, it *matters*," Stogg said, a hangover buzzing off him like high voltage. His eyes were as glassy as two battered red marbles. "It's *his* band friends who've gone missing. You think he'd have the decency to show up. *I* showed up, and I don't . . ." He stopped short when Clausen gave him a threatening look.

This is getting off to a great start, Susan thought. *My God, the man is actually* pouting *like a two-year-old.* How Clausen managed to stop himself from pummeling Stogg each day was a great mystery. "He went into town to hang up missing posters," she explained in an attempt to ease the tension.

"Humph," the sheriff grunted. To Clausen, he said, "Maybe we should reschedule, then, for a time the missing one can be here."

The missing one, Susan reflected with a roll of her eyes. What an absolute ass, inventing any reason possible to hold them up in their search—his sad, small way of punishing them for his dressing down. *Let the drug lab keep on a-cooking, so long as he gets to spite the outsiders.* The mayor had spanked his wittle bottom-wottom, and now the child had to throw a tantrum to get even. Because, at the end of the day, he was under the mayor's thumb, whether he wanted to acknowledge it or not (which must have killed him all the more, with Mayor Moulden being—gasp—a *woman*). While she had no real authority over the sheriff in terms of employment, the mayor could hurt him in terms of town support, particularly during reelection time. She could even see to it that Stogg, an elected official, was impeached, if she rallied enough support.

"He has a difficult time hiking," Susan said in a passive-aggressive, *take that* tone, omitting the *you insensitive ass* she wanted to tack on. "So, there'd be no point in rescheduling."

Clausen scowled at Stogg. As if rubbing it in, he said, "See, no point in rescheduling." He turned to her and Eric as an entirely new person, smiling amiably. "But I should probably call the mayor and let her know. She tends to get cranky when she's left out of the loop." He cupped a hand by his mouth and whispered, "She's kind of a micromanager."

Susan and Eric laughed. "Sure. Take your time."

Clausen stepped away to make the call, but with it being so quiet, they could hear his side of the conversation as well as if they were standing right next to him. "That's right . . . no, not here . . . downtown," he said, repeating every detail for the mayor. He turned to face them a couple of times, raising his eyebrows, as if to say: *See, I told you.* "Yes, I understand . . . absolutely." Finally, he said, "I'll call you in forty-five minutes or so to confirm." He hung up with a broad smile and gave them all a thumbs-up. Eric and Susan flashed him their thumbs in return while Stogg only glowered back at him, as if he was secretly (or maybe not so secretly, given his unmasked hostility) wishing the man would drop dead.

"We good to go?" Susan asked.

"Yep, good to go," Clausen beamed. "Now, let's go find ourselves a drug lab."

CHAPTER 28

Jake had witnessed a fair share of rejection in his life, yet he'd never encountered anything quite like the locals in Clancy.

Not just one uncooperative business but *several*—hardware store, realty office, outdoor goods, bakery—turned him away when he asked if he could hang a flyer in their establishment. Their responses had varied, but all were as equally perplexing and, he suspected, intentionally deterring. The employees at both Clancy Realty and Ah, Nuts *and* Bolts! had claimed that he'd need to speak to the owner before he could post anything because, yah, sorry, it was company policy. Yet, the owner wouldn't be in until . . . they just didn't know—oh well, too bad. Then, at Outdoor Lifestyle, when he *did* finally manage to speak to the store owner, a shaggy naturalist type who wore a ponytail and knee-high tube socks with Birkenstocks, he was told that the information on the missing posters might send out the "wrong kind of message" and scare off potential customers. Although, from what Jake could tell, the guy hadn't sold anything since the late nineties, given the state of the dusty shelves and dated merchandise. And then there was the last and oddest response he'd received at Debbie B's Bakery. After he'd finished giving his spiel, she'd only stared at him coldly until he eventually backed his way out the door.

Which was why he was now focusing on poles outdoors. He couldn't possibly encounter any problems there, right?

Wrong. He hadn't been at it for more than five minutes when a group of teenage boys in matching wrestling hoodies—*Feel the roar of Clancy High Tigers!*—strolled by and bumped right into him. Intentionally, he suspected.

Though he was aware it wasn't his fault, Jake provided them an easy smile and muttered a quick apology. He extended a flyer to the kid in the middle, a tall boy with squinty eyes and a chin speckled with pimples. "Hey, guys. I'm looking for my friends, who went missing—"

"Dumbass midget!" the kid jeered, and his buddies laughed on cue, as if they'd scripted the interaction before making their approach. They kept walking, which Jake supposed was better than getting his ass kicked by a crew of sixteen-year-olds.

Oh-kay. The sad thing was that he was becoming accustomed to the abuse in Clancy, and the slur had hardly fazed him. He tacked a few more flyers up on the old-timey streetlamps that lined the main drag— these with tape, since the poles were metal—and promptly decided that it was time for a late breakfast after an angry-faced woman with a stroller strode past and clicked her tongue. *What's your problem?* he wanted to ask, but he *knew* what her problem was. She lived in godfor-saken Clancy, a place so unpleasant that it'd turn the Dalai Lama bitter.

He went into Scramblers, the greasy spoon that sat on the corner directly behind him. It was a lucky coincidence, as he'd merely picked the first restaurant he'd come across. Had it been a pizzeria, he'd have eaten a slice of pepperoni for breakfast.

The waitress wasn't outwardly hostile toward him, which was a pleasant surprise. She did, however, say, "You got a permit for those?" as she gestured toward his flyers, which immediately put him on guard. "Only reason I ask is because I put a bunch of posters up for the holiday craft fair a while back, and somebody came by and tore them all down."

"Great," was all Jake said. Normally, being as chatty as he was, he would have asked her all sorts of things—what sort of crafts she made, what holiday they'd been for, where the fair had taken place—but he was in no mood for chitchat. He couldn't even bring himself to ask if she'd seen Chuck or Madison, though he figured that, if she had, she would've said something after looking at his flyers. After she brought his food—omelet, hash browns, toast—he ate in broody silence. Taking the hint, she stayed away, only returning occasionally to refill his coffee cup.

With the waitress's warning in mind, Jake paid and left the restaurant, doubling back down the street to check on his posters. He didn't need to go far before he saw that his efforts, like the waitress's, had been sabotaged.

"Aww, man," he said, standing over a metal garbage can. His flyers sat on the very top, crumpled into sad little balls, flaps of tape hanging out the sides. While he was upset, there was something deeper vexing him. What it was, he couldn't grasp. Obviously, he had his missing friends to think about, but it was something . . . more. He stopped at a bench, sat down, took a moment to really *think*.

When he opened his eyes, he understood that what ailed him was not mental. Or even physical. No, it was somebody else—*two* somebodies, actually, who whipped their heads away and focused their gazes on *anything but him* in a gesture so obvious that they might as well have walked up to him, extended their hands, and introduced themselves.

Being the size that he was, Jake had gotten used to stares and whispers—people weren't as sly as they liked to think they were. But this was different; these two men, both wearing baseball caps pulled down almost to their brows, as if that somehow made them invisible—it did quite the opposite, because who wears a hat that way unless they're up to no good?—were staring at him with *purpose*. There was that, plus the fact that they'd also dined in Scramblers when he was there.

But had they come in *after* him? Or had they already been there—which might suggest that he was being paranoid?

No, he decided, they'd come in after. And he was fairly positive that they'd gotten up to leave right when he had. It was a movement he'd registered on a subconscious level, though, at the time, it hadn't sunk any deeper, because why should such a thing bother him?

Now, it bothered him plenty. Why would two complete strangers be tailing him—was this about the flyers? Seemed a bit of an overreaction, particularly since they'd already been trashed. He thought back to the night he and Eric had gone to the bar, picturing the faces of the men who'd tried to get them to step outside to brawl. These two were nothing like them, out-aging the bar thugs by about twenty years.

With indifference he had to force, Jake got up from the bench and stretched, behaving as if he didn't have a care in the world. He grabbed his flyers from the bench, his pulse thudding in his ears and his mouth going dry when, from the corner of his eye, he saw the two men shift. He walked about a half block down and then stopped at an antique store, gazing into its window casually, as if something had caught his eye. He pretended to suddenly notice that his shoe was untied, and only then did he allow himself a look over his shoulder—an urge he'd forced himself to ignore during his walk.

Any hope he'd been harboring about his paranoia vanished in the course of a half second. The two men were still behind him. And now they had stopped too.

Jake took his time with his laces, debating what to do. There was no doubt in his mind that, if he did try to seek help from the locals, they would only turn him away. Worse, they might even know his two new friends, and then where would that leave him—how outnumbered?

His best chance, he decided, was to give them the slip.

CHAPTER 29

Eric had feared that the hike would be filled with spells of awkward silence, but Clausen was as chatty and fluttery as a mad parrot.

They hadn't been hiking long, yet he'd already informed them of his plans to flip a seventy-year-old fixer-upper at the edge of town—*wood paneling from floor to ceiling, but there's original hardwood floors!* Then there was his arduous journey from Texas—*damn moving van broke down in the middle of hell's half acre;* his displeasure toward the equipment at the only gym in town—*everything's so rusty that it sounds like a haunted house door opening when you lift it;* and his plans to get a pet—*always been more of a dog lover myself, though cats are okay too.*

He and Susan could hardly get a word in edgewise. Stogg also hadn't gotten a word in, but this had more to do with the fact that he wasn't making any real attempt to join in on the conversation. His only contribution thus far had been the intermittent huff and puff of air, accompanied by a grumble about the distance they were hiking (ridiculous, since it wasn't far), the early hour (Eric had to side with Stogg on that one, though he refused to give the sheriff any credence with an endorsement), and how much he was sweating despite the bitter cold (ditto). Stogg made a big show of removing his jacket, which he stuffed dramatically into his pack, as if to underscore his torment. Eric felt great satisfaction when Clausen peeped at him with a face laden with mockery and then cast his eyes skyward.

Eric managed to sneak in a quick directive once they neared the area where Susan had initially gone off the trail when nature called. "It's just up here. Through that small clearing in the trees," he said, looking to Susan for confirmation. He was surprised to see that she was staring back at him worriedly.

"You okay?" she asked quietly.

"Sure, why?"

"You're as white as a sheet."

Was he? Come to think of it, he did feel a little off, but it was less in his body and more in his head. That sick, panicky feeling was returning swiftly, and it was only when Susan brought up his well-being that he realized it.

He opened his mouth to tell her that he was getting another one of his bad feelings, but then he remembered their present company. Had it been just the two of them and Clausen, he probably would have spoken up. But with Stogg scowling at him the way he was, like the word *crackpot* was tickling the tip of his tongue and he only needed the slightest nudge of provocation to utter it—and lest he forget the fiasco with the stump—he felt it wiser to suffer in silence. But then—

(*Run! For God's sake, man, RUN! Run!*)

—about halfway to the clearing with the lab, Eric received a warning. It was chanting, from where he didn't know. His head snapped back.

(*Run-run-run-run!*)

The voice was so close that, for a moment, he thought that it had been Susan who'd spoken. It wasn't. He knew this because her gaze was focused straight ahead. There was that, plus the other voices, male and female of all ages, that were joining in.

(*Get out!*)

(*You're in danger!*)

(*Save yourself!*)

(*Go! Please!*)

The voices, so many, screamed at him from all directions: next to his earlobe, in front of his face, where he could've sworn he felt hot breath against his skin, from within the trees. The words made it past his eardrum, tangling up inside his brain. It didn't hurt; it *throbbed*. His urge to break down in sobs was tremendous, a straitjacket of emotions constricting his insides.

He stopped and bent at the knees, clutching his head as if trying to stop it from bursting. And he almost *did* break down, until Stogg's voice sliced through the shrieks, silencing them at once.

"You coming or what?" he demanded. With a jerk, he brought a hand up and slapped at his bicep. "*Great,* now we've got to deal with goddamn mosquitoes."

And then Eric saw it as Stogg clawed at his arm. The Sailor Jerry tattoo of a pinup girl. It was an exact match to the one he'd seen in his vision—the vision where Chain Saw Man—*Stogg*—took the rifle from his accomplice and shot him—*Miguel*—in the chest as he begged for mercy.

His mouth dropped open, and out fell a silent scream. His eyes moved to the very big and very deadly gun sitting at the man's hip.

Stogg frowned down at him. "Is there a problem?"

Eric straightened. *Play it cool as if your lives depend on it,* a voice commanded. It was his own. He smiled. "No, no problem. Sorry, just felt a little nauseous for a minute. The altitude, I think."

With a grunt, Stogg continued forward, quickening his step to catch up with the overzealous Clausen. Once his back was fully turned and he was a few feet away, Eric caught Susan's attention and gave her a pained, meaningful look, which, of course, she had no way of interpreting—he could've been mocking Stogg or trying to communicate that he had to urgently use the bathroom, for all she knew. He didn't dare voice his concerns out loud; as he'd recently been made aware, sound carried in the forest. He thought about asking her for her pack, so that he could get her gun inside it, but he was so shaken that he feared he would not be able to make the request without sounding suspicious.

A dead woman materialized at the sheriff's side and walked next to him. Earth soiled her dress and skin, but her decay was minimal. She mustn't have been dead long—maybe a month or two. She smiled up at the sheriff lovingly, raised a hand, and softy caressed his cheek.

After a moment, she stopped in her tracks and stared directly at Eric. It felt as if she was seeing *into* him, sifting through his innermost thoughts. It warmed him, put him at peace.

He felt the moment she pulled herself back, as his anxiety returned as quickly and bitterly as a shot of cheap tequila. *Tell him it's not his fault.*

Eric shook his head to indicate that he did not understand.

Tell him he's not to blame—he's a good man who only lost his way.

Eric didn't dare speak up, his terror too great over the discovery of Stogg's tattoo. Now was not the time to be spouting messages from the dead.

The woman was losing her patience. *Say it!* She charged forward, shouted in his face: *Tell him Honeybee says it's not too late! Honeybee! Honeybee!*

"Okay! I'll do it—Honeybee, Honeybee!" Eric muttered loudly in frustration. The woman disappeared.

Clausen and Susan gave him a funny look, but Sheriff Stogg spun around, looking as if he, too, had seen a ghost. "*What* did you just say? Where did you hear that?" He shot an angry look at Clausen. "You tell him to say that? Because I don't think that's funny—"

"Relax," Clausen said, looking genuinely confused. "I didn't tell him to say anything. I don't even know what that means."

"Honeybee says it's not too late," Eric said quickly, and Stogg looked more startled than ever. "She says you're a good man."

"You know what he's going on about?" Clausen said with a snort. When Stogg didn't answer, he shook his head and gave them a wave up by his shoulder. "Whatever. Let's go."

They continued on their way. Eric expected the woman to return, but she was nowhere to be found. Soon, they reached the clearing, which was now devoid of the platform and the lab. Eric wasn't too shocked.

The look on Susan's face indicated that she wasn't either. "Damn—I can't *believe* it! Thwarted again. Always a step ahead!" she said, sounding very much like a Bond villain. Eric might have even laughed, had he not been so worried that Stogg might have it in his sights to murder the three of them where they stood.

It occurred to Eric, then, how isolated they were. And who, really, knew where they were? He felt a little better when he remembered the conversation Clausen had had with Mayor Moulden, and he'd had it right in front of Stogg too. Which, he supposed, was great and all—at least their bodies might be discovered and Stogg would be brought to justice, should he decide to shoot them now—but would that really matter that much if they were dead? Perhaps, though, Stogg would think twice about launching an attack—if that's what he was planning now—if he was provided a little reminder.

To Clausen, he loudly said, "When you talked to the mayor earlier about us hiking out here—"

"Sorry, amigos, but this is where we part ways." Clausen grinned at him and Susan.

Amigos? Eric's blood ran cold as he remembered Rifle Man's words to Miguel: *"Sorry, amigo, but there ain't no way around it . . ."*

Susan let out a gasp when Clausen calmly extracted his gun from his belt and aimed it in their general direction. "Don't even think about it," he drawled when she went for the gun in her backpack. He took the bag from Susan. To Stogg, he said, "You waiting for a written invitation or what?"

There was a split second when Eric considered rushing the sheriff, but his hopes were dashed when Stogg pulled his gun too. He would risk his own life, but no way was he going to put Susan in danger with some half-cocked plan of attack.

"You want to do him or her?" Clausen asked.

Stogg sighed deeply, his shoulders hunched. "I'll take the girl." They switched positions so that each man stood in front of his respective target.

"Good. You know the gentleman in me hates killing the ladies. And you owe me after that last time."

"No!" Susan cried. "Wait!"

Clausen gave her a lazy smile, as if this were all a big game. "It's like my old man used to say—"

CHAPTER 30

Jake was under no illusion that he'd be able to outrun two large men. Particularly not these two, who were twice his size. He'd already made up his mind to lose them, and that had been the easy part. He had no fears of freezing up when push came to shove; courage had never been a trait he'd struggled with, perhaps to his own detriment.

He grappled, however, with figuring out the *how*; he had the will, but could he find the way? It was an especially difficult task, given the time constraint he was up against. His two friends were looking squirrelly, and they wouldn't wait much longer to make a move.

Which gave him all of sixty or so seconds to devise a plan.

Downtown Clancy was a far cry from dense. Most of the buildings that formed individual businesses didn't touch each other. Rather, they sat in small clusters, mini malls of mom-and-pop establishments. Beyond that was the dense forest that encircled downtown, as well as Clancy as a whole.

The one advantage he had over the two goons was his size. Perhaps, he thought, he could slip down one of the few alleyways downtown had to offer. Then, he could lure them off the main drag and get them to embark upon a search while he hid in a nook. With them distracted, he'd slip out of his hiding spot, double back, and beat feet. He'd be in serious trouble, however, if he turned down an alley only to discover that there *were* no nooks for him to hide in, not even a dumpster for him to squat behind.

Well, never mind about ifs and buts. It wasn't as if he had an alternative, right? He nodded, endorsing the thought.

His pulse quickened when he noted that they were on the move, but not in the direction he'd been anticipating. One of the men moved toward him, and the other headed up to the opposite end of the street. With horror, he realized what they were doing, splitting up—they were covering both the top and the bottom of the street, which almost guaranteed that they'd nab him no matter which direction he ran. Which also meant that they were onto *him* being onto *them*. The alleyway idea was not going to work. *Fine,* he thought in a frenzy, *it was a stupid idea anyway.*

Panicked, he gaped in both directions. One of the men, the meaner looking of the two, was closing in. The other . . . who knew where he was heading, probably on his way to sneak around the back. Jake's eyes traveled toward the forest, which seemed to be beckoning him with a promise of safety.

He saw it, like a life raft floating toward him in open water. A path that jutted off the main drag. It led right to the forest.

Before he had a chance to change his mind, Jake ran toward the trees. He was far too frightened to look behind him, though he could sense the men chasing after him as much as if he could see them. Before he knew it, he reached the edge of the forest.

He dashed off the trail, which offered little cover and left him vulnerable. He had no clue where he was running to—he was seeing the world down the end of a 3D tunnel, operating on sheer instinct. Unfortunately, his instinct did not remind him to watch his step, and his foot caught on an exposed root. He lost a shoe as he tumbled forward, rolling, rolling right down a steep slope. The pain in his foot, as well as the rest of his body, was excruciating, yet he knew better than to cry out.

He came to a stop at a small plateau. Though he was dizzy, he quickly surveyed his surroundings, finding a fallen, moss-covered tree with a gap underneath large enough for him to scramble under. It hid him perfectly.

One of the men showed up only moments later. Jake held his breath, under no illusion that they only wanted to talk. If they found him, they would kill him. It was as simple as that. Why, he had no idea, but indiscriminate killing seemed to be the way of life in Clancy.

Not too far in the distance, he heard the other man call, "Found his cell phone. He's got to be around here somewhere."

Jake squeezed his mouth together, cursing silently. Holding his breath was becoming painful, but he didn't dare make a sound. He allowed himself a tiny inhale when the man closest to him walked away to meet up with his partner with the cell phone.

They were close enough that Jake could hear the soft murmurs of their conversation as they began their search for him. While he wanted nothing more than to stay hidden, he knew that they'd find him eventually if he didn't make a move. Not too far away at the edge of the forest came the soft hum of an automobile. The highway, *of course*. If he could make it to the road, he could (hopefully) flag down a passing car. He'd be taking a risk making a run for it—and also risking that the car he flagged down would contain men worse than the ones who were chasing him—but it was better than staying there, waiting to face imminent death (and probably a horrible beating prior).

Jake slithered out from underneath the tree on his belly and slowly got to his feet. He began creeping his way toward the highway with a step that was ninja quiet. He was over halfway there when one of the men shouted, "Over there! Grab 'im!" and he took off so fast he suspected that he might have broken every existing Olympic track record known to man, as well as ones that had yet to be created, despite his pain and missing footwear.

One of the men's fingertips grazed his back just as he shot out through the trees and onto the highway. With a petrified shriek, he whirled around as he saw that the man had gotten tangled up in the trees that he'd been able to easily clear—there was a win for Team Little

People if he'd ever seen one. He turned his attention back to the road and the approaching semitruck.

He flapped his hands over his head in an X shape. "Hey! Stop! Please!"

The semi didn't stop, but two other vehicles were approaching about fifty yards behind it. With the man in the trees just about free, he ran toward the car in the front, jumping into the middle of the road when he feared it wouldn't stop, deciding that he'd rather be killed by a machine than a maniac—*two* maniacs—any day of the week.

The car came to a screeching halt. So did the one directly behind it. Jake, wasting no time, ran to the passenger side and attempted to wrench open the door. It was locked.

"What the hell are you doing?" shouted a familiar voice.

His breath hitching, Jake looked into the face of Mayor Moulden. He rubbed his chest, having difficulty breathing, a mixture of exhaustion and panic seizing his lungs. "Unlock . . . the . . . door!"

The mayor's hand hovered over the control. She rolled the window down half an inch. "What's going on?"

"Please! They're . . . coming." And, yes, the entangled man had cleared the trees and was rapidly closing in on the mayor's car. Hearing the blessed clicking sound of the locks disengaging, Jake pulled the door open and scrambled into the vehicle. "Drive! Please!"

The car behind them laid on the horn. At a maddeningly slow rate, Mayor Moulden frowned at the car in the rearview mirror and then turned her gaze on the man, who was now just outside her window. He examined her with his fists clenched at his sides, as if unsure what to do.

Honk-honk-honk . . .

"All right!" The mayor shot another angry look at the review mirror. She glared at the man on the street and then put the car into drive.

God bless American road rage, Jake thought, easing back into the seat and catching his breath as they sped off. It would be another minute before he calmed down enough to speak.

Chapter 31

Bang!

Clausen groped at his abdomen with his free hand, his skin immediately dyeing red. He gaped at Stogg uncomprehendingly—*How dare you,* his eyes seemed to say—then raised his gun weakly to fire at the sheriff. Stogg pulled the trigger of his gun and shot Clausen again, this time hitting him in the center of his chest. Clausen stumbled forward and fell to his knees.

Bang!

It was the final bullet that did it, a shot to the heart. Clausen fell flat on his stomach, twitched grotesquely. Finally, he lay motionless.

Eric and Susan raised their hands when Stogg turned on them. Susan said, "You don't have—"

Stogg's eyes brimmed with sorrow. "They already got my wife. I told them no, and they got to her . . . I should've done what they . . ." He shook his head, his voice choked. "But my goddamned pride . . . and now she's dead because of me, my sweet Honeybee."

"Sheriff, please—"

"It'll never end." The sheriff raised the gun toward his face, staring down the barrel. "And I won't let them take my son too . . . tell him I'm sorry."

"*No!*" Eric and Susan shrieked as Stogg pressed the gun under his chin and pulled the trigger. Eric squeezed his eyes closed as the sheriff's brains launched out the top of his skull. He ran to Susan and cradled her in his arms, though it was really she who was comforting him.

Eventually, Eric asked, "What do we do now?"

Susan stepped back, her expression blank as she surveyed the two dead men. It made Eric feel an uneasy mixture of pride and apprehension, her ability to hold it together so well when *he* felt like screaming.

She pulled her phone from her pocket, nodded. "No cell service here. I expected as much."

"What do we do about . . . *them*?"

She glanced at the bodies and then reclaimed her gun from Clausen. "We shouldn't move them—not that we'd be able to haul their dead-weight back to the car. All we can do is hike back and then make our calls." Without another word, she started for the car.

Eric wanted to say something, but he couldn't find the right words—were there any right words for times when a man committed murder and then shot his own brains out? He silently followed her out of the clearing.

At the car, Susan made several calls, reaching not a single person.

Her first call was to Howell; she left him a voice mail, outlining what had happened in a strong, steady voice. Her second call was to Jake; his phone only rang and rang, ultimately going to voice mail. She began to summarize the events for him as well but then stopped and simply told him to call her back. "Where *is* everybody?" she asked, frustrated.

"Cell phone service is spotty here," Eric pointed out. "And Howell is on his way, right? You saw how remote that drive is."

"Good point."

"I think you should call the mayor. She's going to wonder where we are, and she should probably be in the loop about Clausen and Stogg."

Susan nodded and made the call, using the number on the card the mayor had given to them on the morning of the search party. She didn't seem to know what to say once voice mail picked up. "Hi, Mayor

Moulden," she began and then paused awkwardly after identifying herself. "I just thought you should know . . . I appreciate you believing us about the lab, and the four of us hiked there . . . but, Stogg and Clausen are dead. They . . ." She looked to Eric helplessly, and he raised his shoulders at her. "I think this would be better to discuss in person. Eric and I are heading to your office now. Uh, thanks, bye."

She called Howell back and left a voice mail informing him of their plan and of the address of the mayor's office. "This day sure has turned upside down."

"Imagine what the night will be like," he answered with a dry smile.

CHAPTER 32

Mayor Moulden held up a finger to silence Jake while she listened to her voice mail. Her face remained impassive, and then she hung up.

"Man, was I ever glad to see you," Jake said, still sounding a little breathless. His hands still shook, but he imagined they would for quite some time. "I would've been killed had you not stopped."

"You didn't give me much of a choice. No, you didn't," Mayor Moulden said offhandedly, keeping her eyes on the road. "It's all about choices, isn't it?"

"Sure . . ." *What a weird thing to say,* Jake thought. "I appreciate it, whatever the reason. I owe you one, big-time. Those guys, they started chasing me—I have no idea why. They have my cell phone too."

"Your friends chose to go hiking that night, didn't they?" she said, as if he hadn't spoken.

He smiled uneasily. "What do you mean?"

"That's the thing; they *chose* to go hiking, just like they *chose* to stray off the path to *my* lab. Nobody *invited* them—I wouldn't show at *their* place without an invitation. That would be rude, and we live in a world where rudeness has consequences." The mayor shook her head and then glanced over at him casually. "And how *rude* were *you* to stay in town? You and your *rude* little friends. You were told to leave, and yet . . ." She shrugged, clicked her tongue.

Jake sat up straight in his seat, sensing that there might be something wrong with the woman. The hairs on the back of his neck began to stand at attention. Had he heard her right—*her* lab? Maybe he would've been better off in the forest with the thugs.

"People always get upset when things don't go their way, yet nobody ever wants to accept personal responsibility. Do they?" She shook her head. "No, they don't."

He slowly moved a hand toward the door handle, closed his fingers around it.

She arched an eyebrow and smiled over at him, almost as if she were flirting. "Won't do you any good. I had the interior mechanism removed—it can only be opened from the outside. Go on; try it."

Frightened, Jake pulled on the handle, letting out a confused cry when it gave, yet . . . nothing happened. "What is this?" he yelled, yanking hard on the handle. He smashed all his weight against the door, grunting.

Nothing happened.

She laughed. "You can beat away at it all day, but it won't do any good. And, trust me, bigger men than you have tried. Broken." Broken separated into two words—*bro-ken*—to antagonize him.

"What's *wrong* with you?"

She calmly reached into the compartment on her door and extracted a pistol. Keeping one hand on the wheel, she aimed it right at his face. "This, though, works just fine. You don't want to be rude again and find out how fine, do you?"

Jake slowly raised his hands. "I do not."

"Good boy."

CHAPTER 33

Eric and Susan arrived at Mayor Moulden's office and found, not surprisingly, that she was gone. Only her admin assistant was in attendance.

The assistant was about as helpful as the rest of the town. "Mayor Moulden isn't here," he repeated, as if they hadn't heard him the first time.

"We understand that," Susan said. "But do you know where she is?"

The assistant gave them a shrug that was about as close to passive aggressive as a shrug could get. "No idea."

"Aren't you her assistant?" Eric asked tartly, and Susan gave his hand a squeeze beneath the counter. *You catch more flies with honey than vinegar,* he could hear her say. She'd said it to him on more than one occasion, though sometimes he felt she misinterpreted his tone.

The assistant gave Eric a hard look. "Exactly. Her assistant. I work for *her.* If the mayor doesn't want to tell me where she's going, I'm not going to question her. It's not my place."

"Fair enough," Susan said with a pleasant smile. "May we wait in her office?"

The assistant shook his head. "I'm sorry; that's not allowed."

Eric and Susan exchanged a look. They'd expected as much. They returned to the Jeep to decide what to do next. It was freezing inside the vehicle, with the windows having been shot out. They'd taped plastic over the gaps, which was hardly weatherproofing, with the intention of getting new windows once they returned to Perrick. It would be a chilly drive home.

Eric said, "It's like the aftermath of a nuclear catastrophe here. The whole town has either gone insane or is MIA. Look, there's hardly any people on the streets. Ghost town."

"You want to hear something crazy?" she asked with a sad smile. "For a split second—maybe not even *that* long—I thought that I should call Ed for advice, because he always seemed to know what to do in these sorts of situations. Nuts, right?"

Eric shook his head. "It's okay for you to miss him, you know. Even with what happened, it's okay for you to feel . . . *things*. You're only human. Nobody expects you to behave otherwise."

Susan began to speak, but then her phone binged with a voice mail notification. "Must've gotten a call while we were inside." She listened to it and then said, "That was Howell. They should be here any minute."

"What did he have to say about the shoot-out?"

Susan shook her head. "Funny enough, he didn't even mention it."

"He's all business, that one."

"He is."

After that, they gave up on making small talk, the events of the morning sinking in. Whenever Eric closed his eyes, he pictured the incredulous expression on Clausen's face as he realized that Stogg had turned his gun on him—that he, the would-be murderer, had become the soon-to-be murdered. He saw the expression on Sheriff Stogg's face just before he placed his gun in his mouth and pulled the trigger—*I won't let them take my son too . . . tell him I'm sorry.* He saw the back of his skull explode outward, his body collapse lifelessly onto the earth. These events replayed in his mind over and over, a record player needling the same measure of a song. As much as he'd been haunted by actual ghosts, he imagined that the sight of Stogg taking his own life would be something that would truly haunt him forever.

As promised, FBI Special Agent in Charge Denton Howell and presumably DEA Agent Mark Kinger pulled up next to them in the parking lot in a nondescript rental sedan. "Kinger isn't what I expected," Eric said quietly once they got out.

"Me either."

Kinger was a string bean come to life. He stood well over six feet, yet he probably weighed no more than 165 pounds soaking wet. He was pale all over: thin, pale-blond hair; pale-blue eyes; pale skin. Though boyish in frame, he had the hardened face of a man of excess: a man who stayed up too late, stressed too much, smoked too much, worked until he collapsed behind his computer. Eric saw that he wasn't wearing a wedding ring, something he'd started noticing on other men after his own divorce.

Howell, also not wearing a wedding ring, was exactly the sort Eric could envision kicking ass and taking names. His scalp was shaved smooth, and his gaze was razor sharp; Eric imagined that he was the sort of person who could be blindfolded thirty seconds after arriving at a new place yet still be able to describe the room right down to the artwork on the walls and the color of the tie a person wore on the opposite side of the room. His eyes were as dark and clear as his ebony skin. He was about as tall as Kinger, but twice as wide, with lean muscles gently straining the seams of his clothing. Eric felt shrimpy and inadequate by comparison.

Both men had identical bulges at their hips, which Eric interpreted as guns. He'd been wondering why Susan wasn't also carrying, but she'd changed the subject whenever he'd tried to ask her about it. Susan, as he'd learned in their time together, tended to only shut down further when pressed about something she did not wish to discuss. It was better to let her open up on her own timeline.

After a brief introduction, Eric, Susan, and the agents went into Mayor Moulden's office to speak again to her administrative assistant. His attitude hadn't changed much. "I already told you—"

The agents pulled out their badges and practically shoved them under the assistant's nose. His eyes went wide, and then his gaze shifted to the mayor's office. *He's hiding something, all right,* Eric thought.

"DEA?" he asked, bewildered, completely omitting the part about Howell being with the FBI. Interesting, Eric thought, since it showed where his main concerns rested.

"Listen to me carefully, you little pissant," Agent Kinger said in an intimidating voice that did not seem possible for a man so slight. "If you know where the mayor is and you aren't telling us, you're obstructing justice. As much as you want to keep your job, I imagine you want to keep your freedom more. So help me, if I find out that you're hiding information, I'll see to it that you're locked away with some very unpleasant characters. You may not go away for long, but a lot can happen in lockup overnight."

Eric wondered how much of the statement was true, since he was aware that Howell and Kinger had flown to Clancy unofficially. Still, while even Eric was shocked by Kinger's boldness, the assistant didn't seem fazed. "I told you, I don't *know.*"

"This her office?" Howell asked, gesturing toward the closed door at the far end of the room.

The assistant folded his arm across his chest. "You got a warrant?"

Howell turned to the couple, though he seemed to be speaking mostly to Eric. "As an agent of the law, I'm unable to open that door. Physically, I can open it, but whatever I find would be inadmissible in court, since it would be an illegal search. Because the door is *closed,* see."

"Right . . . ," Eric said slowly. "So, we have to wait to get a warrant or . . . ?"

Susan looked into Eric's eyes hard. "We cannot enter that *closed door* because we are aware of the law as *officials.* But if a *civilian* took it upon himself to open the door . . ." She shrugged. "We'd be viewing the scene differently—in a *legal* sense."

"Oh, geez, I'm an idiot," Eric said, and he immediately strode across the room toward the mayor's door.

"Hey! You can't go in there!" the assistant shouted once he realized what was happening. He scrambled out from behind his desk, but then, oops, Kinger, Howell, and Susan accidentally on purpose got in his way.

"This is the exit, right?" Eric said loudly and in a confused voice. "I think it's the way out." He opened the door to the mayor's office and gasped. "You guys are going to want to see this."

The assistant made a panicked noise and fruitlessly attempted to flee through the real exit, the only door to the outside in the entire building, which was also the way in. "Sit your ass down," Howell said through clenched teeth, and then Kinger rolled the chair out from behind the desk and pushed the assistant down into it. Maybe harder than necessary, not that Eric was going to notice such a thing.

"Look there," Susan said to Eric. "Do you see the keys?"

He nodded, acknowledging the same neon-green dinosaur key chain they'd seen inside the mobile drug lab in the forest. It was hanging from the lock of an open and empty file cabinet drawer.

"The whole office has been ransacked," Howell commented behind them. Some of the desk drawers had been pulled out completely and spilled out onto the floor. The ones that remained had the contents inside jumbled. There were also papers and files galore spread all over the floor and chairs. A coatrack sat on its side in the corner, as if a jacket had been ripped from it in a hurry.

"Where is she?" Howell demanded of the assistant.

He shook his head, looking on the brink of bursting into tears. "You don't understand. I can't tell you! She'll kill me!"

"The mayor?" Kinger asked.

"Her or one of her cronies," the assistant said with a sniff. "She runs the town."

"It seems more like she's running *out of town*, and she's left you holding the bag," Susan said. Quietly, she added, "Look, I know it must be scary to be in your position, but you've run out of options. The mayor left you high and dry, so you'd better start thinking about saving your own skin, because you're looking to go away for a very long time."

"But I didn't do anything!"

"You're withholding," Susan said, "which is the same as obstruction of justice. And I'm sure they're going to try to pin all sorts of other things on you, like conspiracy and fraud for starters. And the DEA? You obviously know about the mayor's extracurricular activities, and, hey, they might even assume that you helped."

"I didn't!"

"But they don't know that, see? And you might be facing distribution charges on top of everything else." She shot Eric a quick look, which told him she was probably winging it. Howell and Kinger seemed impressed by her quick thinking, as well as her ability to disarm the assistant. Eric could practically see his apprehension melting away, his tongue loosening. "Now, I'm sure if you cooperate, the DEA and FBI will go easy on you—isn't that right?"

Howell and Kinger nodded. Lies? Eric didn't know.

"And I'm guessing that they would try their hardest to keep you protected as a witness."

More nods.

"Now, look—what's your name?"

"Brian."

Susan smiled gently, just two buddies having a chat. "Now, look, Brian, we're running out of time. If the other agents in town get to the mayor first, you're going to lose your chance at striking a deal. Because you'll no longer have a bargaining chip, understand?"

The assistant twitched in the seat uncomfortably. He had no way of knowing that there *were* no other agents in town. He nodded.

"So, let's see if you can answer us this time, okay? Where is Mayor Moulden?"

CHAPTER 34

The assistant had informed them that Mayor Moulden kept a small airplane at the local airstrip. He'd also hinted that they'd better hurry, since she was planning on taking off soon. He couldn't say where, but he suspected that it might be Texas and then ultimately Mexico, where she had other contacts. Or, it could be in the opposite direction, up to Canada. It was a wide range, but Susan was inclined to believe that he was not trying to mislead them. Whatever the case, they needed to hurry, since the mayor would be in the wind if she managed to make her escape.

Howell, Kinger, Eric, and Susan sped toward the airstrip in Howell's rental sedan, going about seventy miles above the posted speed limit, which was fifteen miles per hour in the more populated areas. There weren't too many cars on the road, which kept their speed high and steady, but whenever they did encounter one, Howell skirted it with the expert skills of a Formula 1 driver.

Susan glanced at Eric next to her, who seemed frightened by Howell's driving but who had also stubbornly refused to be left behind. "I won't get in the way," he'd snarled when she'd dared suggest it. Howell and Kinger had stayed out of that one, probably wanting to save time by avoiding an argument.

Eric was having trouble fastening the bulletproof vest Howell had insisted he wear, much to Susan's relief. "Here, let me help you," she said, her hands steady and confident as she tightened the straps across his body. Though she was anxious, a great part of her was relishing the rush of adrenaline. Her head was buzzing, and she felt almost . . . *excited*, a sensation she hadn't experienced on the job for quite some time. This, she understood, was where she wanted to be. *This* was where she thrived—right in the thick of it—not working as a beat cop writing speeding tickets and settling petty disputes between neighbors over things like barking dogs and roaming livestock.

"You have your piece?" Howell asked.

She nodded.

To Eric, he said, "Sorry, no gun for you."

Eric held up his hands, shook his head. "That's okay—probably wouldn't know how to use it even if you did give me one."

Kinger grinned. Susan realized that Howell had been teasing Eric a little with the gun thing—of course he wouldn't be getting one—but he'd been so deadpan in the delivery that it hadn't seemed the case. Howell had a sense of humor after all.

"We're carrying only as a precaution," Kinger said. "Remember, we're here unofficially, so hold your fire. We only fire after they fire the first round."

"Hopefully it won't come down to a shoot-out," Susan said, thinking that Kinger might also be teasing like Howell.

He wasn't. Kinger glanced at her over his shoulder. "You never know with these sorts of things."

This is like something from a movie, Susan thought, suddenly nervous. She realized then that Eric's bulletproof vest might actually prevent him from getting killed, and she fiddled with it again. "Hey, you got this," Eric said to her quietly, as if sensing her fear.

"Look, over there!" Howell said as they pulled through the airstrip gate. The tarmac beyond them was blocked off with two large concrete barriers. Mayor Moulden was on the airstrip, her plane geared for takeoff. She was approaching the door in a sprint, cradling a purple brick in her hands.

Eric squinted. "What is that?"

"Pop C," Kinger said with a nod. "That's the same wrapping that I've been seeing down south."

The mayor scrambled onto the plane and whipped the door shut when she saw them coming. Seconds later, the plane started to move.

"Dammit!" Howell spat, pounding a first on the wheel.

"What do we do?" Susan asked, raising her gun. Had they only arrived two minutes earlier!

"Hold your fire," Kinger warned.

"Hang on," Howell said. He floored the gas and drove them off the tarmac and onto the field, attempting to skirt the concrete blockades. The car bounced roughly through mud and potholes, the rear end fishtailing. He maneuvered around the barriers, and it looked as if they just might make it; however, on the other side was a deep depression that they hadn't seen from their approach. The car dropped into it and skidded to a halt.

"Shit!" Kinger cried. "Gun it, Howell!"

"I'm trying!" Howell shouted, the car making an ugly grinding noise as it worked overtime. It made it up the side of the ridge a few feet and then skidded backward at an angle. "It's not working."

"We're out of time! We go on foot!" Kinger shouted, and then he launched from the car. Howell followed immediately.

Susan hesitated, looked to Eric for guidance. "Be careful!" he told her, his tone frantic. Calmer, he said, "You'll do great."

His words and support had the soothing effect she'd been seeking. She made a move to get out of the car, and from behind her she heard, "I love you!"

"Love you too!" she replied, and then she sprinted to join Howell and Kinger.

They were crouched behind the concrete blockades. They had their weapons out, steady and poised to fire. "I thought we wait for her to fire first?" she asked, having to shout to be heard over the plane's engine.

"Change of plans!" Kinger said. His finger moved to the trigger. "On my go—"

"Wait! Don't fire!" she shrieked. "The back window, look! She has a hostage!"

Howell lowered his weapon, but Kinger hesitated. This was his case, she knew, and he would be reluctant to let the perpetrator go so easily. "Could be one of them."

Susan spoke fast. "It's not! That's my friend—that's Jake Bergman! I know him." His eye was puffy and his head bloody, but there was no mistaking that it *was* him. He placed his hands, tied together with a rope, against the window and then dropped away. His palms left behind a smear of blood.

Kinger didn't lower his gun.

"Don't risk it," Howell said. "He's a civilian."

"I can hit the engine," Kinger said crazily.

"What if you miss?" Susan shouted.

Howell was starting to look worried. "Lower your weapon! Agent Kinger!"

Susan let out her breath as Kinger finally lowered his gun. "Car!" he shouted.

They ran back to the car, cognizant that the mayor might still open fire on them. It didn't seem likely, as the plane was starting to make its way down the runway.

Inside the car, Howell said, "I'll make a call to Fort Lewis-McChord."

"The air force?" Susan said, surprised, though it made sense. "Please tell them about the hostage," she said.

Howell nodded. "Of course."

"I'll call the FAA. We'll get her, we'll get her," Kinger said, though he didn't sound optimistic.

CHAPTER 35

The crazy bitch had hit him hard on the head.

So, take her down, a voice inside his skull commanded.

Jake eased on his side, his head swimming and body rumbling all over. He bit his tongue hard to stop himself from vomiting. Where was he? What was that sound—what was it pressing against his aching body at such strange angles?

Focus.

He remembered putting up the flyers downtown . . . the chase through the forest with the men. Then . . .

He got into the mayor's car; later, a gun was pushed into his face.

He recalled that he was *angry,* wanting to *fight.* But . . . no, he couldn't. Physically, he couldn't.

Paralyzed?

He focused hard, remembering-forgetting-remembering that, only seconds ago, he'd sat up and placed his hands on a very cold and very tiny window.

It was coming back . . . pieces, pieces.

Airstrip.

Moulden belting him with a gun multiple times—unnecessarily, since he hadn't put up a fight. His face . . . his skull . . . his gut.

Were there others? No, it was only her. Then . . . what?

Rope. She tied him up, called him . . .

Collateral.

She'd dragged him from the car and then stuffed him someplace quiet. She'd left him for some time but had returned—he'd heard her cursing.

He peeped his eyes open ever so slightly, finding that he was in the back of the tiny airplane. His vision went temporarily red as a glob of blood dripped into his eye. He blinked it away, squirmed to ease the pressure against his sides. He saw that he was lying on a pile of purple bricks.

Mayor Moulden was at the wheel, preoccupied with . . . yes, now he remembered. She was making an escape. He'd heard her on the phone, screaming that shit had hit the fan in Clancy. She said she was making her way to . . . Vancouver?

What would happen to him if she made it to Canada?

Hands aching, he rotated his wrists. In her haste to do evil deeds, Mayor Moulden had done a terrible job tying him up. The ropes were slackening even with the slightest of movements. But he didn't dare move faster, lest she realize that he was awake. Would she shoot him now that they'd gotten away? What would happen if she opened fire in an airplane? Would they go down—hadn't he heard or seen something about that on TV?

It was a struggle to move slowly, not only because of his nausea but also because of his nerves. But he managed. It didn't take him long to free himself, maybe a minute, though it was difficult to keep track of time. He focused on his burning rage—rage for his missing and pre-sumably dead friends, rage for the way they'd been treated in Clancy, rage for being chased, threatened, and tied up like an animal. His anger solidified into a hard core that burned through his center as he remem-bered the smug way she'd called him and his friends *rude*, justifying her insane crusade as the teaching of lessons.

He made a slow move to get up on all fours. He lost his balance and fell on his side as the plane began to pick up speed. *Stay calm, stay calm,* he told himself.

But we're taking off! shouted a voice within his head. *She's going to kill you when she lands—you know this, right?*

Yes, he thought, his anger swelling. He knew this.

She might continue to use him as insurance for a short time after they landed, but once she got to where she needed to go, she would execute him. And she'd do it with all the remorse of a camper swatting at a mosquito.

No, if he was going down, this bitch was going with him.

Jake wiped the rest of the blood from his forehead with the back of his forearm. He got to his feet, slowly made his way up to the front of the plane. He got close enough to see a bead of sweat trickle down the back of her neck, to hear her frenzied breaths. Through the front window, he saw the scenery change from ground to clouds as they became airborne. Beneath them was the thick green blanket of the forest, void of any humanity.

This is for you, Chuck and Madison, he thought.

And then he launched his attack.

CHAPTER 36

After Kinger and Howell finished making their calls to the air force and the FAA, the car fell hopelessly silent.

Howell said nothing as he calmly maneuvered the car out of the hole they'd driven into in their desperation to get to the plane, which was all the more galling now that they'd calmed down—so, it had been possible, after all, to get them out. How different would the outcome have been, then, if they'd been able to drive all the way on the tarmac—would they have been able to drive in front of the wheels of Moulden's plane and block her escape?

Nobody wanted to voice it, but they knew they'd been beaten in a bad way. Mayor Moulden, drug kingpin of Clancy, kidnapper of Jake, murderer of countless individuals, was getting away. No, Eric thought, she'd *gotten* away. If she managed to flee the country, she'd probably stay gone forever.

And it all came down to the minute or two that they'd arrived too late.

What will happen to Jake? Eric wanted to ask, but he knew the answer. He suspected they did too.

"Dammit!" Kinger shouted out of nowhere, pounding a fist on the dashboard. "Three years of my life—so close! I should have opened fire—I wouldn't have missed. If we hadn't—"

"Don't go there," Howell said sternly. "There's always going to be an *if we hadn't*: *if we hadn't* gotten there so late, *if we hadn't* stopped for coffee, *if we hadn't* hit that red light, *if we hadn't* ceased fire—it'll do no good, and you'll only make yourself crazy." He placed a hand on Kinger's shoulder. "We'll get her." His voice contained far more optimism than Eric felt. "Maybe not today, but we'll get her eventually."

"So, that's it?" Kinger spat, as if trying to start an argument with Howell. He flapped a hand a moment later, as if losing the will to continue.

"They're airborne," Susan said, sounding utterly defeated. She reached across the seat and took Eric's hand. Her eyes were about as sad as he'd ever seen. He wished he could take the pain away for her.

"Jake will be okay," he said, more to himself, though no part of him believed it. He'd seen the way he'd been beaten, and he couldn't bring himself to think what would come next.

"What the . . ." Kinger gasped, sitting up in his seat. "Did you guys see that?"

"See what?" Howell began to ask, but Kinger was already getting out of the car. Everyone else followed suit.

"There," Kinger said, raising a hand and pointing at the plane. "The plane wobbled. Did you see that?"

"Yes! Oh my God!" Susan said. "What's going on? Think she doesn't know how to fly a plane?"

"No idea," Howell muttered, placing a hand over his brow to shield what little gray, Pacific Northwest sun shone in his eyes.

Kinger said, "There it went again! She'd better straighten out, or they're going down."

"Jake . . . ," Susan said.

Eric huffed out an incredulous breath as the mist about the forest thickened and swirled. It was moving far faster than any cloud he'd ever seen in real life, and maybe even in movies. It didn't seem possible, that nature could create something so grand. "Do they get tornados here?"

"Tornados? No, I don't think so," Howell answered. "Why?"

"The mist. Look how fast it's moving." He was mesmerized by its sheer force, which was frightening, yes, but also beautiful. It was gaining speed, swirling and churning up-up-up like a tidal wave. "I've never seen anything like it! Have you?"

When he didn't receive a response, he tore his eyes away from the sky and met his companions' gazes. They were all staring at him, perplexed. He turned his attention back to the angry sky.

And it *was* angry, he understood. He heard its rich, primal roar deep in his ears, felt its teeth sharpening against the air, ripping at the atmosphere. "It's the forest," he muttered. "I thought it was the sky, but it's the forest."

"What's he talking about?" he heard Kinger ask.

"They want her," Eric said, unable to tear his eyes away from the magnificent spectacle. He was entranced, and nothing in the world could make him want to look at anything else. "It's a reckoning. They want her blood for all the lives she's taken . . ."

"Eric?" Susan this time. *"Eric?"*

Eric gasped as the mist whooshed up and enveloped the plane. The vapor was so dense that he could barely make the plane out within it. One of the men at his side let out a sound of disbelief—or was it awe?— as the plane sputtered and then made an impossible horizontal 360.

Then came the lights from the forest below, every color of the rainbow. Looking at it was like experiencing love and hate simultaneously. "Awesome," he murmured, forgetting momentarily about his battered friend on the plane, their failed attempt at a rescue, his girlfriend's anguish. For a moment, it was only the light that possessed him. He wanted it, wanted it to take him. Nothing else mattered . . .

Eric clamped his hands over his ears as the mist roared furiously, swirling in all directions around the plane, as if it had sprouted tentacles. It tugged at the wings and the tail of the plane, pulling it down, down into the forest.

The plane, as if accepting defeat, sputtered helplessly and then gave out. It fell in a shriek that was both soundless and piercing toward the woods, taking out treetops in its wake. Moments later came a crash.

The dead in the forest howled in victory.

"Jesus Christ . . . ," he heard Kinger say. "Think they could've lived through that?"

"We're going to find out. Quick, get in the car!" Howell commanded.

"What made them crash, I wonder?" Susan said, and Eric understood that he'd been the only one who'd seen the spectacle of lights and fog.

"It was the forest people," he said anyway. "Justice. They wanted justice."

"Looks like they got it," Howell said, and then they raced toward the trees.

CHAPTER 37

Locating the plane wasn't too difficult. They only needed to follow the smoke and look for the remnants of broken trees.

There were also lights—not from the forest this time, but from the firetrucks, ambulances, and police vehicles that raced toward the scene. A few were parked, and once again Howell skirted around them like a professional stunt driver, ignoring the angry shouts of those he passed, until debris prevented him from going any farther. They ran toward the plane on foot, Kinger and Howell flashing their badges as they sprinted past, whenever they were hassled.

Susan let out a horrified cry as they came upon a small battered body inside the plane. "Jake. Oh God, no!"

Jake moved ever so slightly. "I took that bitch down," he said and then laughed crazily. He rubbed his ribs. "Ouch."

He had a large gash on his scalp that was probably going to need stitches; the entire left side of his face was crimson from the bloody waterfall oozing down on it. They stepped aside so that the EMTs could enter the plane and do their thing.

"Where do you hurt?" one of them asked.

"Everywhere," he said. "My arm, I think it's broken. My head, it hurts too. *A lot.*"

"At least you're alive," Eric said, choking up. He couldn't before, but now that he'd confirmed Jake was okay, he could admit to himself that he'd been preparing for the worst—to find Jake, not just dead, but mangled. "If you've got nine lives, you must've used about eight of them."

Jake smiled weakly. "Better be careful from now on, then, eh?"

The EMT poked and prodded Jake, checking his blood pressure and his eyes with lights and by asking him to follow her finger, murmuring to her partner every so often. Jake screamed in agony as they jostled him slightly to place a brace around his neck. "I know, it hurts," she soothed. "Just a little longer, and we can give you something for the pain." She didn't look too worried, which Eric took as a good sign.

Finally, they administered morphine, injecting sweet relief into Jake's veins. His eyes rolled back into his head in ecstasy. "Oh yah . . . that's the good stuff."

"I think he's ready," the EMT said, and then she and her partner went about the laborious task of extracting Jake from the airplane on a gurney. It was slow going, but they were being careful not to jostle him or, worse, lose their grip on the thing and drop him altogether. Better safe than sorry.

"Jake?" Howell asked.

Jake's face was 90 percent smile. "Yo! That's my name," he said and then giggled.

"Where's the mayor?"

"Ghosts took her. They're do-diddly . . . dead . . ."

Howell and Kinger exchanged a look that said: *This guy's out of it.*

Jake's eyes slid closed. Kinger snapped his fingers, pulling Jake from his high. The EMT shot him an annoyed look. "He's in extreme pain and needs to rest."

"Won't be a minute," he promised her. "Jake, this is important. Where's the mayor? She take off on foot or in a car or . . . ? Did somebody pick her up? Focus."

"Told ya already! Dead people pulled her right from the plane. She fought like . . . the . . . devil."

Howell put a hand on Kinger's arm. "We're not going to get anything out of him. Kid's doped out of his mind."

"Yep." Jake shook his head lazily. "But . . . look by the door. Clawed to stay . . . inside. Ripped her out . . . night-night." Jake's eyes slid closed.

This time, they let him sleep.

Susan, who'd witnessed more unexplainable things over the course of a few months than most people did in their entire lifetimes, weaved around the EMTs and the agents to examine the door. She frowned. "Guys! Over here."

Kinger, Howell, and Eric scrutinized the area Susan pointed to. Long claw marks ran along the interior of the plane—not deep, but enough scratches to give Jake's claim some credence, though maybe not entirely in the way he'd insinuated.

"Look at this," Eric said, holding up a small pink object.

"That a fingernail?" Kinger asked.

"Just like Madison's," Susan said.

"Justice," Eric whispered.

EPILOGUE

Ben Harvey was walking out of Jake's hospital room just as Susan and Eric were walking in. He stopped in the center of the doorway, blocking their path, and abruptly flung his arms around them both and pulled them in close for a group hug.

"Hi, um, okay, great," Susan said, patting his back gingerly, while Eric thanked him with an awkward smile that was smooshed by Harvey's shoulder. After a few uncomfortable seconds too long, they parted.

"You guys!" he cheered, as if some kind of congratulations were in order. He reached up and pinched Eric's cheek. "I could kiss you."

"Please don't."

From his bed across the room, Jake snickered wickedly and egged Harvey on. "Tell them about the free passes."

"Yes, yes!" From his pocket, Harvey extracted a couple of photocopied tickets that took up an entire page of paper each, like something taken from a children's coloring book. "I was actually just heading to your hotel to give these to you."

"We checked out," Eric said, and then he and Susan accepted the tickets.

"Back to California?"

"As soon as they discharge Jake," Eric said.

"It's been a week. If I was going to die of internal bleeding, I would've done it on the first day and saved myself from this god-awful food," Jake said, plopping down a fork of what looked like mashed potatoes mixed with some kind of minced meat. He pushed the tray on the table by his bed away from him. "I can't take anymore."

Susan read on the ticket, "Good for life on any Ben Harvey bus tour. Drinks included." She scanned the ticket to the bottom of the page, finding a limitation denoted with an asterisk. "Excludes alcoholic beverages. Alcohol?"

Harvey nodded. "Just added to the tour—it's been a big hit. Costs add up fast on those, though, if I don't watch it."

"Oh, I can imagine," Eric agreed.

"But I'm sure I could sneak a couple to you guys, since I know the owner," Harvey said with a wink. "Business is booming now, thanks to you guys. I've added some new stops on my tour. People are calling from all over, overseas even—Australia, Britain, China, you name it—to book a place. And here I thought I was going to have to close up shop soon! Now, I'm thinking I might even expand into the hostel industry."

"Glad we could help," Susan said dryly.

"The forest is the last stop on the tour—where Moulden *met her maker*," Harvey said, wiggling his finger in a manner he probably intended as creepy.

After Jake had been taken to the hospital on the day of the mayor's momentous plane crash, Eric, Susan, Howell, and Kinger had searched the woods for their missing villain. The foursome all had their own theories about how the claw marks had gotten on the plane's interior, none of which included ghosts ripping the mayor away, like Jake had so vehemently claimed in his drugged-out state. The most plausible theory they could come up with was that a hungry mountain lion had smelled Mayor Moulden's blood, attacked her, and then dragged her back to its den to finish its meal.

At least, this was the theory Eric and Susan endorsed out loud; they had their own versions of what might have happened, otherworldly events that they dared not try to rationalize to Howell and Kinger, for fear of looking crazy (Eric) and hurting any future career moves (Susan). Eric believed that the spirits of the dead who'd been long ago buried in the forest had sought revenge for all the evil deeds the mayor had perpetrated. Susan simply didn't know *what* to think, though she was unwilling to quickly dismiss the uncanny. Not after her experiences at Death Farm.

They found Mayor Moulden a few yards away from the plane in a crater that had been left by a fallen tree—what was left of her, anyway. Her body was mangled so badly that they initially questioned if it even was her. Closer examination, and then later dental records, confirmed that it was. Nearly every bone in her body had been broken, and her kneecaps had been removed. Strangest of all, she was missing her tongue; it had been ripped clean from her mouth.

It was never found.

Inside the plane, they discovered forty-five kilos of Pop C, wrapped and ready for distribution. Kinger gave it an estimated value that stretched into millions—it was difficult to give it an exact value, he said, since the drug was so new to the market and the formula was ever changing. Had Mayor Moulden succeeded in escaping, the drugs would have been distributed throughout Canada and into new markets in the eastern United States. Mayor Moulden was expanding her empire, "going national" as she'd said; a map found in the plane showed as much. Testing of the bricks revealed that the supply contained toxic levels of chemicals that were unlike anything Kinger and the rest of his partners at the DEA had ever seen. The death toll would've likely been in the hundreds. Maybe thousands.

Harvey said, "I sell little vials in my store for people to take on the tour—for the forest part."

"Vials? Why?"

Harvey frowned, as if the answer should be obvious. "So they can take dirt from the site of the plane crash. People are far more macabre than they like to think. They love those sorts of death souvenirs."

"You don't seem very broken up about the mayor's passing," Jake commented.

Harvey shrugged. "Eh," he said. *Can you blame me?*

They couldn't.

Once word of Mayor Moulden's death had spread, Clancy locals began to come forward about their involvement in the Pop C trade. Many sought immunity deals in exchange for their testimony, which authorities had anticipated. The DEA was more focused on busting the big fish of the operation, so they obliged.

There were also those who only wanted assurance that they were now safe to live their lives as peacefully as they had done before the mayor's operation had taken over. The individual experiences varied, though the general claims were the same. Mayor Moulden was at the head of a small-time drug cartel—small time *initially*—that had moved into Clancy a few years prior. She'd exploited the town's Darkest Thrills fame to bring in her crew of workers unnoticed. As her operation grew and she required more minions, she began to recruit locally. Some of the locals had jumped at the chance to join up with Moulden. Clancy's economy had been suffering for years, and she'd offered what seemed like a great deal of money in a short amount of time.

Moulden had been clever in her recruitment. She hadn't skimmed from the dregs of society—not *only* from the dregs, anyway. On the contrary, she'd targeted everyday individuals like failing business owners and single parents who were struggling to put food on the table for their children. She'd employed teachers whose minuscule salaries hardly covered their basic necessities, and loggers whose bodies were spent from years of abuse in the harsh Pacific Northwest environment. She'd even taken on a few younger employees from the high school, teenagers with high GPAs who needed money to go away to college, which she'd claimed to encourage.

These were salt-of-the-earth individuals who had the respect of the community—hardworking locals who'd been struggling for years to get ahead, with no foreseeable escape from poverty. Moulden, it had seemed, had offered them a way out.

Most important of all, the worker bees justified, Moulden had instituted a strict policy against her employees using Pop C. It was an offense that would see them terminated from their duties (though they later learned the true meaning behind "terminated"). It was bad for business, she'd said, and it made them untrustworthy. The locals liked the rule, as they'd foolishly believed that it would keep the drug from infiltrating their wholesome town.

There were also those who were not onboard with Moulden's town domination, yet they were forced to go along with her plans anyway. These folks tended to fall into the categories of the elderly, staunch religious followers, and righteous individuals whose job it was to uphold the law. Individuals like Sheriff Stogg.

During their interviews, the DEA and FBI were told of the intimidation tactics used by Moulden. Loved ones of the rebellious were frequently taken hostage and forced to make batches of the drug, thus involving them in the operation. Or they were simply killed outright, like Stogg's wife, forcing those left behind to invent stories to explain the disappearance. Anyone suspected of talking to outsiders or the authorities, like Big Ian, was silenced through death and typically buried in the forest under the stumps of large trees. Sometimes, Moulden would order her lackeys—Clausen, a drug runner she'd imported from Texas, being one of them—to do a random execution as a reminder to townspeople to watch their step.

She never, ever let them forget who was in charge.

Moulden hadn't, of course, always been mayor. But, like her Pop C operation, over time her political standing grew. So did her ego and her demands. Those who'd practically begged to be on her staff at the beginning of her reign grew weary over time. They were scared by the rumors they heard—rumors that, deep down, they knew were true—and they wanted out. However, by then it was too late, as the one key piece of information the mayor had neglected to tell them was this: there was only one way to leave her operation, and it was through death.

The forest was searched after a couple of the mayor's henchmen—mostly loggers and foresters with extensive knowledge of forest topography—came forward with crudely drawn maps of where the bodies might be buried. They couldn't say where exactly, but they had a general idea.

It was slow, difficult work upending the trees stumps. Thus far, the bodies of twelve individuals had been found, including a man named Miguel Juarenz. He'd been shot three times in the chest.

Chuck and Madison were not among the twelve, but they were found at the bottom of a dry riverbed deep in an area of the forest that nobody ever used. They had both been bludgeoned to death, and Madison was, indeed, missing a fingernail.

The henchmen claimed that there could still be dozens more out in the forest waiting for discovery. With the mayor's identity out of the bag, they were willing to provide the names of the locals who'd "gone missing." The names of other victims they simply *couldn't* provide, if they'd been brought in from out of town or were unfortunate tourists like Chuck and Madison.

"People on my tours also place memorial items in the forest," Harvey said, defending himself against the trio's frowns. "Gifts for the dead and their spirts. Biodegradable, of course." He did not make it clear if he believed that it was truly helping these "spirits" in whatever quest they were on in the afterlife or merely helping his wallet. They suspected the latter.

"Of course," Susan said, and with nothing else for Harvey to contribute to the conversation, he bid them all farewell.

Once Harvey was gone, Eric crumpled his and Susan's free tickets and tossed them into the garbage can.

"Oh, you two don't think you'll be vacationing up here again? After you had such a lovely time, it would be a shame," Jake said bitterly, and then he crumpled his own ticket and threw it at the same garbage can from across the room. He scowled when he missed the basket. "I'd rather eat a bucket of glass than come back up here."

Susan said, "I'd eat a bucket of glass before going on the *tour*. What was he thinking with those free passes?"

"Will wonders never cease," Eric said.

Jake held up a couple of newspapers. "Harvey brought these too. We're front page on both."

"I'm shocked, I tell you, shocked," Susan deadpanned.

Not surprisingly, the story had made national headlines. Once again, Eric and Susan—and, now, Jake as well—had received media attention. So had Kinger and Howell, who'd been invited to assist after they handed over their findings to larger authorities at the DEA and FBI.

Eric sighed. "Might as well get it over with."

Jake unfolded the top newspaper, cleared his throat, and with faux cheer said, *"Psychic Eric Evans lends his skills to authorities to help locate murder victims in the Pacific Northwest!"*

Eric held up a hand. "I'm going to stop you there. I think I'm good with just the headline. How the hell do they expect me to work after this?"

His enrollment for the upcoming semester had crept so high—well into the thousands—that he'd begun to question whether he'd be able to continue teaching at Perrick Community College at all. The media had made his life on campus difficult after Death Farm. Now, with his new and unwanted fame, they'd most likely make it impossible. If he were in the mood to face facts, he'd begin to look for an alternative line of work or, at minimum, a new teaching gig.

But he wasn't in the mood, so . . . later. As he'd learned, life usually worked itself out in the end.

"What does it say about me?" Susan asked.

"Which version do you want?" Jake asked, giving both papers a little shake. "The one where you're a modern Joan of Arc—a *bold female*, their term—refusing to back down in the face of threats and resistance?"

Susan rolled her eyes. "God."

"Or do you want the other: *Who* is *this strong beauty who constantly lands herself in hot water?*"

"Because that's not sexist. Did they actually *write* that?" Susan said, incredulous.

Jake nodded, understanding her sarcasm. "Verbatim."

"What does it matter anyway? It's only a matter of time before the press turns on me again. Well, they can say what they want, as long as it doesn't hurt my chances with the FBI."

"You think you're going to work for them, then?" Jake asked.

"I'm pretty sure, yah. What's that phrase—once you've been liberated, you can never go back to confinement? I just don't think I'd be happy at Perrick PD anymore. I've put the work in, and now it's time to move on to something bigger. I didn't realize it until I was away for a while, but I haven't been happy there for some time. Maybe happy isn't the right word. *Fulfilled.*"

"Maybe we should write a tell-all after all," Eric said with a chuckle. "At least then we'd be able to tell our side of the story."

"At least then I'd have something to do," Jake joked, though his voice was tinged with sadness over the loss of his friends. "Besides write letters."

He'd received the most media attention out of the three, mainly because of the band. Tabloids and news stations exploited the "rising stars shot down during their glory" angle when reporting the murders of Chuck and Madison. Jake had been flooded by thousands of emails from individuals who wanted to extend their "thoughts and prayers." The last album the band released had become a chart-topper. Even though Jake and John could theoretically find new band members, they agreed that Chuck and Madison were irreplaceable. Augustine Grifters was officially done.

"Let's get ourselves home before we start making big plans for the future," Eric said. And home they went, once Jake was discharged from the hospital.

They didn't talk much during the journey, though occasionally one of them would make a strained comment about how they'd need another vacation to recover from the one they'd just taken—wasn't that funny? They would laugh, as if it was the first time they'd heard the joke. However, underneath the cheer, they thought how lucky they were to have survived their very own Darkest Thrills misadventure.